LIGHTER THAN AIR

LINDA HOOVER

For everyone who isn't afraid to step out in faith to do what they feel God is leading them to do. Adventure awaits you.

CHAPTER ONE

Early summer, 1900

*P*hineas Higgins was a petty, grudge holding, mean-spirited man. He knew it and made no excuse for it. But tonight, the smile that split his face felt right as he swaggered through his smoky tavern toward the bar. The bartender drew a mug of ale and set it in front of him. "A good night at the gaming table, Mr. Higgins?"

Phineas wanted to shout, but he settled for a triumphant laugh and a slap on the wooden bar top instead. "Best night I've ever had." He chugged the cold, crisp ale, swiped at the foam on his upper lip and thunked down the mug. "Give me another." The exhilaration of his success brought on a rare moment of generosity. "A round of drinks for everyone!"

A cheer went up as two curvaceous barmaids passed out mugs of ale, one tall with long red hair and the other petite and blonde. Some of the customers slapped him on the back as he made his way to his customary table in the corner of the crowded room, while others raised their drinks to him. He leaned back in the chair, and watched with satisfaction, as the girls served the customers.

The blonde barmaid came close, her skirt swaying as she walked. With a leer, he reached over and pinched her round bottom, making her squeal.

He cackled and rubbed his hands together in a celebration nobody else in the room understood or cared about. Phineas knew those around him had no idea what the celebration was about. They merely enjoyed getting a free drink. And he wouldn't announce the reason for his glee, either. He couldn't take the risk.

He surveyed the common room of his tavern, proud of his accomplishments—. The fire in the hearth burned against the chill of the night. Gas fixtures placed evenly around the room reflected warmly against the polished wooden floor and furnishings. The number of people frequenting the tavern gave testimony to the good food and drink served here. A person had only to take a whiff to start his mouth to watering.

Business was good and the income from his gambling meant he had a tidy sum in the bank. It should have been enough to make him happy. And it might have been, until the night the squire came into his establishment for a drink and a game of faro.

Phineas drained his mug, then smiled as he remembered that night. Turned out the man had a weakness for both, and Phineas knew just how to exploit it. He still couldn't believe his luck. After several evenings in a row, it had come down to tonight, when the squire had left as a beaten man. The fire of satisfaction burned in his middle. In only a few months' time, he would go from being a mere tavern owner in Brighton to possessing a beautiful country estate. His father would have been proud.

Despite that his smile faltered and his hands curled into fists as he remembered the squire's daughter, smart enough to manage the estate. He would need to keep an eye on her. He'd take whatever steps necessary to make sure she didn't interfere.

Phineas held the thought for a moment then forced his hands to relax. He'd deal with that problem later. His pretty red-headed barmaid passed with a tray full of mugs, and he grabbed one. Tonight he would celebrate.

CHAPTER TWO

"There's something I need to tell you, Elena. You'll want to have a seat."

At the tone of Papa's voice, Elena Bishop's gaze shot to her father. What disastrous news might he deliver? Too much food, drink and too many late nights had taken their toll. His once-fit body was now overweight. His thinning hair was white, and there were perpetual bags under his gray eyes. Today his eyes were red-rimmed, and instinct told her it had nothing to do with drink.

In their study, a place she wouldn't normally find him, he stood on the business side of the big desk, books and ledgers littering its walnut surface. She set her basket of roses onto the floor and sank into a chair across from her father.

Sorrow replaced the hardness she usually saw on Papa's face, and it frightened her more than the anger and bitterness that came soon after her mother was killed in the ballooning accident.

She swallowed the anxiety threatening to close her throat. "What is it, Papa?"

He sat with a heavy sigh. "This is all my fault. You've kept excellent records, and it's thanks to your hard work that the estate is in such fine shape. Unfortunately, we have only until the end of the summer to enjoy our home. At that time, we'll need to find somewhere else to live."

"What do you mean?" Elena shook her head. She must not have heard him correctly.

Papa slumped back in his chair and rubbed his face. Letting his hands fall to his lap, he met her eyes, and she saw no hope. "I've gambled and lost. One drink too many, one game too many are merely excuses. The fact is, I must come up with the money to pay my debt, or I'll forfeit the estate."

"There must be some mistake." With shaking hands, Elena pulled the ledgers toward her and began leafing through the pages. "By the end of summer, the estate will have produced a good amount. And the hotel you invested in in Brighton will have made a tidy profit from the tourist season."

Papa gently pulled the book away and closed it. "It won't be enough." He propped his elbows on the desk and rested his head in his hands.

Elena stared at him. It wasn't fair. How could she lose both her mother and her home? Despair stood at the door. She could give up and let it in or slam the door in its face.

Her gaze dropped to her hands clasped in her lap. Losing their home was unacceptable. And what of the staff? She and Papa both thought of them as family. What would God want her to do?

She drew a deep breath and stood. "I'm not giving up. I've managed this estate by God's grace these last ten years, and I doubt He's provided for us so it can be lost now."

"I'm truly sorry, Elena. I only have until the end of August to wallow in my misery not come up with the money needed. There's nothing like spending time with the people and things you love, knowing you're going to lose it all. Ten thousand pounds cannot be raised in a few months, and I won't go begging to family and friends for it."

She felt the blood drain from her face and fell back in her chair.

"Ten thousand?" she whispered. "How could you think of making such a wager?"

"It doesn't matter. The deed's been done, and I don't think you could ever know how sorry I am for it."

She closed her eyes, shutting out the hint of tears in her father's eyes. But resolve stiffened her spine, and she leveled a gaze at him. "I refuse to be defeated. With God's help, we'll figure this out." She stood and left the room.

Without pausing, she went out the French doors leading to the terrace and the garden beyond.

Her shoes tapped out a quick rhythm as she marched over the sunny flagstones, down the steps and then crunched along the gravel path. On most days, she could find peace in the clean lines and symmetry of her well-tended garden. Today, she needed the comfort of the old oak by the spring. The flowering shrubs and trees surrounding it made it the perfect place to think and pray in solitude. She'd spent a lot of time there since her mother's death.

Elena dropped to her knees when she got there and dipped her cupped hands into the spring. She took a long drink of the cold, sweet water. Then, she sat with her back against the rough bark of the oak tree and waited for the wild beating of her heart to slow. When it did, she gazed up at the green leaves and patches of blue above her head. "Well, God, what are we going to do now?"

Bees buzzed amongst the fragrant primroses and bramble rose bushes and birds twittered in the trees. She let her eyes close and soaked in the peace of this place for several minutes. There had to be a way to save their home.

Getting on her knees, she got another drink. As usual, the water refreshed her, made her feel better. Even her father always said it helped to lift his spirits.

That's it.

She sat back with a bump. People went to Bath in Somerset County to take the water for their health. And families were already coming to nearby Brighton for summer holiday.

In her imagination, brightly colored tents dotted the lawn. Families played croquette, badminton or went for a stroll. She could even provide picnic food, and of course, they'd want to drink the water. It would be a rustic, yet peaceful holiday for families who wanted to get away but couldn't afford to stay in a hotel in Brighton.

She drew up her knees and wrapped her arms around her legs while considering what would be involved. Tents, recreation equipment, and food didn't come without cost. How much money could they spend to increase their income? And what of the extra work she'd be asking of the staff? They all, herself included, might end the summer exhausted with nothing to show for their efforts. But what if they didn't do anything—?

Elena lifted her face to the sky again. "Lord, I believe you've given me this idea and You will help us. Thank you."

Giddy energy filled her. She jumped up, lifted her skirt, and ran all the way back to the house. Hair pins came loose along the way, allowing her hair to tumble around her shoulders.

She made it all the way to the house without tripping and falling. Amazing, considering her tendency toward clumsiness. In her mind, it was a sign that this idea came from God.

Her father was right where she'd left him. Elbows on the desk, head in his hands.

"Papa, I know what we can do."

He didn't lift his head. "There's nothing to do. We're ruined."

Elena pulled a chair around the desk and drew it up close to him. "Do you remember the spring and how good the water is?" He didn't answer, so she went on. "We can turn the estate into a resort. If we host ten or twelve families a week for the rest of the summer we should be able to raise the money we need."

He dropped his hands and stared at her as if she'd lost her mind. "A resort? Here? You plan to keep ten or twelve families here in this house at one time?"

"Of course not." She laughed, then explained her idea

7

regarding the tents and the recreation, but his expression didn't change.

"Have you given any thought to how the earl will feel about this, with his estate bordering ours?"

That gave her pause. The Earl could be a bit stuffy. However... "If he was privy to your debt, he'd be glad to know we're doing something to raise the money ourselves rather than asking him for it."

"Ha! He'd never give it, anyway. He's tighter than his father ever thought of being."

"Let's not worry about the earl right now." Elena made a shooing motion with her hand, as if to sweep the thought away. "We'll deal with issues as they come up. For now, we must remember it's God's will for us to keep the estate."

"You can't know that for sure."

"I have no doubt this is where we're meant to be."

At least she hoped so. Because, if she was wrong...

CHAPTER THREE

a man's homecoming was supposed to comfort him, cheer him. Not make him fear for his future.

Justin Ramsey paused outside the study door and sent up a hasty prayer for the right words. He gave his damp palms a quick swipe on his pant legs and crossed the threshold. His older brother, Richard, the seventh Earl of Kinnley, sat writing at the desk in the center of the room.

"Richard, I thought I'd find you here."

His brother glanced up from his papers but remained seated. "You're finally home. I trust you've made your hellos to Mother."

"You know I'd never hear the end of it if I hadn't gone to her first."

His brother gestured to the seat on the other side of the wide mahogany desk, and Justin slid into it.

"Now that you've graduated, what do you plan to do?"

Straight to the point as always. But no matter. This was the moment Justin had been looking forward to—and dreading—for the last six months. His grandmother's last wishes had ensured that. And if Justin never did another thing, he'd be sure he fulfilled them, even though it meant a trip to the United States of America to search for a man in California. And, typical for Grandmother, she'd made it even harder by insisting he keep it a secret. Although the whole scheme would be easier if he could tell Richard.

He regarded his brother, who sat with his elbows propped on the arms of his swivel chair, his fingers steepled in front of him. It rankled to be of age and still be subject to someone else's control over your life.

Justin cleared his throat and ordered his thoughts. "I would like to go to America to see the country and get to know the people. There's a great story waiting to be written and I believe God has given me the talent to do it."

Aside from the letter, this was the truth. Writing a book had been a dream of his for a long time. The adventure of going from the east coast to California would give him plenty of material. Just the thought of it made him tingle with anticipation.

Richard shook his head. "Lots of books have already been written on that subject. I doubt you'd find anything new to say. It sounds like a waste of money."

Justin pushed away his resentment. "Has something happened that I should be aware of? Are we running low on funds?"

"Of course not." Richard frowned. "We're financially sound, but that doesn't mean we should throw money around willy-nilly. I think you should join the military. It's a perfectly respectable occupation for a second son."

Justin took a deep breath and counted to ten. "The military is a fine thing, but it isn't for me. Writing, on the other hand, is something I love. You've probably noticed in the papers that America is beginning to take the lead in new innovations. I believe first-hand investigation may give me an idea for an enterprise that will add to *our* family fortune."

Richard relaxed back in his chair as Justin talked, his expression going from forbidding to calculating.

Justin loosened his grip on the arms of the chair and watched. Of all the arguments he could make, this one should tip the decision in his favor. His brother never failed to take interest in adding to their financial holdings.

Richard placed both hands on the desk and leaned toward him. "I'll make you a bargain. You keep things quiet and dignified while I'm gone, and by that, I mean keep our good neighbor Elena out of trouble, and I'll grant your request. However, if I find things in chaos when I return, you will agree to go into the military." Richard leaned in as if he'd just finished plotting Justin's entire future and couldn't wait to give him the details. "I'm sure our uncle can arrange for you to be assigned in India. He would no doubt be happy to have a member of the family there with him. And if seeing another part of the world is what you need to write a book, I'm sure India would make a more interesting topic than America."

Justin stared, chilled to the core. He wanted no part of the military, and he had no reason to believe Richard wouldn't follow through with his threat. However, his brother always did have a tendency toward exaggeration. They were talking about Elena, for goodness sake. How hard could it be to keep her in line?

The ice in his middle thawed and he grinned. "Going to London for the summer season, I suppose. Sounds like Mother finally convinced you to find a wife."

"I'll be gone until the end of summer, most likely, but not to London. I'm going to America to marry, and when I return with my bride and her family, I expect to find everything and everyone in order." With a sigh, he added, "It would be a plus if all the buildings are still standing."

Justin's jaw dropped. He hadn't known his brother was courting anyone. "Who?"

"Elena Bishop. Really, Justin, try to pay attention. I was just speaking of her. Her father has never recovered from the loss of his wife, and she needs watching after."

Justin stared at his brother. His childhood friend had only ever annoyed Richard. How could he think of marrying her? Of course, she was a lovely girl. The dimple in her right cheek gave her a merry smile, and the golden highlights in her brown hair had always fascinated him.

Wait, he'd said something else. "What's this about an American bride if you're marrying Elena?"

"Marry Elena? Are you mad?" An expression of horror crossed Richard's face. He pointed at his head where silver threads could be seen in his dark hair. "Where do you think these gray hairs came from?"

Justin stifled the chortle that threatened to escape from his throat. "Elena couldn't have given you those. She's just a sweet girl. Besides, they're barely noticeable."

"While you were finishing up at Cambridge, I've had to rescue her from a tree after she tried to save Mrs. Jones's cat. I fished her out of the pond when she somehow managed to fall out of a rowboat." He stood and paced from one end of the book-lined study to the other. "She twisted her ankle while delivering soup to the Smith cottage and I had to transport her home. And she nearly burned the village church to the ground when she brought a donation of flowers for the communion table and knocked over some candles."

Justin watched his agitated brother in amusement, not feeling one bit bad that Elena had disrupted Richard's ordered world.

His smile slid away when Richard came to an abrupt stop and pointed at him. "You will keep the young lady from ruining the countryside while I'm gone."

Justin stood to face his brother. "Oh, come now. I know she has a tendency to trip over her feet, but aside from the church incident, she's generally more a danger to herself than anyone else."

Richard shook his head and jabbed a finger at him again. "I'm telling you, if you want your trip across the ocean, you will make sure Miss Bishop stays at home and out of trouble. No missions of charity. No home remedies for people, livestock, or agriculture. Otherwise, it's the military for you. Understand?"

An easy task. "You have nothing to worry about. Now, tell me who your bride is."

Richard's rigid posture relaxed, and he strolled over to a couple of leather wingback chairs near the fireplace. When Justin joined him he said, "Her name is Melissa Worthington. You met her at Christmas."

He had a vague recollection of a Worthington family, but no one face came into focus. He shrugged. "Can't say I remember her."

"She's blonde, blue-eyed. Perfect picture of lady-like decorum."

"That could describe any number of ladies."

"True, but I expect you'll recall the unfortunate lady whose lap received the contents of Miss Bishop's cup."

The picture was clear now. In his mind's eye, he could see Elena tripping and eggnog flying. She had felt awful, but the young lady was gracious. Miss Worthington would probably be a good choice for a neighbor to the Bishops.

"I know who you mean. She's an heiress, isn't she?"

"She is. She also has a desire for a titled husband. We believe we suit, so we're to be married two weeks after I arrive. I'll leave first thing in the morning."

"Congratulations." Justin leaned forward, holding out his hand.

"Thank you." Richard gripped his hand in a firm shake. "Remember what I said about Miss Bishop. I want to see nothing but peace and tranquility when I get back. And one more thing. Don't mention this to Mother. You know what a soft spot she has for Elena. She may misconstrue our good intentions."

"Don't worry." He smiled as he leaned back in the chair and stretched his legs out in front of him. "Mother will never know, because I've always been able to handle Elena."

CHAPTER FOUR

"You resemble your mother more every day."

Elena looked up from her list of needed resort supplies to see Justin Ramsey, with those unruly dark curls, arms crossed, shoulder propped against the doorway. As a young girl she'd made daisy crowns just as an excuse to touch his hair.

She followed his gaze to the portrait of her mother hanging over the fireplace. The study was the only room in the house where her picture could still be found. People said she resembled her. They had the same petite build, oval face and brown hair, but Justin often said Elena's hair looked as though streaks of honey ran through it.

Her eyes met Justin's and he grinned and came into the room. Just the sight of him made her heart lighter. Her childhood friend, her co-conspirator, confidante and protector when others made fun of her clumsiness.

He held out his arms as she came around the desk to greet him. To her consternation, she tripped and fell against him. He gave her a hug and set her back on her feet. "Do you have time for a walk?"

She pushed hairpins back in place, looped her arm through his and started for the door. "I always have time for you. I want to hear about your last semester at school. Any jaunts about the country-side seeking inspiration for a book?"

In the garden, she gazed up at him and he stared back at her with a dazed expression.

"Justin? Are you all right?"

He blinked. "Yes. No. When did your eyelashes get so long?"

"What? My eyelashes? Maybe we better sit down."

"I'm fine, really." But he sank onto a marble bench next to the rose beds. He closed his eyes and took a deep breath of the warm floral-scented air.

When he turned to her again and grinned he was the same Justin she'd known for years.

"To answer your question, yes. I have a book in mind. I want to write about what's going on in America. I want to see everything—the cities, the countryside. Get to know the people."

A twinge of jealousy bristled through her. She'd love to go on a trip like that. "What a wonderful idea. Will you go after the Summer Season?"

"I'll be here for the summer. But I have news about Richard. He surprised me by announcing his engagement to an American heiress. He plans to leave tomorrow. Mother and I will stay here to make everything ready for their return."

Her eyes widened and she suspected her eyebrows were in the vicinity of her hairline. "Anyone I've met?"

"You met her last Christmas. Her name is Melissa Worthington."

She tried to recall which young lady he referred to. Several American families had attended the gathering. But now that she thought about it one did stand out. She groaned as she remembered the incident and shook her head. "Don't tell me."

He chuckled. "That's the one."

"Then I suppose she must have some idea of what she's getting into."

"It'll be fine. While we're waiting for Richard to come back with his bride we can enjoy the countryside."

"I'd love to spend time with you, but I'll be rather busy."

"Not getting into trouble, I hope. Richard says you've had a few mishaps while I've been gone."

She felt a flush creep up her neck and onto her cheeks. "I'll admit the occurrence at the church was unfortunate, but as far as I'm concerned, anything else he may have been referring to was overreaction on his part."

Justin raised one eyebrow and she frowned. She'd never been able to accomplish the eyebrow trick, and it was even more annoying because it meant he didn't believe her. He was a wonderful friend, but he tended to be bossy on the pretext of keeping her out of trouble. Maybe it would be best if she didn't share her plans for the summer.

He smiled. "I'll admit that sometimes Richard takes things out of proportion, but I plan to stick close just in case."

"I'm sure that won't be necessary." She resisted the urge to squirm under his amused gaze. "There must be any number of other things that require your attention or enjoyment."

"You're my friend, Elena, and I want to help with whatever will keep you so busy."

My, but he was persistent. "I'll manage fine on my own. And with Papa, of course."

"Of course. If you change your mind, let me know."

Thank goodness. It would be bad enough working around Papa's objections. She certainly didn't want Justin giving opinions, instructions and overall supervision. She grabbed his hand and stood. "Come on. Let's go to the spring."

He grinned and stood with her. "It seems like forever since we've been there."

They took their time strolling through the park. She let herself imagine they were children again, when nothing was more important than chasing butterflies, picking flowers and inventing games.

When they stepped through the foliage that surrounded the spring, she drank in the fragrance of pine mixed with primroses. Justin kneeled to get a drink, then dipped his face in the water.

He came up dripping, and she backed away with her hands out in front of her. "Don't you dare." He sprang at her and shook his head, showering her with icy drops of spring water.

His laugh rang out. "You should see your face."

She smiled and dried her hands on his coat.

"Hey, not my jacket."

"Serves you right." She laughed at his offended expression, but he still followed her to the old oak and sat beside her. When she turned to him she caught her breath. A ray of sun shone on his handsome face, making his eyes sparkle like sapphires. Had his eyes always been such a dark blue? And why did her heart suddenly want to gallop out of her chest?

"Elena. Are you all right?"

She blinked and realized he was studying her, his brow wrinkled.

"I'm fine." She forced a smile. "Tell me more about what you'd like to do in America."

He leaned back against the tree and talked about his dream. She listened with one ear while she tried to understand what had just happened. Until now, her friend's familiar eyes had never caused her pulse to race.

With a mental head shake she brought her attention back to Justin's plan to go from the east coast to the west coast of America. Maybe someday she could do that, but right now she had other things to worry about.

And Justin's tug on her heart wasn't the least of them.

CHAPTER FIVE

"*D*id you say Higgins?"

Elena squeezed her hands together in her lap at her attorney's words the next morning.

Mr. Atwood's brow furrowed. "Yes, I'm afraid so. Phineas Higgins has won other sizeable wagers under questionable circumstances."

Elena leaned forward, her hands clutching the edge of the desk. "The Higgins whose mother used to live in the village? The mother we took care of after her husband went to prison?"

"Phineas is a bitter man, like his father. After his father's death he's only gotten worse.

"To date, no one has been able to prove him guilty," Counselor Atwood said, his kind brown, grandfatherly eyes conveying his sympathy. "I'm looking into it, but the situation appears grim."

"I agree, but I have a plan to—" Elena cut off her own words as a cold chill washed over her. How long had this man waited for an opportunity? Evicting her father from his home must seem the perfect revenge for his own father being sent to jail. Never mind that her father had only been doing his job, as squire, to keep the peace.

"Are you all right, Miss Bishop? Shall I have my secretary get you some water?"

Elena brought her focus back to Mr. Atwood's concerned face. She let go of the desk and stiffened her back. This was bigger than she'd imagined, but nothing God couldn't handle. "I'm fine, although I wasn't expecting to hear a crime may have been committed. I can imagine Mr. Higgins cheating to get his revenge, and frankly, I'm not sure if that makes me feel better or worse about Papa, but he takes the blame on himself. Please know, I'll be praying for God's help in your investigation."

"Thank you, and I'll be praying, as well."

"In the meantime, here is my plan for the summer." Elena outlined her idea, including how much she hoped to raise and waited for a response. His eyebrows steadily climbed his forehead until it looked as though they might be stuck at the top.

He stared at her for what seemed like a full minute, then asked, "Does your father support this?"

"Unfortunately, no, but he won't stop me. He said something about having nothing more to lose. I feel confident my idea came from God, and I fully intend to carry it out."

He opened a desk drawer, pulled out a sheet of paper and a fountain pen and scribbled down names and addresses. "Go to these men for supplies. I also recommend you talk to Mrs. White. She's a member of the church I attend and the owner of one of Brighton's finest boarding houses. I'm sure she can give you some good advice."

On the way home, Elena looked again at the list Mr. Atwood had given her. Every line had a check mark, and every check mark represented a step toward accomplishing her goal. Supplies would begin arriving tomorrow, and Mrs. White had been wonderful. Elena's stop at the local newspaper office ensured an ad describing the resort and where to send reservations would begin running the next day. Mr. Atwood had even called the *Times,* in London, and placed an ad.

Elena sighed and leaned back against the carriage's cushioned seat with a smile. She'd accomplished a lot, in spite of an all-day rain, which caused the fabric of her clothes to cling to her skin. She couldn't wait for a nice long soak in a warm tub.

Closing her eyes, she breathed in the scent of honeysuckle growing in the hedgerows. It was one of the things she loved about living in the country. The possibility of having to live somewhere else made her pay attention and enjoy it while she could.

CHAPTER SIX

*T*he next morning, Elena had an almost irresistible urge to jump up and down and clap her hands. A line of five wagons lumbered up the service drive. The resort was no longer an idea or lists on paper. It was real and the chance to save her beloved home started today.

The wagons came to a stop as close to the service door as they could get. Elena eagerly joined the staff as they carried boxes and bags of food to the kitchen, as well as other supplies needed for the guests they hoped to have.

Gratitude warmed her as she worked with the men and women who served in their household. For all their reluctance last night, if their laughter and chatter were any indication, they'd accepted and even embraced the idea of turning the estate into a resort.

Movement on the terrace caught her eye. She turned to see Papa watching the activity, his face as gloomy as yesterday's rain.

She hurried toward him, waving to get his attention. "Papa, come see what we have."

He turned and plodded into the house, head down, shoulders slumped. She stopped and watched with a heavy heart. To his credit, she hadn't seen any signs that he'd been drinking. At least that was something.

Putting on a smile, she turned back to the busy group behind her. She needed to talk to old Bill about the best layout for the tents. After a quick search, she found the small, wiry man on the far side of the wagons pacing, waving his hat at the men and shouting.

"Watch where you're putting your feet, boys. You're trampling the foxgloves. Ho. Daniel. Get out of the herb garden."

When she came into Bill's line of vision he hurried to meet her. "Miss Bishop, these great louts are ruining the borders. Can't they unload these wagons farther from the house?"

"Don't worry, Bill. This is the last big delivery. Tomorrow the tents arrive, and I need you to help me mark out where they'll go."

He turned and trudged beside her, still shaking his head and muttering about the damage being done.

When they reached the park, Bill surveyed the entire area, then pounded a stake into the ground and paced off the distance to where he thought the next tent should go.

After they had twelve places marked, their head gardener tossed the mallet to the ground. "What happens if nobody comes? Or if only a few come?"

Elena hesitated, unsure and wishing for discretion.

"Why do you ask?"

"Some of us have heard that your father may be in a bit of financial trouble. None of us likes the thought of losing our jobs."

"I don't like the thought of losing you either. Many of you have been with my family all my life. I intend to do everything I can to make sure none of us lose our home." She shaded her eyes and gazed out over the park, seeing tents instead of stakes. "It wouldn't hurt if we had at least ten families per week, though."

Give us the strength to carry out your plan, dear Father. We're going to need it.

Keep the neighborhood quiet or join the military.

As the line of slow-moving wagons turned into the Oakwood drive ahead of Justin's carriage, he could hear his brother's warning as clearly as if Richard stood next to him right now.

Prickles of apprehension crept up his arms and across his shoulders. Elena said she'd be busy this summer, and he could only assume the contents of those wagons were part of it.

As she'd done for the past two miles, Mother kept her rather nearsighted gaze on the wagons that turned into the drive as if connected like train cars. "What do you suppose the Bishops are going to do? Have a circus?"

"I suppose I'd better find out."

He'd find out all right. As soon as he had his mother safely home, he'd head right back over and have a talk with Elena.

And like it or not, she would listen.

CHAPTER SEVEN

$\mathcal{J}$ustin couldn't get to Elena's house fast enough. Whatever in the world she was up to, he'd handle it. Immediately.

He spurred his horse up the drive, followed the wagon tracks around the garden to the park, stopped and stared. His brain didn't want to acknowledge what lay before him. Men scurrying about, unloading wagons, Old Bill barking commands—was that a tent rising at about the midpoint of the park? More tents going up, fifty feet to either side?

Justin held in the groan pushing up from his middle. This scene was exactly what his brother had demanded he prevent. Quiet and dignified? No, this was chaos and confusion in the making. He blinked and gave himself a mental shake. Where was Elena?

She appeared from the other side of the middle tent, and he urged his horse to a trot toward her. He reached Bill first and dismounted.

The man smiled and gave him a nod.

"This activity has to stop. Please let the men know."

Bill took his hat off and scratched his bald head. "Miss Elena has her heart set on getting all these tents up today. I'd hate to slow the progress."

"It's all right, Bill. I'll handle Elena."

He strode toward her with grim determination, leading his horse behind him. Bill called to the men to take a rest.

She saw him coming and met him halfway. Her smile was polite, but her eyes told a different story. Probably afraid he would interfere with another one of her grand schemes.

When they were close enough, she began speaking before he had a chance to start. "Justin, it's nice to see you, but I don't have time to talk. I need to have a word with Bill."

Elena started to move around him, and he stepped in front of her. "I'd like to have a word with you first. What are you doing here?"

With hands on hips, she said, "I live here. What are you doing here?"

"You know what I mean." He pointed at the tents behind her. "What are you planning? As your neighbor, I have a right to know."

She frowned, then narrowed her eyes. "Are you responsible for the men stopping their work?"

"There's no point in them putting the tents up when they'll just have to take them back down."

"Is that right?"

He crossed his arms. "I don't know what's going on here, but I believe it has the potential to disturb the peace." *And keep me from going to America.*

Elena mimicked his pose. "I don't remember anyone giving you the job of keeping the peace. I believe that position belongs to my father."

"Then your father isn't doing his duty."

She stiffened and dropped her arms to her sides. "I'll have you know my father is fully aware of what's going on, and I'll thank you to stay out of it. Now, if you'll excuse me, I need to get my men back to work."

She moved to his right, but Justin held up his hand, palm out. "Richard has given me the responsibility of keeping the neighborhood quiet while he's gone. I intend to do that."

She stared at him until he dropped his hand. Without a backward glance, she marched toward Bill, head high. He hoped she wouldn't trip on some unseen object and fall, as usual.

With jerky movements, Justin mounted his horse and headed home, his neck and shoulders stiff with angry tension. He tried to relax, but he could feel it creep up the back of his skull and settle into a band wrapped tightly around his head. She may have won this round, but he wasn't going to let it go.

How dare Justin come over and tell her staff what to do. Elena got the men going again, then went to the garden and sat on a bench amongst the roses. What nerve to think she would simply call everything off just because he said so.

She stood and began to pace, hands clenched at her sides. Pieces of gavel flew up behind her with each indignant step. Justin would not stop her from doing what she could to save her home and staff. She came to an abrupt stop and stared at the gray clouds gathering to block the sun. "Lord. Please forgive me. I know you gave me this idea and that you'll help me. I'm going to trust that you'll take care of Justin."

She closed her eyes, drew in a deep breath and blew it out, feeling the tension drain out of her. Lady Ramsey had taught her the technique several years earlier and it had come in handy more times than she could count. When she opened her eyes she saw Papa standing on the veranda, and hurried to talk to him. This time he didn't walk away. He had half a smile as he waited for her, hands clasped behind his back.

When she reached him he said, "I saw Justin ride by looking none too pleased. And then I saw you in the garden with the same expression. Shall I assume you two talked?"

Elena huffed out a breath. "Well, I wouldn't say we actually talked. More like he gave orders. He's sure I'll be disturbing the peace and wants everything to come down."

Papa turned to gaze out over the park beyond the gardens. The voices of the men and the thwack of hammers against tent stakes drifted to them on the rising wind, along with the scent of rain. "I expect the thunder shower we're about to get will be a good test of the weather-worthiness of your tents."

Her gaze had gone back to the park with Papa's, but now she turned and studied him. She had expected an, "'I told you so'" regarding Justin. "He's not going to stop me, you know."

Papa chuckled. "As I recall, he has always had the last word."

Her hands clenched for a moment, then relaxed. "Not this time. I'll admit he upset me at first, but then I realized he's not my problem. I need to concentrate on making this a fun experience for the families that come. I could still use your help."

His face turned serious, and he shook his head. "I don't have the heart to be part of a losing venture."

He crossed the terrace and entered the house. With a sigh, she gazed out toward the park again. A gust of wind gave her a push and whipped the canvas of the last tent being raised. The men struggled to stake it down then gathered their tools into the wagon and headed back to the stable just as the first fat drops of rain fell.

Elena stood where she was and watched the tents. The scattered raindrops soon turned into a downpour, but she didn't move. Her hair became a sodden mess and the large puff sleeves of her blouse stuck to her arms like a second skin. The loose folds of her soft, green skirt were soaked and wrapped around her legs, thanks to the wind. But getting wet didn't matter. She wanted to see how the tents stood up to the test.

The worst of the storm moved on and left a steady rain. All the tents remained standing, as if there'd never been a storm. This was surely a blessing from God and she breathed a prayer of thanks.

The tents had survived a rain storm, but would they survive Justin?

CHAPTER EIGHT

*J*ustin plodded from the stable to the house in the pouring rain, his mood as dark as the clouds overhead.

He could see his trip to America, and his mission for his grandmother, sinking beneath the waves of the Atlantic. Instead he'd surely soon be headed to a guaranteed post in India. It would probably be the hottest, rainiest spot they could find. He stepped through the front door and stood, fuming in a growing puddle of water.

"Lord Justin, I'll call your valet immediately." Their butler hustled down the hall.

Grashel hadn't told him to stay put, but Justin knew better than to traipse through the house in wet boots. Dripping on the tile was one thing. Muddy footprints on the carpet was quite another.

"Justin, whatever happened?"

He glanced up to see his mother descending the stairs. She had changed out of her traveling clothes and already appeared refreshed from the trip. She wore her prematurely white hair in a loose twist, and her round cheeks glowed a healthy shade of pink. Dark blue eyes shone with concern.

"Hello Mother. I got caught in the rain."

"I can see that." She stopped at the edge of the puddle. "Why didn't you stay at Elena's until it stopped?"

"I wasn't invited."

"Since when do you need an invitation? You two have been under each other's feet since childhood."

His valet and several maids hurried toward him. One maid carried a towel, which she handed to him for his face and hair, and the other two with a mop and bucket. When the water was taken care of, Grashel stepped in, laid a copy of the *Times* on a hall chair and Justin sat while Martin began the process of pulling off his boots.

His mother asked, "Did you talk to Elena?"

"Of course I talked to her. That's why I went over there." When she didn't respond he glanced up to see her disapproval. Mother didn't deserve that. "The rain seems to have dampened my manners."

She smiled and he knew he was forgiven. "Did she tell you what they're doing?"

Justin held onto the arms of the chair while Martin tugged on his riding boots. "You wouldn't believe it, Mother. There were tents going up all over the park. I told the men to stop, but I'm sure she got them started again as soon as I left."

"But what did you find out?"

"I found out Elena has a stubborn streak. She ignored my request to cease the activity."

As Martin headed toward the kitchen with the soggy boots, it occurred to Justin that he still didn't know what Elena was planning. Instead of giving her a real opportunity to tell him, he'd given her orders to stop.

"Well?"

He sighed. "To be honest, I don't know what she has planned, but I do know it has to stop. I'm sure Richard wouldn't like it." He shifted his gaze to one of the landscape paintings hanging in the hallway. He hadn't told his mother about the agreement he had with Richard, as per his brother's instructions. He knew she wouldn't approve of him "managing" their neighbor.

"You're as bad as your father."

His chin dropped to his chest. That phrase was usually directed toward his brother. From the corner of his eye he could see her frowning at him, hands on hips.

"I admit I handled things badly today. I'll visit her again."

"Never mind. I shall invite her to tea and talk to her myself."

When she'd gone to the morning room, he turned back to the landscape. The lake surrounded by trees probably depicted some location in America. Justin heaved another sigh. He was acting pathetic and it needed to stop. He'd make a point of being present when Elena came for tea and find out just what she was up to.

With trembling hands, Elena opened the morning post: two letters addressed to Oakwood Resort.

She hurried to the terrace, where Papa sat having tea and scones. "Look. We have two families. They want to come next week to 'enjoy the healthy air of the countryside,'" she read from one of the letters. She danced around the small table where he sat. "Isn't it wonderful?"

"You'll have to stay busy all summer even to think of raising what we need. I hate to see you work so hard just to meet with failure. You might as well relax and enjoy what we have while we have it."

He picked up a scone and dolloped on a generous serving of lemon curd then took an appreciative bite. He closed his eyes and smiled. Opening them again he gestured for her to join him. "Everything tastes sweeter when you're not taking it for granted."

His repast looked inviting and her stomach reminded her she hadn't eaten yet. "Okay. I'll join you, but not because I'm going to sit here and wait to be removed from our home. You can be gloom and doom if you want. I prefer to thank God for the beginning of our rescue."

She slathered lemon curd on a scone and took a bite. The sweet, tartness melted in her mouth. "We'll have to serve these to our guests." She finished it and reached for another. "I received an invitation to tea with Lady Ramsey this afternoon. You're included, if you'd like to go."

"Thank you, but I've never enjoyed hen parties." He finished his tea and settled back in his chair. "And you might not like this one. She'll probably try to talk you out of this resort foolishness just like Justin did yesterday."

"Lady Ramsey is a practical and sympathetic woman. She's never been one to spout off orders."

Papa leaned toward her, his expression serious. "You're not planning to tell her our circumstances, are you?"

"Of course not. However, I do think she'll get into the spirit of it."

He relaxed back. "We'll see."

If only she could get Papa involved. His negative attitude was draining.

Justin paused outside the drawing room door to make sure Elena was there. He'd rather be mucking out the stable than interrogating his friend, but at least today he had a plan. Be polite, so she'd tell him everything he needed to know. Her soft, feminine voice remarking on the raspberry tarts was his cue.

"Good afternoon, ladies. It's nice of you to make room in your busy schedule to visit, Elena. Maybe we can actually have a conversation."

Elena eyed him warily as he strolled across the room and sat beside her on the rose damask sofa.

A frown flitted across his mother's brow. "Justin, I hope you're planning to be civil."

He turned on what he hoped was a charming smile, but it felt more like a grimace. "You know me, Mother."

"Yes, well, I thought I did." She passed him a cup of tea and a plate of tarts from the teacart next to her matching damask armchair.

He took two and handed back the plate, then turned to Elena. "Has Mother asked you about the activity in your park?"

"We haven't discussed the plans I have for Oakwood, but I can understand why you'd both be curious."

Elena turned to his mother and gestured toward him. "I imagine Justin told you about the tents in the park. I believe God has inspired me with the idea of a resort this summer. Some families can't afford a holiday in Brighton but would still like to get away from the city. I'll offer a rustic experience including fresh country air and exercise. I'll also make available the energizing waters of our spring."

This resort idea was worse than anything he could have imagined. Elena was guaranteeing noisy pandemonium right next door.

His mother clapped her hands. "How wonderful. What fun that will be. Do you need any help?"

What—his mother was offering to help? The tension headache came back with a vengeance.

Mother jumped up in alarm and hastened to him, laying her hand on his forehead. "What is it dear? Are you ill?"

His face must appear as hot as it felt. "I'm not ill. I'm shocked." Pushing her hand away he stood and looked from her to Elena. "A resort next door does not sound like fun. It sounds like a lot of noise and commotion. Richard wouldn't allow it, and since I'm representing him while he's away, I say you can't do it."

"Now Justin—"

"I mean it, Mother. There will be no resort."

Elena came to her feet. "You have no right or authority to stop

33

me. You won't be fighting me on this. You'll be fighting God."

"I hardly think God has told you to do something that would be an inconvenience to others. There must be some other place better suited to providing for those in need of a country holiday."

Now her face was flushed, but he admired her ability to keep her voice calm. "I don't see how my resort is an inconvenience to you. I've already made it clear I don't need your help. And besides, today we received two reservations for next week."

"You'll have to go home and write to them and cancel. Then tell your men to tear down those tents. I'll be over tomorrow afternoon to check on your progress."

"Elena is my guest. You have no right to tell her to leave." He glanced at his mother. The steel in her voice matched the hardness in her eyes.

"That's all right, Lady Ramsey. We'll take tea another time. Apparently, the art of being pompous was one of your son's courses of study this past year. I imagine he received high marks."

She brushed past him, crossed the room and stumbled on the threshold. He winced and started toward her, but she steadied herself on the door-jamb and continued on.

He turned to his mother who glared at him.

"For goodness sake, Mother. It's not as though she wants to open a hospital or feed the poor. Keeping Richard happy is more important than a few families coming to the country."

She didn't comment and her expression didn't soften. There was nothing he could say in his defense that she would sympathize with, so he excused himself and headed for the study.

Justin knew he was on the right side of this. Elena might think God had told her to make a resort, but his going to America at his grandmother's request was more important. His mission didn't involve anything as frivolous as tourists taking a holiday.

With his hands clasped behind his back he paced to the window and gazed at the tree line separating their property from Oakwood. Elena had to come to her senses.

CHAPTER NINE

*T*he next morning, as the first rays of sun peeked in his bedroom window, Justin fought through layers of what felt like suffocating cobwebs. His head throbbed as if someone pounded on it. He rubbed his gritty eyes and scrubbed his hands over his face. For some reason his mouth hung open. He snapped it shut, promptly cutting off his air supply.

Water should help. He struggled to sit. Every single part of him ached. Finally, he could reach the cup on his bedside table. One sip took his mind off his aching person and placed it squarely on his raw throat. This must be what it felt like to swallow broken glass. He set the cup on the table and carefully inched his way back down.

Wonderful. He'd caught a nasty cold and it was all Elena's fault. If she hadn't been so stubborn, he wouldn't have been caught in the rain. He groaned. When she received news of his cold, she'd say he'd gotten what he deserved for trying to interfere with God's plan.

He shivered under his blankets and tried to ignore his pounding head. But was it a feeling? He strained to listen. No, it was a sound, the sound of hammer against stake. Not only had the tents not been removed, more were going up. When had his pleasant childhood friend turned into such an independent and stubborn woman?

A soft knock on the door interrupted his gloomy thoughts. His mother came in with the doctor close behind. "Dr. Parsons is here to see you. Martin told me first thing this morning you'd need to see him, and when I checked on you I agreed."

She crossed the room with amazing speed and cradled his face with her cool hands. "Oh, my poor Justin. You're burning up. You'll have to stay in bed for at least a week."

He gently pushed her hands away. "I can't stay in bed," he croaked. "I have to talk to Elena."

"I'll be the judge of how long the patient is confined." Dr. Parsons set his bag on the bed, opened it and pulled out a thermometer.

Justin fumed while holding the glass tube in his mouth. He couldn't afford to waste time lying around.

The doctor read the thermometer and frowned. "You have a fever, and a sore throat, I'll wager. Let's have a look."

He sighed and allowed the doctor to peer into his throat, push on his neck and poke and prod in general.

Dr. Parsons closed his bag with a snap and gazed first at him and then Lady Ramsey. "Steam treatments twice a day, using two or three drops of eucalyptus oil, plenty of liquids, including beef broth and tea with lemon and honey, and lots of rest. I'll check on him in a couple of days."

He struggled to sit up. "But—"

"No buts." Dr. Parson patted him on the shoulder. "You'll live. However, if you don't take care of yourself now you could be sick most of the summer. I'm sure you don't want that."

Justin shook his aching head and slumped against the pillows. One of his friends at the university had come down with a fever a few days before Justin came home, and he'd received the same instructions—and prognosis.

He didn't have the strength to move anyway. Maybe a couple of days in bed wouldn't be long enough for Elena to cause a disaster next door.

The next day, Elena kept glancing toward Justin's estate, both hoping for and dreading another confrontation. She'd spent the morning outside, watching and helping when she could, as the men set up another tent for the game equipment. Her handsome neighbor hadn't put in an appearance by lunchtime. Something must be wrong. Justin wouldn't issue an ultimatum one day and forget about it the next.

She entered the dining tent and saw the first table sat at an odd angle. As she struggled to straighten it, Daniel came by and trotted over to the other end. "Miss Elena, we can get these tables. There's no need for you to trouble yourself."

"I'm asking a lot of extra work from all of you this summer, and I don't mind helping." She hefted her end of the table.

When they'd lined it up to her satisfaction, Daniel cleared his throat. "Begging your pardon, Miss. It isn't my place to ask, but we're wondering about Lord Justin. We've heard he wants to stop your resort, and we're thinking we may be taking all this back down in short order."

Daniel reminded her of a gentle St. Bernard with his strapping build, thick, unruly, brown hair and big brown eyes. "Lord Justin feels a resort isn't necessary, but I'm sure he'll come around." She squared her shoulders. "Even if he doesn't, it won't change anything. We will go forward as planned."

Daniel grinned, slapped his cap back on his head and left the tent.

She closed her eyes. "My heavenly Father, please continue to show me what to do." She opened them in time to see Daniel stick his head back in the tent.

"Thought you'd like to know Lord Justin is laid up with a cold. He won't be over to bother you for at least a few days." He gave her a conspiratorial wink and disappeared again.

Well, now she knew the answer to her question. Served him right. There was a time when, if she'd heard that news, she'd rush over with a pot of Cook's delicious chicken soup. She had no such desire today. He could just stay in bed all summer.

She left the tent at a brisk pace; her heart lighter than it had been for a few days. Her steps slowed as guilt set in. She wasn't being kind. All right, she thought, as she continued on toward the house, maybe he can stay in bed for a week. That might be enough time for him to come to his senses.

She smiled and quickened her steps. But then that pesky guilt nudged her again. She'd have to take the soup or there'd be no living with herself. She wouldn't stay long, however. A lot of work needed her attention before Monday.

A knock on the door gave Justin something other than his misery to focus on. "Come in." When there was no response he cleared his throat and tried again. This time a young maid entered, bearing a tray with a bowl on it. She brought it to his bedside table, then went to stand by the open bedroom door.

Elena followed right behind her and studied him as if he were a specimen under a microscope. He tried to sit up straighter, against the pillows layered behind him. If only he could breathe through his nose. He had no chance of appearing dignified with his mouth hanging open.

"You look pathetic."

He viewed her through watery eyes. "Thank you. I feel worse than pathetic." He grimaced and swallowed carefully. "Did you bring your cook's chicken soup? All I've seen here so far is beef broth."

"You poor thing. Your throat is sore too, isn't it?" She brushed back his hair and put a cool hand on his forehead and then his cheek. "And you have a fever. Maybe you'll be better in a week or so." A smile tugged at the corner of her mouth.

She pulled a chair up to the bed, tucked a napkin under his chin and picked up the bowl and spoon to feed him. He could have done it himself, but as long as she felt sympathy for him maybe it would sway her to his way of thinking. At least he hoped it was sympathy and not an opportunity to gloat.

The sun shining in the window made the golden highlights in her hair shimmer. *Beautiful. She* was beautiful. He squeezed his eyes shut. Don't lose sight of your goal.

After the first savory spoonful, he said, "This is your fault, you know."

She narrowed her eyes but continued to bring the soup to his mouth. "I'm going to assume your condition is muddling your mind, so let me clear it up for you. I believe you were the one making threats about something that's none of your concern. It's certainly not my fault if you can't get yourself home before it starts to rain."

He held up a hand and blocked the next spoonful. "It is my concern, when it's happening on the property next to ours." He dropped his hand and opened his mouth.

Elena stuck the spoon in it, let go and sat back. "Are you saying you still intend to stop me?"

Justin shrugged and took the spoon out of his mouth. "I have to."

"And I have to follow through with my plans." She stood. "I trust you can eat the rest yourself."

She turned to leave and he grabbed her hand, causing warm tingles to race up his arm. From her startled reaction he wondered if she might have experienced the same thing.

"Thank you, Elena."

"For what?"

"The soup."

She stared at him, then shook her head. "You're welcome." She pulled her hand free and left.

Justin sagged against the pillows. What had just happened between them? He sighed. He'd have the rest of the day to think about it, while things next door got more and more out of hand.

CHAPTER TEN

*W*ithin ten minutes of her first guests' arrival, Elena had begun to question the wisdom of this idea.

Not because she'd bumped the tea table on the terrace and toppled the cream pitcher onto the fresh white linen tablecloth. Not because the four little Smith boys had plucked half the blooms from the shrubs lining the flagstone path from the terrace to the drive. Not because Justin had shown up and greeted each guest with a silent, dark scowl that had surely made them feel as welcome as a swarm of mosquitoes.

No, her guests themselves had made her doubt her ability as hostess to these city-weary families.

Excited little boy voices filled the air, while their bodies filled the drive with activity, running circles around the carriages, their parents and the staff as they unload the wagon. In constant motion, the Smith boys ignored their mother's pleas to calm down.

The Clark family stood back a safe distance, their disapproval lining the parents' faces. Two little girls with golden curls peeked out from behind them and watched the boys' every move.

Finally, red-bearded Mr. Smith, shouted, "That's enough!"

The boys ran to stand beside their father like soldiers.

When she'd settled the two families at tables on the terrace and the staff had served tea and hot scones, Elena welcomed them and invited them to make use of the activity tent, walk along the park paths to the spring, and enjoy picnics in the oak grove. Justin stayed in his spot at a table just a little apart from the group. He wasn't smiling, but he wasn't frowning anymore either, so after a slight hesitation she continued.

She tried to ignore Justin as she talked, but she couldn't—not with those little waves of awareness constantly rolling off of him and bumping into her.

The Smith boys distracted her too, with their whispering through huge bites of strawberry-jam-covered scones and gulps of tea. When they'd finished, their little red heads disappeared one by one under the table, where their whispers turned to snickers and giggles.

One of the boys crept out and crawled toward the Clarks' table, his right hand clenched shut and a mischievous grin on his face. The girls ignored him until he edged toward the older girl's chair and opened his fist.

"Spider!" The girls' blond ringlets bounced as they knocked over their chairs and made their escape. The Smith boy retreated to his hideout under the table.

Mr. Smith stood and bellowed, "That's enough!"

In the resulting silence, he plopped back into the chair, making it creak under his excess weight. "Boys," he said, "come out from under there and apologize."

The boys came out, stood in a line and took turns saying they were sorry. This satisfied Mr. Smith, who reached for another scone.

Elena stole a glance at Justin. He had a thunderous scowl on his face. And if she wasn't mistaken, his left eye twitched. She didn't have to guess what he was thinking.

She cleared her throat. "Daniel, please take everyone to their tents."

Chairs scraped over flagstone as the families stood. The spider-wielding Smith boy ran over to Elena and gazed up at her with a grin, showing a gap where his two front teeth used to be. "My father says if we like it here, we're going to stay all summer."

"Oh, my. How nice."

He waved and ran after his family.

"Excuse me, Miss Bishop."

Mr. Clark approached, doffing his bowler hat and revealing a receding hairline. "I don't want to make a fuss, but are our accommodations anywhere near the Smiths? If they are, I'd like to request a change."

The poor man. His shiny suit told her he wasn't wealthy. He'd spent what he could afford on a nice holiday for his quiet little family, and it was up to Elena to make sure the Smiths didn't ruin it.

"Six tents separate you from them. And we'll put more distance between you if we must."

When Daniel had taken them out of earshot she turned to face Justin, who still glowered. Taking a fortifying breath and straightening her shoulders, she joined him at the table.

She could sense his lecture coming before he uttered a word. "This is just the first week and already it's a disaster. You should have done what I told you and taken it all down before you had to deal with this. It's beyond me how your father could allow you to take your scheme this far, but if he isn't going to watch out for you, I will. You could get hurt."

A familiar frustration squeezed her heart. Once again Justin stepped over the boundary of protectiveness. She folded her hands on the table in front of her and looked him in his stormy blue eyes. "In case you haven't noticed, I've grown up. I am the one who manages the estate, and I'm the one who takes care of me, with God's help of course."

"Certainly I can see you've grown up. However, you haven't thought your plan through. There must be a quieter way to spend your summer." His face relaxed into a smile. "I'll be glad to help you put everything back to rights."

She wanted to smack him. Instead she leaned back in her chair and studied him through narrowed eyes. "Is there something you're not telling me? I don't remember noise being a problem for you."

Justin surveyed the tents. "It's not a problem for me, per se. I'm merely trying to follow my brother's instructions to limit noise. Richard wants a quiet, peaceful neighborhood when he returns."

When he turned his attention back to her she gave him a reas-suring smile. "Things will be fine as soon as the guests settle in. Anyway, you know I'm not one to give up at the first sign of trouble."

An explosion of shrieking brought them both to their feet in time to see the Clark tent settling down over the family. A couple of the staff ran toward the area calling for them to remain calm, while four little red heads darted in the opposite direction. Above the cacophony Mr. Smith thundered, "That's enough!"

Elena cringed. From the corner of her eye she could see Justin shaking his head.

"This can't continue, Elena. My offer to help still stands." He turned and left.

She headed to the park. Those tents had withstood a thunder-storm and yet four little boys brought one down within minutes.

Elena arrived in time to see Mr. Clark assisting his wife out from under the folds of canvas, her hat sideways on her head.

"Miss Bishop, we're leaving. Please refund our fee."

"Of course, Mr. Clark. I understand, and yes, your money will be returned. I'll meet you at the house shortly." She signaled for Daniel to put the Clark's baggage back in the wagon. Once loaded, the family climbed in and they headed back to the house.

Her chest ached as if someone had piled rocks on it. She didn't blame the Clarks for wanting to leave, or for wanting their money back. But this wasn't the way she'd imagined their first week beginning.

Elena went in search of Mr. Smith. She found him at the edge of the tent area watching his boys trudge toward the trees at the back of the park. Every line of his large body appeared tense, his face matching his red beard, which bristled out in all directions.

He gave her a quick glance, then continued to watch his sons. "I'll keep a close eye on the boys from now on. I apologize for the trouble they've caused you and I assure you they will be punished."

She scanned the park and saw that the boys had covered very little ground. "Where are they going?"

"To get a switch."

"What's a switch?"

"A switch is a slender branch from a shrub or tree, which makes an excellent instrument of discipline. Once applied to their backside, they're not likely to repeat the same offense."

Her eyes widened. "Do you mean to say they break off a branch, bring it to you and you strike them with it?"

He smiled grimly. "You have the right of it."

She turned her gaze back on the boys. No wonder they slogged along so slowly. She wouldn't have been in a hurry, either.

Elena hurried back to the house where she knew Mr. Clark would be waiting for his refund. Hopefully Bill wouldn't hear about the switches. She didn't want to have that conversation with her gardener.

CHAPTER ELEVEN

*W*hat had possessed him to give Bishop the whole summer to pay his debt?

Phineas heaved himself out of his chair, maneuvered around the desk to the open sitting room window and peered to the right and the left. Cool air from the sea caused the curtains to flutter inward and brought some relief to the stuffy room. Of course, having the window open also meant he had to endure the noise of hawkers and other amusements on the pier and the commotion of horse traffic and raised voices in the street below. Not to mention the harsh cries of seagulls.

His nephew should have been here by now. He rested his palms on the frame, leaned close to the glass on the upper half of the window and squinted, hoping that would allow him to see farther. He'd given Ronald one little job; find out what the squire might do to raise money.

No sight of the young man. Phineas straightened and clasped his hands behind his back while he continued to watch.

He remembered that some tavern customers mentioned seeing a number of wagons full of supplies and colored fabric going out of town in the direction of the Earl's estate and had speculated on the possibility of a circus. More than a week had passed and he'd heard nothing new. Would the Squire try to host a circus? It seemed best to check it out.

Phineas replayed Ronald's good points while he waited. The seventeen-year-old followed orders without question—an excellent trait in an employee. He also had a rather common appearance. Someone people didn't take notice of. Depending on the information Ronald brought him, blending in would be a useful asset in this situation.

With a scowl, he returned to his desk and sat in his chair, with an exasperated humph escaping him. Another five minutes, and Phineas would start deducting from the boy's pay.

The gold watch he pulled from his vest pocket was a thing of beauty; the etching on the cover a small masterpiece. When he pushed the button, the lid sprang up to reveal a family crest engraved on the inside of the cover, and it always gave the correct time.

Phineas didn't know why men of nobility came to his tavern, but he wouldn't complain. He allowed himself a chuckle as he remembered the surprised and then angry expression on the duke's face. He should have quit when his money ran out instead of wagering a family heirloom.

Thinking about how he'd acquired the watch hadn't kept him from keeping track of the time. As the second hand made its final sweep around to the twelve, a knock sounded at the door. Phineas snapped the lid shut and put the watch in his pocket. "Come in."

Ronald ambled in, shutting the door behind him with a bang. He jumped and spun around then with a sheepish look, turned back to Phineas. "Sorry about that, Uncle."

Phineas drew in a breath and let it out slowly. Becoming a businessman had taught him about the importance of conducting oneself with decorum. Ronald had a lot to learn, but he wouldn't take the time now to discuss the proper way to close a door.

He shook his head and motioned his nephew to a chair near the desk. "What did you find out?"

Ronald slouched in the chair, his legs stretched out in front of him, his arms lying on the arms of the chair. He shrugged. "Not much. Only that the squire's daughter wants to have a country camp for folks from London. The colored cloth in the wagons that people thought might be used for a circus is really for tents the families will sleep in. One delivery boy I talked to said he took two wagons full of stuff to Oakwood."

Phineas narrowed his eyes. It appeared the squire's daughter would indeed be a problem. But how could she possibly expect to raise the sum needed by offering a country camp?

He leaned back in his chair and tapped his fingers on the armrest. Most men wouldn't worry. They'd laugh at her attempt. But he wasn't most men. The success he enjoyed now wouldn't have been achieved if that were the case.

He brought his attention back to Ronald, who had taken out a pocketknife and worked on cleaning the dirt from under his fingernails. Phineas clenched his fists and bit back the words he wanted to shout. Ronald worked best when you didn't yell at him.

Phineas cleared his throat. "Ronald, I have another job for you." Ronald regarded him with half closed eyes. "I want you to go to Oakwood and find out about this country camp, and I want you back here by the same time tomorrow to report. Do you think you can do that?"

"Sure." Ronald gave him an easy smile and slipped the knife back in his pocket. "Can I get something to eat before I leave? Cook's roast beef and onions sure do smell good."

"Yes, but make it fast."

Ronald unfolded from the chair and left, banging the door behind him. A muffled, "Sorry," came from the other side.

Phineas resisted the urge to throw a paperweight at the door.

The next day, Phineas again sat at his desk, watch in hand. The mantel clock ticked while rain drummed against the window. He had discarded his jacket and rolled up his sleeves in an effort to endure the airless room.

Brighton's daily newspaper lay open before him. He'd skimmed through it, but only one thing interested him.

He didn't understand what made him so anxious over the little bit of information he had, but truth be told, he couldn't wait for his nephew to arrive. Not even the fragrance of Cook's lamb stew and fresh baked bread could distract him.

He snapped the watch closed, put it in his pocket, then picked up his teacup. As he raised it to his lips, Ronald rapped once, entered and slammed the door shut behind him.

Phineas jerked, sloshing tea out of the cup. He glared at his nephew as he set the cup in its saucer and pulled out a handkerchief to mop up the spill.

"Sorry uncle, I—"

Phineas held up his hand to stop the repeated apology, then gestured to the chair in front of his desk. At least Ronald arrived on time today. He flopped his wet jacket over the back of the velvet loveseat, removed his flat cap and tossed it after the jacket, then shook the water out of the hair his cap hadn't covered. When the boy was slouched comfortably in his chair, Phineas asked, "What have you learned?"

"I talked to some of the boys they got working in the stables. They started with two families, but only one stayed." Ronald laughed, seemingly oblivious to his uncle's mood. "The one family ran the other one off before they had a chance to settle in. Kids knocked the tent down over them."

"Hmm." Phineas gazed at the gray sky outside the window. "Not a good start for the resort."

He tapped his index finger on the maple desktop while he mulled over what he'd learned. The news reassured him somewhat, but it might not be a bad idea to make a visit himself.

Ronald now had one leg thrown over the arm of the chair.

"Sit up, will you?"

Ronald shifted around to a sitting position.

"I want you to get a job at the Bishop estate. I may need you to do some work for me from the inside."

His nephew's half-closed eyes flew wide. "You mean like mucking out stables?"

"You'll take whatever you can get."

"What if there's no jobs to be had?"

"Then create an opening. First thing Monday morning."

Phineas dismissed his nephew then rested his elbows on the desk and tapped his fingers together. Monday afternoon he'd pay a visit. Maybe he could convince the squire his daughter's little camp resort idea would only waste their time and what little resources they had left. His brows drew down into a frown. More importantly, he didn't want a bunch of people milling around, doing damage to his property.

Sunday afternoon, Elena's spirit drooped like a flower that had been deprived of sunshine and rain. The sun warmed her face where she sat on the terrace, and a gentle breeze carried the fragrance of roses. Why was she melancholy?

The week with the Smiths had finished well, possibly because they had no other guests to bother. And they had decided they would stay only two weeks rather than the whole summer, for which she was extremely grateful.

"It's been only one week, dear. You're not thinking of giving up are you?"

Elena straightened her posture and turned to Lady Ramsey. Over the years, this kind woman had been like a mother to her, and was her one source of human encouragement. She found strength in the scriptures each day, but it gave her comfort to be able to see and touch the person she spoke to.

"I have no intention of giving up. I'm puzzled, though, about what to expect from our guests. The Smith family certainly took me by surprise. In my mind, I saw everyone conducting themselves with manners and consideration for others." She shook her head and relaxed in her chair. "Obviously, people don't always behave the way you expect."

"Including my son. I must say, I don't understand his behavior."

Elena sighed. "He's always been a little bossy."

Lady Ramsey's dark blue eyes crinkled at the corners as she laughed. "That's true, but he's gone beyond the usual." She sobered. "It's as if he has something personal to gain by stopping your wonderful resort idea. I plan to get to the bottom of this. I wouldn't be surprised if Richard is involved, but to what end?"

The next day, Elena heaved a sigh of relief, and strolled toward the spring. Three families had arrived, and settled into tents, which she'd been careful to place some distance from the Smiths. No incidents and no Justin.

A splash and a little boy's cries for help sent her heart racing and feet flying to the spring. She arrived in the clearing, panting for breath. Three little redheads yelled and ran frantic circles around the water. Their brother's head bobbed up in the middle of the spring, then went under.

Elena froze, her pulse pounding in her ears. The water was cold and deep, and she didn't know how to swim. She closed her eyes. "Father, please show me what to do."

The image of Mr. Smith came to her mind and she shouted, "That's enough!" The boys stopped and stared at her with huge eyes and tear stained cheeks.

"Find a stick long enough to reach your brother." They dashed into the surrounding trees and bushes, and ran helter-skelter, sometimes running into each other.

Elena made a desperate search and found a branch that might work. The poor little guy's head still bobbed up but stayed under longer each time he went down. She hurried to the edge and held out the branch. "Grab it, Noah."

He thrashed around, trying to get a hold on it, but it remained out of reach. The ground around the spring had turned into a slippery, muddy mess from splashing water and little feet running on it. In spite of that, Elena moved a little closer to the edge, and held the branch out further. Noah lunged and grasped it. She fought to stand firm against his weight, but teetered forward, until her feet flew out from under her, and she plunged head first into the icy water.

From under water she heard wavery voices and foliage crunching under running feet. She tried to get her head above water, but Noah clamped on and plastered himself against her face. Her full skirt wrapped tighter around her legs with every kick.

Her lungs burned and head ached. She wouldn't be able to hold her breath much longer. Suddenly the weight lifted. Her head bobbed above the surface long enough to gasp for air and go under again. A heavy stick passed in front of her face and she grabbed it with both hands. Strong arms hauled her up and out of the water.

Elena pushed wet hair out of her eyes and looked for Noah. The sight that greeted her could only be called pandemonium. Guests and staff crashed through the undergrowth to get to the scene. Women and children cried, and men shouted.

Someone had wrapped a jacket around her and held tight, but uncontrollable shivers still shook her body. *Noah.* She struggled to get up, but a familiar voice spoke close to her ear. "Don't worry. His parents have him."

She turned and saw Justin's face, mere inches from hers. Why did it have to be him?

CHAPTER TWELVE

*E*lena muttered to herself as she sat propped against pillows in bed, holding a bowl of chicken soup. "I could be outside right now helping the staff if Papa hadn't insisted on getting the doctor. All I needed was a hot bath and I was ready to go, but no, the doctor sided with Papa and here I am in bed for the whole day."

A knock sounded on the door and Papa stuck in his head. "Elena? May I come in?"

Without waiting for an answer, he strode across the room, and pulled up a chair beside the bed. "Your face is flushed. Are you sure you're all right?"

She resisted the urge to roll her eyes. "There's nothing wrong with me, but what about Noah? What did the doctor say about him?"

"He said Noah needs a proper bed until he's well enough to travel. From the looks of him, I'd say it won't be anytime soon. For now, the boy is in one of the guest rooms."

Elena groaned inwardly, remembering how she'd promised no one would stay in the house. And it would be one of the Smiths, no less. How much more trouble could they cause?

Her father continued. "Thank God he's alive. If he had drowned it would have put a quick end to this enterprise of yours. Not that it will bring in the money we require, anyway. And paying for doctors to see guests doesn't help."

"We can be thankful he's alive because Noah has his whole life in front of him."

"You're right. It's a blessing to have you both alive."

With a frown, Elena handed Papa her bowl of soup. "This never should have happened. Different staff members are scheduled to watch the spring to prevent this kind of accident."

He set the soup on the bedside table, kissed her on the forehead then stood. "I'll check on it. Get some rest."

Elena watched in amazement as Papa left the room, shoulders squared and purpose in his step. Did he actually plan to help?

Justin stepped through the front door just as Elena's father came down the stairs like a man on a mission.

He gave Justin a cursory glance. "Are you still here?"

"Yes—no." How did Squire Bishop's glare always make him feel ten years old again? "I've come back as you suggested the last few times I was here."

"Oh. Well, you can see Elena tomorrow. I won't have you badgering her today."

The squire passed him and headed for the back of the house.

"May I at least ask how she's doing?"

"She'll live."

He stared at Squire Bishop's retreating back. When he'd carried Elena in this morning her father appeared shaken to the core, and his thank you had been distracted to say the least. Maybe the possibility of losing her, after he'd already lost his wife, caused his behavior.

Justin let himself out the front door and ambled down the steps leading to the circular drive. It wasn't hard to understand how frightened her father must have been. The sight of Elena going under the water had almost caused him to panic, but common sense, or more likely God's leading, moved him to do the right thing. The memory still made his stomach queasy.

He stopped and stared at the three-tiered fountain in the center of the circle. This could not be allowed to happen again. Justin turned and marched around the outside of the house in search of Wilson. As head of the male staff he would be responsible for what happened.

When Justin came to the back corner of the house, he overheard Squire Bishop speaking to Wilson. The squire made no effort to keep his voice down, so his words carried easily.

"I appreciate your apology, but it doesn't change what happened. The possibility of someone falling into the spring is one of the reasons I objected to this resort idea in the first place."

Justin rounded the corner and saw Wilson and the squire standing almost toe-to-toe. Wilson stood the same height as Squire Bishop and had a sturdy build. Justin knew from long acquaintance the man was as comfortable doing his job outside as in.

Wilson nodded with respect, while the older man yelled in his face.

The squire jabbed a finger toward the back of the park. "Elena assured me the staff would watch the spring at all times. Who was supposed to be on duty?"

"Toby should have been there, Sir, but one of the young ladies who arrived today asked him to help with a stubborn catch on her luggage. He lost track of time and as a result will be disciplined."

"And what of the man Toby was to replace? He shouldn't have left."

"That's why both men will share a most unpleasant task for the next two days. They won't forget their duty again."

The squire stepped back. "From now on I expect someone to

watch the spring around the clock. This incident will not be repeated."

"Yes, sir."

Squire Bishop's shoulders sagged and the sternness left his face. "This is all a foolish waste of time. But my daughter is much like her mother. When she has an idea, it's next to impossible to talk her out of it. Especially if she believes the idea came from God." He put his hand on Wilson's shoulder. "You've been with the family a long time. I know I can count on you to take care of the situation."

By now, Justin had almost arrived at the steps leading to the terrace. The squire went in the house and Wilson came down to the lawn.

"Is there something I can do for you, Lord Justin?"

Justin squirmed a little inside. Wilson should chastise him for shamelessly listening in, but at least he understood Elena's father better now.

"Uh, yes. You may have noticed I heard some of your conversation."

Wilson waited for him to continue.

"All right. I heard most of it, and to tell you the truth, I had hoped to speak to you for much the same reason. Now I'm intrigued. What punishment do you have planned?"

With a humorless smile, Wilson said, "They'll be mucking out the privies."

Justin grimaced. "That should be effective. I'll leave you to it then."

When Wilson left, he gazed up at the back of the house. Elena chose a room on this side because she loved to gaze at the garden. She might be at the window now. Or maybe stewing in her bed, frustrated over being restricted to her room. He could imagine that to be the case, and liked the idea of her well and irritated rather than sick in bed.

With nothing more to be done, he started the long trek to the front of the house. He rounded the corner in time to see Squire Bishop ushering a man out the door. The man didn't appear at all happy about it and said so in a voice that carried to Justin.

He clapped his hat on his bald head. "Now see here, Bishop. I have every right to be on this property, and I demand to know what's going on."

Justin stopped. What were the odds he'd stumble onto two private conversations, shouted for all to hear, in less than five minutes? When had he signed up to be an actor in a melodrama?

Turn back or go on? His horse waited for him in the drive and once again he stood in plain sight. I'll go on. Squire Bishop might need my help.

"You have no right whatsoever, Higgins." Squire Bishop took the apple-bodied, spindle-legged man by the arm and steered him to his carriage. There he propelled him up to the seat. "I don't want to see you here again."

The man spit and sputtered, his red face causing him to look even more like an apple. "I will be back. You can count on it."

Justin reached the drive, and even though his boots crunched on the gravel, neither man noticed him. "Can I be of assistance?"

Both turned in surprise, but Squire Bishop recovered first. "Lord Justin. Thank you for the offer, but Mr. Higgins is just leaving. There's no need to trouble yourself."

The apple man regarded him through narrowed eyes. "Lord Justin?"

"Yes, yes." Squire Bishop waved his hand in the general direction of the Ramsey estate. "You should remember the Earl's property borders ours."

The man's red face drained of color. "Very well. We'll speak another time." He picked up the reins and slapped them on the horse's back, causing the animal to jerk the carriage forward.

Justin watched it rapidly disappear up the tree-lined drive, before turning to Squire Bishop. The older man also stood watching. When Higgins disappeared around the wall at the end of the drive, the Squire heaved a sigh and his shoulders slumped.

"Is there something I can do to help you, Squire?" He closed the space between them and the man turned to him with a start.

He straightened. "Lord Justin, I'd forgotten you were here."

"Who was that man?"

"No one important. A man I used to play cards with."

"It sounded like he was threatening you."

"I appreciate your concern, but I can handle him." He turned and started up the steps to the door. "Come back tomorrow and see Elena."

Once again Justin had gotten no answers.

He mounted his horse and started home. It appeared the squire planned to take responsibility again. Maybe he'd put an end to this resort as well.

When Justin got home his mother greeted him at the door. The sight of her worry lined face caused a knot to form in his middle.

"A telegram from your brother came an hour ago. They always bring bad news." Her hand trembled as she gave it to him. "It's addressed to you."

CHAPTER THIRTEEN

*P*hineas muttered to himself, as his carriage took him away from Oakwood. Bishop had some nerve treating him that way, lording it over him as if he were a peasant who still lived in the village. He turned, shook his fist in the direction of the house and shouted, "You can't tell me what to do!"

Birds flew up out of the hedgerows. The horse whinnied and reared up on her hind legs. As soon as her front feet hit the ground she took off, throwing Phineas against the seat. He dropped the reins, but scrambled to pick them up again, and pulled back hard. "Slow down, you stupid horse!"

The horse slowed to a stop. Phineas took off his bowler and used his handkerchief to wipe his face and head. His heart knocked painfully against his ribs. Bishop had almost caused him to be killed.

He stuffed the handkerchief in his pocket and got the carriage rolling again. The squire still thought he was better than him, but that would change. It hadn't taken Ronald long to put one of their staff out of commission and fill the opening. With him at the estate things would go from bad to worse.

The information Ronald had given him before he'd even gone to the front door made him smile. The boy and the daughter falling into the spring without any help from his nephew meant the Bishops might cause an end to the resort on their own. Phineas didn't like to take chances, though. Stacking the deck, so to speak, in his favor had always been his practice.

He relaxed into his seat. The daughter was another angle to keep in mind. Next time he came by, he'd try to have a word with her.

Elena retreated to her room, her bare feet making no sound on the thick hall carpet. She carefully closed the door and forced herself to put one foot in front of the other before collapsing in the rocking chair by the window.

She wrapped her mauve, satin dressing gown tighter around her and stared past lace curtains to the ordered flower garden below. It wasn't the garden she focused on, however. A round man waving a walking stick at her father filled her mind's eye.

Her father's raised voice along with that of another man demanding admittance had drawn her from her room to the top of the stairs. The man had pushed his way inside the front door, but Papa hadn't let him in beyond that.

He had a bushy brown mustache and large muttonchops, probably to make up for the lack of hair on top of his head, where a few strands had been combed over the crown. He had little raisin eyes, a bulbous nose and no chin. Elena shuddered.

Her enemy now had a face. A face she hadn't expected to see until the end of the summer. Another chill washed over her and she rubbed her hands up and down her arms, then reached for the tea cozy on the marble-topped occasional table beside her. Fragrant steam rose as she filled her cup. The lump of sugar she dropped in quickly dissolved as she stirred. If only Mr. Higgins would disappear like sugar in hot tea.

The next morning Elena got up, feeling none the worse for her icy plunge in the spring. Thank you again, God, for your gracious mercy. Please bring Noah back to health soon.

She found Papa at one of the tables on the terrace, enjoying scones and lemon curd. It pleased her to find him out here.

"Papa, do you think Mr. Higgins will return? I thought we had until the end of the summer." She bumped the table causing tea to slosh into his saucer. "I'm sorry."

"It's fine. Please join me."

He wiped his mouth with his napkin and took a sip of tea before giving her his attention. "Mr. Higgins has no right to be here before the end of August. However, I can't promise he won't be back." He frowned. "He's not a man of integrity. I'll never be able to apologize enough for what my foolishness has cost us."

"You don't have to——"

Papa held up his hand, stopping her mid-sentence.

"If he comes back and I'm not close, you are to call for Daniel. He'll deal with him."

"All right. He's obviously not a gentleman, but I have to tell you, part of me would like to give him a piece of my mind." She thought for a moment. "I suppose if I did let him know what I think, I wouldn't be acting like a lady."

Papa laughed. "That doesn't stop you from telling Justin what's on your mind."

"You're right. But that's different. We've known each other for ages."

She felt her face warm under Papa's smiling scrutiny. She'd had some strange feelings where Justin was concerned, but that didn't mean she considered him as any more than a friend.

"Good morning. Do you mind if I join you?"

Elena startled and knocked the table, causing tea to slosh across the tablecloth and onto the plate of scones, which rapidly became soggy lumps of dough. She and Papa sprang back and up. Years of practice made them adept at keeping these types of spills off their clothing. Her blush deepened when Justin's hand bumped hers as they reached for the same napkin to mop up the mess.

"You shouldn't sneak up on people like that. It's not nice." It mortified her to think he might have heard them talking about him.

"I wasn't sneaking, and you wouldn't be so testy if I hadn't caught you talking about me."

She dropped her napkin and faced him, hands on hips. He stood with something between a frown and a grin on his face. It was a comical expression, and she couldn't help smiling. For some reason her brain must have turned as mushy as the tea-soaked scones, leaving her without one intelligent word in reply.

Papa cleared his throat, breaking the awkward moment. "Let's move to another table and start over. And yes, Lord Justin, you may join us. It will give me the opportunity to properly thank you for saving my daughter's life."

"No thanks are needed, sir." Justin held her chair for her and then took a seat. "You're looking well, Elena. I'm glad you've recovered so quickly. Did your father tell you I came by yesterday to check on you?"

She turned her gaze on her father, who only shrugged. "No, he didn't. Why didn't you tell me, Papa?"

"I had other things on my mind, and I didn't want to worry you with the thought of him being here to bother you." As soon as the staff had brought refreshments to their new table, Papa, who didn't look the least bit repentant, reached for a scone and clotted cream.

Elena studied him a moment. More and more she was seeing the father she remembered. She turned to Justin. "It's kind of you to check on my welfare. I owe you my thanks for pulling me out.

And I imagine Papa's fears that you still want to stop the resort are groundless. You can see that I'm serious about making a go of it."

"As a matter of fact, this incident only makes me more concerned. You need to stop now before something worse happens." He turned to Papa. "Don't you agree, Squire Bishop?"

Elena's breath caught. What would her father say?

CHAPTER FOURTEEN

*P*apa's eyes locked with Justin's. "Two days ago, I would have been in perfect agreement with you. Now I have a better idea how much this means to Elena, and I've decided to support her."

Elena gasped, then jumped up and threw her arms around his neck. "Thank you, Papa."

He gently pushed her back toward her chair and shook his finger at her. "This doesn't mean I think it will make a difference. And I still don't want to see guests wandering about inside the house."

Her heart swelled to the point of bursting. She used her napkin to dab at the tears trickling down her cheeks and silently thanked God for answered prayers. "Don't worry. Everything will be fine from now on."

Justin huffed out a breath. "You can't guarantee that. No one can."

"You're right, of course, but we can do our best to ensure there are no more accidents."

"I've had a telegram from my brother reminding me of my

duty to keep the neighborhood quiet. I'm sure he wouldn't be pleased with the job I'm doing."

Pressure built inside her like steam in a teapot, but she reminded herself to be a lady, even though she was talking to Justin. "Your brother isn't here. I fail to see how any activity on this side of the ocean will affect him."

"That's not the point." He closed his eyes and rubbed the back of his neck, then focused on her again. "Since day one, there has been nothing but commotion coming from Oakwood."

"I'll admit it has been somewhat loud, but—"

"It's not just the noise. I've also been charged with preserving life, limb and property. There were very nearly two lives lost yesterday. If things continue on as they have been someone won't survive the summer."

A scream, followed by a crash, came from inside the house. The drawing room door flew open and Noah's brothers ran out, eyes wide and faces white.

The cook's ample form soon filled the doorway. She stopped, took a moment to draw in a deep breath, then shook her fist and yelled, "You boys stay out of my kitchen!"

If God had sent the Smiths to test Elena's faith and determination, he couldn't have picked a better family to do it.

Justin had never been so frustrated. That seemed to sum up his state of mind more times than not as he left Oakwood. His horse, sensing his dark mood, tossed his head and sidestepped into a low hanging branch. His new Homburg flew from his head and landed on its top in the muddy ditch.

He swung down from the saddle to retrieve the soft, felt hat. Mud and water dripped off as he lifted it. He gave it a good shake and slapped it back on his head, then patted his horse's sleek, black neck and rubbed the white stripe that ran from nose to ears. "Next time I'll ride my bicycle."

Justin continued home on foot, leading King by the reins. The telegram he'd put in the breast pocket of his jacket burned like a hot coal against his chest. The message was short and to the point. "Spoke to uncle. Post can await you in India."

Richard hadn't even mentioned if the wedding had taken place. He kicked a stone and sent it flying up the road. His brother obviously had no faith in his ability to take care of things here. The toe of his boot met another rock with a satisfying thwack.

The sun beat down on his slumped shoulders as he trudged along. He had to admit, Elena had turned out to be a lot more difficult than he'd imagined. She was holding on to her resort idea with the tenacity of a bulldog. He couldn't figure it out. In the past, she'd almost always give in and do things his way. Why was this so important to her?

He stopped and sniffed. "Why do I smell ditch water?" His stallion snorted and bumped his hat over his eyes. Oh yes. He pushed it back up and plodded on home.

Send the people home.

A chill crept up Elena's spine as she reread the note that had come with more reservation requests. Nothing on the envelope gave a clue to the sender's identity. The note implied a threat. Mr. Higgins came immediately to mind, but why would he be anonymous when he had already come to the house bold as you please?

She slid the note under the pile of requests on the desk and went in search of Papa. Elena found him in quiet conversation with a woman, who appeared to be about Papa's age, as they came down the staircase to the main floor. The lady was of medium height, had an abundant amount of auburn hair piled up on her head and a sturdy build. Not slender or heavy, sturdy.

When they reached the bottom, Papa saw her and grinned. "Elena, this is Mrs. Turner. She has offered to help with Noah's care. Isn't that wonderful?"

Elena turned to the woman, whose smile made her hazel eyes sparkle. "I hope you don't mind, Miss Bishop. My nephew felt obligated to bring me on holiday, along with his family. They don't need my help and as I have some experience with nursing, I hoped I could be of some use."

"You're a gift from God." Her stiff muscles relaxed a bit as she held out her right hand.While one of the maids showed Mrs. Turner to her room, Elena linked arms with Papa and led him back toward the study. "You appear happier these days."

"I feel a new sense of purpose. I've been brooding in my selfish world for far too long." He patted her hand and gave her a wink. "And once the mud settled I had a drink from the spring. I'd forgotten how refreshing that water is."

"And maybe you're starting to sense God in your life again."

His smile faded, and he glanced away. "Maybe."

When they reached the study, Elena retrieved the note and handed it to Papa. "What do you make of this?"

He patted his pockets, searching for the spectacles perched on top of his head. When he realized where they were he put them on and frowned as he read, then put the glasses back where he found them. "Higgins seems a likely suspect. He's the only one I know of, other than Lord Justin, who would have an objection to your project." Papa slapped the note against the palm of his hand. "I imagine he expects us to be intimidated into giving up."

"Ha. He doesn't know me very well and he certainly doesn't know God. We will not be deterred by a bully."

"You're right. He doesn't know whom he's taking on. It probably wouldn't hurt, though, to have the men take turns watching the grounds during the night. I'll have a word with Wilson."

He handed her the note and left the room. She crossed to the window and pulled aside the heavy lace drapery. The approach to the house had always appeared inviting to her. Oak trees lined the long drive providing a shady ride from the road. The drive flowed into a circle in front of the house, making it convenient for a carriage to come to a stop at the entrance.

A fountain, in the center of the circle, sat within multiple rings of red begonias. Water bubbled up from the small round basin at the top and spilled in a curtain down to the larger basin under it, and on into the basin at the bottom. It was then drawn up to the top to repeat the cycle. As a girl she'd been fascinated with where the endless supply of water came from and calmed by the never-ceasing sound of a quiet rain shower.

She sat in the window seat with a sigh and leaned her forehead against the glass. Circles within circles. Life had been going on here, for the Bishops, for over four hundred years. Father passed the land on to son time after time. Would she be the one to break the cycle?

CHAPTER FIFTEEN

a week later, the note still lurked in the study. Elena strolled in the fragrant garden and tried to make some sense of it. She had no idea what it threatened, and so didn't know what to watch for. Families enjoyed their week and left as new ones arrived. Things appeared as they should, but she found herself peering around corners and jumping at every unfamiliar sound.

"Elena, I've been looking for you."

She gasped, whirled around and fell against Justin's chest. She struggled to right herself, but he easily set her on her feet. Just as he always had. She couldn't prevent the thrill that shot through her when she gazed into his dark blue eyes. A small frown creased his brow.

"What's wrong? Has something else happened? You have dark smudges under your eyes."

Her hands flew to her face, and then went just as quickly to rest in fists on her hips. "Thank you for noticing. However, it's not the resort that's wearing on me. I just haven't been sleeping well."

His face softened and he reached for her hands. "Something else *is* bothering you. Why won't you let me help?"

Justin had been her rescuer for as long as she could remember.

She counted on him, trusted him. He stood here now, holding her hands and gazing into her eyes. It felt so right. If only she could tell him the real reason for all of this. But no, Papa had asked her not to tell anyone. Unless…

She bit her lip as she considered. "Let's talk in the gazebo."

As soon as they were seated, Elena began. "I can't share the reason for the resort, but I can tell you someone other than you is unhappy about it. We received a note saying we should send the people home. That's it. There's no clue who it might be from."

Justin gripped her hand. "That sounds like a threat."

"So far, nothing unusual has happened. I don't know what to guard against. Maybe if you help keep an eye out, we'll get to the bottom of it."

He closed his eyes for a few seconds, then gazed into hers. "I don't like anything about this. Since I've been home I've noticed a difference between us. I don't understand it, but I know, more than ever, I don't want anything to happen to you."

Elena swallowed past the lump in her throat. "I've sensed it, too, and I don't want anything to happen to me or our guests, either. The problem is we need to continue on. As for your brother, the families should be gone by the time he comes home."

"I'm no longer certain he'll wait until the end of the summer."

"Why has the state of the neighborhood taken on such importance to him? I can't remember him being concerned before now." She paused then frowned. "He isn't blackmailing you, is he? I remember him doing that once when we were children. I can't think now what it was about, but he had something unpleasant hanging over your head if you didn't follow his orders."

Justin stood, stepped to the edge of the gazebo and focused on the coral-bells in the flowerbed next to them. "You know Richard. He can be quite insistent when he sets his mind on something."

"You're not telling me everything."

He gave her a wry grin and shrugged his shoulders. "This is something Richard and I have agreed on together."

Elena raised her hands, palms up, and let them drop. "Then I guess we're right where we started, other than the matter we spoke of. You might not need to be here every day, though."

"In the times I've been here so far, I've either witnessed a disaster, or rescued someone from one. I'd think you'd be glad to have me around."

She squirmed inside. It was the annoying truth, but if she gave even a little ground, he'd take more, until everything was the way he wanted it in the first place. She lifted her chin. "I believe I've already expressed my thanks for the rescue. Now if you'll excuse me, I need to check on Noah."

"Fine." He stepped to the side as she stood, allowing her room to pass. "I think I'll have a look around to make sure there are no disasters in the making."

"Fine." Without giving him another glance, she stepped with a little more force than necessary toward the house. His footsteps crunched in the opposite direction until she heard the firm close of the gate. She slowed and took a quick peek over her shoulder. He was gone.

Justin realized he was striding in quick time toward the tents and forced himself to slow down and take in the view before him. Over half the colorful tents were occupied this week. Families were in evidence everywhere. Parents and children batted a badminton birdie back and forth over a net. Some strolled across the park toward the spring and others read or played games on blankets spread on the grass.

Happy voices called out to each other and croquet mallets whacked against balls. He narrowed his eyes and observed more closely. It appeared tranquil now, but things had a way of happening when least expected.

"That's enough," boomed Mr. Smith.

Justin jumped and saw the same startled reaction from others. All activity ceased for several moments, then some began to mutter, and others shook their heads and laughed good-naturedly. Soon everyone returned to what they'd been doing.

Amazing. These people seemed to accept Mr. Smith's jarring interruption as part of a relaxing week in the country.

Elena's face came to mind and he sat on one of the benches scattered around the park for the guests' convenience. Her lovely eyes hid a troubling secret. Something she couldn't let him help with. But…what? Did it have to do with the man he'd seen the squire arguing with? But how could the resort and that ill-tempered fellow be connected.

Warmth filled him at the thought of her hands in his. He wanted to see the dimple in her cheek when she smiled and hear her light-hearted laugh. An overwhelming urge rose inside him to protect her. He wanted to make everything all right, but how? The one thing Justin did know with certainty was that if this resort continued, he'd be on his way to India.

Movement at one of the unoccupied tents, located along the outside edge, drew his attention. A young man squatted at one of the stakes, fiddling with the rope. Justin stood, put his hands in his pockets and ambled in that direction. His arrival went unnoticed until the toes of his shoes came into the lad's line of vision on either side of the stake. The hands stilled, and wide brown eyes, in a chalky, white face, slowly rose from the hem of his trousers until their gazes met.

CHAPTER SIXTEEN

*H*e let go of the rope and fell with a thump on his backside. His mouth opened and closed like a fish out of water, but no sound came out. He appeared to be around twelve-years-old.

Justin offered him a hand and pulled him to his feet. "Are you a guest here?"

He nodded. "I didn't mean anything wrong. I'm just interested in how the knots are tied. Me Mum told me I better quit working on the ropes of our tent. She said she didn't want it falling down on her head."

"So you thought you'd try it here, where no one would complain if the tent fell."

"Yes, sir." He hung his head and straight brown hair swung forward, covering his face like a curtain. He took a step back. "I should get going. Me Mum'll be worried where I've gotten to."

He took another step and turned, preparing to run. Justin clamped a hand on the boy's shoulder and spoke to the back of his head. "If you want to see how the knots are tied, I suggest you ask one of the male staff. They won't be happy if they have to set tents back up."

His head bobbed up and down double time. "Yes, sir. Thank you, sir."

Justin released him and the boy took off, making a beeline for the center of the tent city. The rope and stake appeared secure, but it occurred to Justin, it wouldn't hurt to check all the stakes along this side.

He patted himself on the back, as he made his inspection. Elena didn't know how lucky she was to have him here. Another calamity had been averted, thanks to him.

Elena stopped in the doorway to Noah's room. He stayed awake a little more each day and the doctor was encouraged with his progress, but right now he slept. A male and female voice murmured together. She looked for the source, and her mouth fell open. Papa and Mrs. Turner sat next to each other in side chairs facing one of the bedroom's windows. They both smiled as they carried on a companionable conversation.

She stepped out of the doorway, and leaned against the wall, hands pressed flat on either side of her. Her heart pounded in her chest as if she'd been caught in some mischief. But that was silly. Papa wouldn't care if she saw him talking to Mrs. Turner. As a matter of fact, it was about time he noticed a woman again.

A deep breath helped to calm her. Once steady, she pushed away from the wall and stepped into the bedroom.

Papa saw her and stood. He assisted Mrs. Turner to her feet, then escorted her to where Elena stood. "You just missed the doctor's morning visit. He feels it should only be another week or two until Noah will be well enough to travel. Isn't that wonderful?"

Her face relaxed into a smile. "You've been a good nurse, Mrs. Turner.

The lady's cheeks turned pink. "I'm happy to do what I can,

but the good Lord has more to do with it than me. Noah's mother has been here as much as she can, too. I know that makes a difference."

"Just the same, we've appreciated your help and generous spirit."

"You're very kind. Just think, soon you'll have everyone out of the house, and out from under foot."

Papa harrumphed. "We don't need to worry about that right now."

Rosie paused in the doorway. "Excuse me, Mr. Bishop, Miss Elena. You asked me to let you know when the post arrived."

Papa held his elbow out toward Elena. "Shall we?"

She smiled and took his arm as they started for the corridor. At the doorway, they stopped and turned back to Mrs. Turner. "I'll come by at noon," her father said, "to see if you're able to accompany me to the terrace for lunch."

Mrs. Turner smiled and lifted a hand in farewell. Elena's gut clenched. What was going on? Okay, just a few minutes earlier she'd told herself he should be interested in other women. It had been ten years, after all. But the idea of someone taking her mother's place just didn't feel right.

She glanced at him as they descended the stairs. The changes were undeniable. A smile lit his face and he even hummed under his breath. This was the man she'd known and loved as her father ten years ago. No doubt Mrs. Turner was, at least in part, responsible for it. Elena only hoped he didn't plan to have her stay on in the house after Noah left.

The post lay on a silver tray on the hall table in the entryway. Papa gathered it up and they proceeded to the study to sit at the desk; he behind it and she across from him. A spring wound tighter and tighter inside of her, as she tried to work up the courage to say something. He picked up the first of many envelopes and reached for the letter opener.

"Wait."

He froze and met her eyes.

She twisted her hands together in her lap. "I believe there is something you might want to consider."

He laid down the envelope and studied her with concern. "What is it, Elena? I don't think I've ever seen you in such a state."

"It's nothing really." She flapped her hand back and forth as if shooing away a triviality. "I'm concerned about Mrs. Turner."

Papa crossed his arms on the desktop and leaned toward her. "Why, exactly?"

His tone made her blush. Who was she to be telling Papa anything? But, now that she'd started she needed to finish. "It seems to me you may be thinking she should stay in the house even after Noah leaves. I'm afraid that will give our other guests the wrong idea. We'll want to be careful of her reputation."

"I'm aware of how to conduct myself with propriety. You have enough to concern yourself. Please don't add Mrs. Turner or me to your list of worries. Now may we get on with it?"

She leaned over and scooped half the envelopes toward her.

Time ticked by as they went through the requests. It shouldn't be long before all the tents were filled. Her grumbling stomach let her know it was almost time for lunch, when Papa opened the last envelope. His eyes widened and then narrowed as he read.

She jumped up and came around to read over his shoulder. Another anonymous note. "You should have sent the people home."

CHAPTER SEVENTEEN

*E*lena's voice shook. "What do you think it means?" She returned to her chair, her knees weak.

Squire Bishop tossed the note on the desk and rubbed his eyes. "I don't know. But it wouldn't hurt to send a letter to the authorities in Brighton, letting them know about the threats."

Elena took a steadying breath and came to stand by Papa again. She put a hand on his shoulder. "I think we should pray."

"I think we need to tell the staff to be even more watchful, especially at night."

"Prayer first."

He smiled and covered her hand with his. "Okay. Prayer first."

Elena asked God to protect the people and show her and Papa what to watch for. As soon as she said amen, Papa left the room. She leaned on the doorjamb and watched him head toward the back of the house. It looked as though Mrs. Turner would have to wait for Papa's return. It was good to see where his priorities lay.

"Thank you again, dear Jesus, for bringing Papa back to life." She pushed away from the doorframe and went to the terrace for lunch.

Early the next morning, Elena had a vivid dream of someone's hand on her shoulder, shaking her, and calling her name. She tried to roll away, but it wouldn't let her go.

Finally, she recognized Papa's voice. "Elena, wake up."

Her eyes popped open and in the dim morning light she saw Papa standing beside the bed holding a candle. He hadn't taken the time to tie his robe shut over his nightshirt or brush down the hair that stuck out on one side of his head.

She struggled to sit up. "What is it, Papa?"

"There's been mischief during the night. Get dressed and meet me downstairs."

"Oh, no. What happened?" She was talking to an empty room.

She pulled a skirt and blouse on over her nightgown and made quick work of lacing up her high shoes. Her hair was already in a thick braid, which bumped against her back as she hurried.

Mrs. Campbell met her when she got to the main floor and directed her to the terrace. Papa waited at the wall overlooking the garden. His focus went beyond that, however, to the line of tents closest to them. She followed his gaze and gasped.

The rosy glow of sunrise clearly showed what Elena didn't want to believe. The last three tents on the right end had been knocked down and waded into a huge ball. Stakes stuck out like pins in a pincushion. She sagged against Papa and he put a supporting arm around her waist.

It took a few moments to process the sight before her, then she said, "Thank goodness no one occupied those tents. No one was hurt."

"None of the guests, anyway. But thanks to whoever did this, Tommy now has a lump on his head. Bill found him inside the tool shed, tied up and gagged."

Her spine stiffened and adrenalin surged through her. Fists clenched, she stepped away from Papa with, "Where is he now? Is he all right?"

"He's in his quarters. He'll be fine." Papa nodded in the direction of the vandalism. "Do you want to have a closer look?"

"Yes." She turned and they proceeded down the steps and along the walk that would take them to the tent disaster. When they got there, she planted her fists on her hips, and stared. The wad of canvas, ropes and stakes could be considered a work of art. The large ball was smooth and symmetrical, while the ropes criss-crossed in a diamond pattern. Even the stakes were placed at even intervals.

A shudder ran through her. Whoever did this enjoyed his work. Would the person responsible use as much creativity if he decided to harm one of their guests?

Wilson arrived with some of the men and they went right to work loosening the ropes. "We'll have this untangled and put back to rights in no time, Sir."

"Excellent, Wilson. Please send word to the house when you're done."

If the guests see this mess they'll wonder what's going on, and maybe begin to worry. Elena bit her lip against the urge to tell the men to hurry. Wilson said they'd have it done quickly, and she needed to leave them to it.

"Any thoughts on who might have done this?"

"No. It was masterfully done, though, wasn't it? I have to wonder at his state of mind."

"It concerns me that he would hurt anyone to make his point."

She tripped and Papa grabbed her arm to steady her, then tucked her hand in the crook of his elbow. "I believe it would be prudent to call an end to the resort. We don't want to chance anyone else getting hurt."

Elena stopped, bringing Papa to a halt with her. She gave his arm a squeeze. "Are you going to be supportive or not?"

He opened his mouth to respond, but she went on. "I don't want anyone else to get hurt, either. Especially any of our staff. They are our family and a large part of the reason I'm trying to save the estate. We're not the only ones in danger of losing our home."

Papa patted her hand where it rested on his arm and tugged her forward again. "We don't know that the staff would be asked to leave. Mr. Higgins may want to keep them."

"I doubt that very much. I believe Mr. Higgins to be a mean-spirited man."

Papa didn't reply to that and they finished their walk without further conversation. The racket the early morning birds made in the trees filled the void, and by the time they reached the house, Elena heard the sound of hammer on stake. Wilson was as good as his word.

Ronald whistled while he threw straw down on the floor in one of the horse stalls. He'd created a masterpiece out of those tents. Even though he knew his uncle wouldn't agree, he hoped the Bishops wouldn't be scared into quitting too soon. He'd enjoy creating some more mischief, and if people got hurt...

CHAPTER EIGHTEEN

"Whatever is the matter, Justin? You've been in a sour mood since your brother left."

Justin cast a sidelong glance at his mother. The peacock blue of her hat and matching walking dress heightened the color of her eyes. He liked it when her eyes twinkled and smiled at him. Now they were filled with concern.

The breeze carried laughter and good-natured shouting to them, where they strolled in their garden. He sighed and let his shoulders droop a little. What could he say? That he wanted to go to America, but because of Elena's resort, Richard would make him go to India instead? That sounded like tattling, and at any rate, he wasn't supposed to mention their agreement.

Before he could come up with a reply, his mother continued. "I've been missing my sister lately and have decided to pay her a visit. I'll expect you to accompany me, as I believe it would do you good to get out of the neighborhood for a while. It won't be for more than a fortnight."

The number of things that could go wrong in two weeks' time spun through his head, leaving him dizzy. He stopped and focused on his mother. "I can't leave. Richard wants me to watch over things here. Elena could get in trouble again."

She tilted her head back to look at him through narrowed eyes. "What is it, exactly, that Richard wants from you?"

He tried for a casual laugh. "Oh, well, you know, make sure the neighborhood is quiet and in order when he returns with his bride and her family."

"And what will happen if it's not?"

He swallowed hard. It was tempting to tell her of Richard's threat to send him to India. She seemed to suspect something, anyway, and maybe she could intervene for him. He took a moment to consider, then did a mental head shake. At his age he shouldn't be hiding behind his mother's skirts, and he'd given Richard his word. He couldn't tell her.

"I suppose we'll have to deal with Richard's disappointment." He let his smile fade. "There is still the matter of Elena's safety."

She chuckled and patted his arm. "Elena has her father and staff to keep an eye on her. The two of you haven't gotten on well this summer, anyway. It would probably be a good idea to put some distance between you. We'll plan to leave tomorrow."

She chattered on about the trip for the rest of their walk. The animation in her voice and glow on her face were evidence of her excitement to see his Aunt Connie again. His mother had never gone anywhere unless accompanied by her husband or one of her sons, so there was no point continuing his objections.

When he got to the house, he found Martin and told him to pack his bags, then went to the study. A large globe, set in a mahogany stand, stood at the far corner of the desk. He rotated it until the North American continent came to rest under his finger-tips. Justin closed his eyes and prayed, "Dear God. I know you want me to go to the United States. Watch over things here for me while I'm gone. And please keep Elena safe. Amen." He gave the globe a spin and left the room.

Elena stood at the terrace wall and observed their tent community. There had been no more artwork that week. Most likely because of the extra staff patrolling the area. She wanted to believe whoever did it had had their fun and would leave them alone.

Another bright spot came a few days earlier in the form of a message from Justin saying he wouldn't be over to bother her for a while. If she were honest with herself, she'd have to admit she missed him a little. She huffed out a breath. He had his nerve telling her to stay out of trouble, though. Did he think she couldn't survive without him?

Turning, she saw Papa come out the door with Mrs. Turner. He held out his elbow and she linked her arm through his. He had to be telling her a story, because he was doing all the talking, while she gazed up at him and nodded or said, "Not really." When they stopped walking on the garden path and laughed at what must have been the funniest thing Papa had ever said, she realized they'd gone right by without seeing her. And here she stood continuing to stare at them like an impolite child.

She swallowed the lump in her throat and went back to the house. I want him to be happy, but... She didn't know how to finish the thought. What was her problem, anyway?

In the study, reservation requests, lists, ledgers and bills covered most of the desktop in a kind of organized chaos. Papa knew exactly where everything was, except his spectacles, and what needed to be done and when, but she preferred neat and tidy. It was hard to think amidst clutter. However, there was work to be done and she'd best get to it.

"Excuse me, Miss Bishop."

Elena saw Mrs. Turner standing in the doorway, then glanced at the clock on the mantel, surprised to see she'd been working for an hour.

"It appears you're busy. I can come back later."

It was tempting to let her leave, but instead she said, "No, no. Come in." Elena got up and led the way to a couple of upholstered chairs situated near one of the windows. "Please have a seat. Would you like some tea?"

Mrs. Turner sank into one of the burgundy silk armchairs, flipped open a fan and waved it with enough energy to blow around the wisps of hair framing her face. "Tea would be lovely. Thank you."

Elena went to a bell pull to summon one of the maids, then joined the older woman. Rosie soon made an appearance and tea and biscuits were requested. She turned to give her attention to Mrs. Turner, who had stopped fanning and was now fiddling with the ribbon wrist loop.

The usually calm, composed lady appeared nervous. Elena couldn't imagine why, until she thought of Noah. She tried to keep panic out of her voice. "Is there a problem with the Smith boy?"

Mrs. Turner shook her head. "Oh, no. He's doing better every day. I should think he'd soon be well enough for the family to stay on and enjoy the rest of the summer."

The tension in the back of her neck and shoulders didn't relax. She wanted Noah to be well, but well at home. Not here. "I'm glad his health continues to improve. I would imagine the family would be ready for their own beds, though."

"You're right, I'm sure. I know I've enjoyed sleeping in a bed, rather than a cot." She flipped open her fan again and proceeded to create a breeze strong enough to blow the wisps of hair back and keep them there. "It's so kind of you and your father to allow me to help."

Her curiosity overcame her reluctance to talk to the woman who had captured Papa's attention. "It was kind of you to offer, and we appreciate your help. Is there something you wish to discuss, Mrs. Turner?"

"As a matter of fact, here's the tea."

"I beg your pardon."

"The tea is here," she said, pointing her fan toward the young woman approaching them with a tray.

When she'd set it on the mosaic-topped table between their chairs and taken her leave, Elena poured tea and handed it to Mrs. Turner. Before she could offer biscuits to the lady, she'd drained her cup and held it out for more.

Elena's eyebrows shot up, but she willed them to come right back down. "My goodness. You must have been thirsty." She set the plate on the table and refilled the cup. This time she kept an eye on her guest to see if she'd need another immediate refill. When Mrs. Turner seemed to be sipping, rather than gulping, Elena filled her own cup and relaxed a bit.

"I apologize. I'm not in the habit of drinking so fast. The tea is quite bracing, though." She reached over and picked out a strawberry shortbread biscuit from the selection on the plate. "Umm. Something else I've enjoyed while being here is the food that comes out of your kitchen."

"I'll pass your compliment on to Mrs. Harris." She set her cup and saucer on the table and waited until Mrs. Turner was finished eating. When the lady reached for another biscuit, Elena's toe started tapping. She forced herself to be still and held back the sigh that tried to escape.

Several biscuits and two cups of tea later, Mrs. Turner set her cup on the table and leaned back in her chair. "Thank you, Miss Bishop. That was refreshing."

"You're welcome." She leaned toward her guest. "You said you had something you want to discuss."

"Oh, yes. You see ———"

"There you are, Candice. Our picnic basket is ready and the carriage waits at the front door."

Elena's mouth fell open. Papa and Mrs. Turner were on a first name basis? From the corner of her eye she saw Mrs. Turner smile at Papa and turn to her with an apologetic expression. She closed her mouth.

"Hello, Elena. It was nice of you to have Candice for tea." He held out his hand to assist Mrs. Turner to her feet. "I hope you saved room for lunch." He tucked her hand through his arm and winked at Elena. "We'll see you at supper time."

She watched them leave the room, then wilted into the chair. What had Mrs. Turner come to tell her? It surely had something to do with Papa. Would he have proposed without telling her? And why would he do that if he were so certain he'd have no place to live by the end of the summer?

CHAPTER NINETEEN

*E*lena was probably reading too much into the situation. A walk with a change of view should help, and their long, tree-lined drive was just the thing. The dappled shade felt good on this warm day. Birds sang to each other in the trees, and the voices of happy guests drifted to her ears on the breeze.

A bicycle bell rang and she looked up in time to see a telegram delivery boy hurtling toward her. His eyes went wide when he saw her. Fine gravel and dust flew as he swerved and brought the bicycle to a stop. He laid it down and hurried over to her.

"I'm sorry about that, Miss. I wasn't expecting to see anyone in the drive. I didn't scare you, did I?"

Elena took in the boy's flushed, dust-covered face. He couldn't be any more than thirteen years old. He wrung his hands and watched her with wide eyes.

"I'm fine, thanks to your skill in handling that machine."

"I'm considered to be one of the best, Miss." The boy puffed out his chest and hooked his thumbs under the suspenders holding up his knickers.

"I believe it. Would it be safe to assume you were in such a hurry, because you have a telegram to deliver?"

"Oh. Right. I almost forgot." He whipped off his cap to wipe his forehead with his sleeve, and a shock of white blond hair fell over one eye. He brushed it away and plopped the cap back on his head. The bike was righted and he was back on it with no break in his stream of conversation. "The boss is always telling me I shouldn't stand around running my yap. I'll just be on my way up to the house."

He took off, throwing gravel up from his back wheel. Elena turned to shield her face, then watched him ride to the front of the house. He could have given her the telegram and saved himself the ride, but she didn't have a chance to offer. It was probably his duty to take it to the house, and since he was one of the best, he'd do his duty.

She turned to continue her walk, and before long the chinging of the bicycle bell sounded behind her. She stepped into the grass as he sped by, his jacket flapping behind him. Their brief contact brought a smile.

The relative quiet returned when the boy disappeared around the corner at the end of the drive. She resumed her stroll to the stone wall that marked the front of the estate. A pool of sunshine beckoned beyond the last oak tree at the end of the drive. She stood in the center of it and closed her eyes. Warmth washed over her, filling her with tranquility.

Meadowlark and red-winged blackbirds called to each other, bringing a flood of fond memories from childhood summers. She took a deep breath of sun-warmed air. The bramble roses climbing over the length of the wall smelled heavenly. Thank you, God, for allowing me to experience these things and for your plan to keep us here.

A horse and carriage approached, and came to a stop, intruding on her moment of peace. Her eyes snapped open when a man's voice said, "Excuse me. Would you be Miss Bishop?"

The man wore a top hat, which he took off when she turned his way, and inclined his head in her direction. Warmth left her in an instant. She stared at the man she'd seen shaking a walking stick at Papa and swallowed hard. Papa's instructions to call for help if Mr. Higgins were to show his face again would do no good from this distance.

She watched his round body climb from the carriage and walk toward her. Instinct told her to run, but her feet wouldn't budge. Oh, Lord. Please tell me what to say and do.

He smiled as he approached, but his narrowed eyes seemed to be assessing her mental faculties. He stopped in front of her, hat in hand. "Are you quite all right? You look as though you've had a bit too much sun."

His breath made her eyes water. The man must live on garlic and onions. At least the odor served to unlock her feet and her tongue. She backed up a few steps and planted her fists on her hips. "Mr. Higgins, I believe my father made it clear you're not welcome here."

"So, you are Miss Bishop."

He slowly eyed her from head to foot and licked his lips. "You're a lovely little thing. Maybe your father and I can come to an arrangement."

Elena had no trouble comprehending his meaning. The thought made her nauseous. She shook her head. "There will be no arrangement, Mr. Higgins. Now I'll thank you to get in your carriage and go back to where ever it is you come from."

The smile never left his face. "Ah, feisty, are we? I think I can handle that."

He put his hat on and took a step toward her. "There are some questions I'd like answered, before I go anywhere." He nodded toward the house. "For instance, what have you got going on in the back half of the estate?"

She crossed her arms over her chest and glared. "It's none of your concern."

His smile disappeared and he stepped closer. "I believe it is my concern. This property will soon be mine, and I don't want what-ever activity it is to ruin it."

She stood her ground, in spite of the noxious fumes he expelled. "As you said, you don't own this property now, God will-ing, you never will. This conversation is over. I insist you leave at once."

His little raisin eyes bored into hers for what seemed an eter-nity, before he turned and left. She didn't move until he climbed back in his carriage and headed down the road. Strength left her then, and she folded onto the ground in a heap.

Her hands trembled as she pushed strands of hair away from her face. How had Papa ever become involved with such an odious man? Thank you, Lord, for being with me.

Elena got to her feet and hurried to the house, taking care not to trip and fall. She wanted the front door between her and that awful experience.

Once inside, she leaned on the door and breathed a sigh of relief. God helped her handle the situation, but she had no desire to do it again. The bravado she'd felt a few weeks ago, about giving him a piece of her mind, had deserted her when faced with a real opportunity.

She pushed away from the door and started toward the stairs. The telegram that came earlier caught her eye on the hall table. Elena picked up the envelope, expecting to find Papa's name on it, but it was hers. She'd never received a telegram before. Who could possibly have reason to send her one now?

The best way to find out was to open it. Standing and staring at the envelope would tell her nothing. She carefully lifted the flap and pulled out the fold of paper. Her eyes went to the bottom first. Warmth rushed up her fingers and settled as a tingling in her heart at the sight of Justin's name. Her face relaxed into a smile. How sweet of him to think of her while he was gone.

Her smile disappeared when she read the short message. "I'll be home soon. Stay out of trouble."

She tossed the paper on the table and turned for the stairs. Is that the only thing he knows how to say, "Stay out of trouble?" Really, he could be quite insufferable. She managed just fine without him this morning, didn't she? Her steps slowed. Still, it would have been nice if he'd been there.

She went back and stared at it. If nothing else it showed he was thinking of her. She picked it up and slid it into her skirt pocket. It was her first telegram, after all.

Phineas seethed. He'd been sent packing by another Bishop. He slapped the reins across the horse's rump and she broke into a gallop. Miss High and Mighty thought he'd left because she told him to. Ha! He'd left because it suited him.

Anger surged from his middle, building pressure and sending tension to every part of his body. No woman told him what to do. Not even his dear old mother, who thought so highly of the Bishops. They might have provided for her, but he had no doubt it was just to appease a guilty conscience. If the squire hadn't sent Phineas' father to prison, she wouldn't have needed taking care of.

His head pounded, and his grip on the reins made his knuckles ache. He forced himself to relax and slowed the horse's speed as he settled back in the seat. There was no cause to be upset. The Bishops had no idea where their troubles were coming from or that they would get worse.

He rolled his shoulders to release more of the tension and recalled Miss Bishop's fine physical form. She truly was a vision to behold. A different sort of pressure began to build. He'd give her the opportunity to stay on her precious estate, if she'd marry him when he took it over at the end of August. Of course, Squire Bishop would have to go. That thought brought a rare smile.

CHAPTER TWENTY

*T*hey wouldn't have enough money. No matter how many times Elena added the figures in the ledger, the outcome was the same. They needed more income.

Two of the maids passed by the open study door, chatting about an upcoming trip to Brighton Pier. Their voices bubbled with excitement.

That's it! For an extra fee, they could offer a trip to Brighton, once a week. Thank you, Lord.

She opened a drawer and pulled out paper and pen. She'd need to add that to their advertising. If she hurried, it could go with Luke when he went in for the supplies. It wouldn't take long for him to make an extra stop at Mr. Atwood's office. He was a wonderful help in this area.

Justin paced the length of his aunt's drawing room. The latest report regarding the situation at Oakwood should have been here by now. Fortunately, one of the stable hands at Oakwood was cousin to one of their footmen. He hated to stoop to spying, but

Elena left him no choice. She wasn't forthcoming and he needed to keep an eye on her.

He stopped in front of the window facing the front lawn. No one in sight. The drive remained as empty as every other time he'd checked. He ran his hands through his hair, then let them drop to his sides. When he'd heard about the tents being knocked down he had wanted to go straight back. The boy he'd stopped earlier came to mind, but the lad didn't seem as though he had the intelligence to create the mess they'd found.

He shook his head and resumed pacing. Just one more week and they'd go back. He'd try again to reason with her.

The beeping of a car horn cut into his thoughts. He went to the window in time to see his cousin and her friend, Lady Howell, drive by. If he didn't have to wait there for his message, he'd find somewhere else to be.

Lilian had been talking non-stop over the past week about this friend who would be perfect for him. No amount of explaining that he wasn't interested in finding someone would discourage her. As soon as her friend returned to her country home she'd bring her around.

He scanned the room and spotted a wingback chair by the fire-place with its back to the door. He dropped into it just as the girls came in.

"I'm sure he's around here somewhere, Iris. I've told him all about you and I know he's looking forward to meeting you."

"I don't know if I can agree with that, Lilian. If he's here he must be hiding."

He grimaced. He should have grabbed a book before he sat down. At least then it wouldn't be so obvious that Lady Howell was right.

"Yoo hoo, Justin. Are you in here?"

He sat still as a statue. There was a *slight* chance they might go away. The girl's skirts swished as they entered the room, but their feet made no sound on the thick Persian carpet. It wasn't until the flowery aroma of Lilian's perfume tickled his nose that he knew he was found. He gazed up into a round, smiling face framed in dark ringlets. "Hello, Lilian."

"Ha. I knew you'd be in here. You've practically lived in this room all week."

"Does it seem that way? I suppose I should get out more." He stood and faced the ladies, focusing on the young woman beside his cousin. She had glossy blond hair, a heart-shaped face, and blue eyes that twinkled with amusement.

Her smile widened when her eyes met his. "You're right, Lilian. He is handsome."

He lifted an eyebrow at Lilian, but she just laughed and said, "Justin, may I present Lady Iris Howell. She and I have been great friends these last two years. And this," she said, turning back to Iris, "is the handsome Justin Ramsey."

He ignored Lilian, took the hand Lady Howell offered him, and gave it a gentle squeeze. "It's nice to meet you."

"Come out with us." Lilian linked her arm through his. "You have to see Iris's motor car."

"I've only had it a month. Papa gave it to me for my birthday. I'm not to drive it too often, but Lilian talked me into bringing it over today."

"It didn't take much talking."

Lady Howell laughed. "She's right. I don't need much excuse to drive it."

"Regardless of the circumstance, I'm glad you brought it." Justin held out his free arm to Lady Howell. She took it and the three of them went outside.

When Justin and the girls arrived, they found his mother and aunt sitting in the vehicle, with his aunt holding the wheel. The ladies relaxed against dark red, leather seats and gazed through the windscreen, as though on a drive through the country.

Justin couldn't help laughing. "Where are you and Aunt Connie going, Mother?"

They turned and watched the young people as they strolled to the driver's side of the car. His aunt ran her hand over the shiny, cream-colored side. "These are marvelous machines. I hope to drive one someday."

"And, I'm sure you will."

"Don't patronize me, Josephine. You know I always accomplish what I set my mind to." She reached over and squeezed the horn's bulb twice for emphasis. The loud blats startled three of the estate's strutting peacocks into flight. They squawked until they were out of sight.

When Justin and the ladies recovered from their surprise they laughed until tears ran down their cheeks. Justin drew in a deep breath and let it go. The laughter had been what he needed to release the tension building inside him.

His mother and aunt got out of the car, and his aunt claimed his arm. "I'm glad to see you out here, instead of inside wearing a path in my drawing room carpet. And since it's such a lovely day I propose we go to the back terrace for tea."

Justin glanced back at the drive. Still empty. "That's a wonderful idea, but if you don't mind, I'd like to have a look at the car first."

"All right, dear. Don't be long."

Lady Howell gestured to the interior. "Have a seat, Mr. Ramsey. My father says the best way to get the feel for it is from the inside."

He stepped up on the running board and slid behind the wheel. One of his school friends had an auto similar to this. He'd been talked into driving it once. It was exhilarating and frightening at the same time. A horse was much easier to control, less likely to stop for no apparent reason, or refuse to start in the first place. He hadn't asked for another opportunity.

"Well, what do you think?" Lady Howell got into the passenger seat and beamed at him. "Isn't it wonderful?"

She pointed out the features leaning into and over him as she described how the pedals and levers worked. He pressed himself against the seat to avoid contact with her arm and shoulder. When that didn't work, he considered sliding out of the car altogether, but then she sat back in her seat and observed him with shining eyes.

"You can see the motor if you'd like." She grabbed his arm with both hands. "You simply must take it for a drive. I will take it as a personal affront if you refuse me."

Justin stared at her. She was without a doubt the most forward young woman he'd ever met. Maybe he should speak with Aunt Connie about the influence Lady Howell might have on Lilian.

He forced himself to smile. "I wouldn't want to offend you, Lady Howell, however I have a feeling your father wouldn't approve if I drove your auto." She started to frown so he said, "I'll be happy to inspect the motor after we've had tea."

She let go of his arm. He got out of the car and hurried around to the passenger side. She was all smiles again as he assisted her out. "I'm sure you're right about Papa. He'll change his mind when he meets you at dinner tomorrow evening, though. I predict we'll be seeing a lot more of each other in the days to come."

Lady Howell linked her arm through his as the three of them moved on to the back terrace. This was turning into the very thing he'd told his mother on the way here that he wanted to avoid.

At least he'd sidestepped having to drive the automobile. The last thing he wanted to do was chance having an accident with Lady Howell's motorcar. The future already looked dismal for his trip to America. Having to pay for repairs or to replace the vehicle would be the last straw.

As they rounded the corner of the house one more glance back showed the same empty drive. He resigned himself to believing no news was good news.

On rainy Mondays, Elena made her welcome speech in the dining tent. This first group had arrived on an early train. She observed their guests as they settled into chairs at the tables and smiled. The weather had dampened the spirits of the adults, but the children were full of energy and ready for a new experience. She turned to Papa, who stood next to her wearing a smile of his own. "I'm glad you agreed to come out this morning. I think you'll be glad you did."

He put his arm around her shoulders and gave her a squeeze. "I should have done it sooner. Candice has helped me see things from a different perspective, and one of them is if I'm going to support you in this effort, I need to be there in deed, not just in word."

Soon the female household staff arrived carrying trays of scones with jam and butter, and pots of tea. The chatter quieted as all eyes followed the young women.

This was the best part of a rainy-day arrival, and she almost giggled with anticipation of the response she knew she'd see. When the coverings were removed from the scones, the fresh baked aroma filled the air, and faces lit up with smiles of appreciation. She had a cup of tea and watched her guests enjoy their refreshments with blissful sighs. Some even licked their fingers. A tea break was exactly what they needed to perk them up.

After the welcome speech, Elena and Papa sat at one of the tables and enjoyed a scone and another cup of tea, while waiting for the next group.

Old Bill ran into the dining tent and skidded to a stop in front of them. He bent over, hands on knees, to catch his breath. In a few moments he straightened, snatched his dripping hat off his head and said, "Squire Bishop, we have a problem."

CHAPTER TWENTY-ONE

*E*lena jumped up, her chair toppling over behind her. "What is it, Bill?"

Papa set her chair upright. "Is anyone hurt?"

"No, sir. It's one of the tents for the second group. We found it in the spring."

"It's not your fault. Someone must have done it during the night." Poor Bill acted as though he was personally responsible for the tent being there.

"Everything was ready this morning. I don't know when it could have happened, but you better come have a look."

She and Papa picked up their umbrellas and followed Bill out the door. The wet grass was slick, so Papa held his umbrella with one hand and cupped her elbow in a steadying hold with the other. He had become the father she needed again. The thought warmed her to her toes.

They arrived to find a soggy ball of canvas in the middle of the spring. Ropes wound around it to hold its shape. More ropes, attached to tent pegs, driven into the ground kept it afloat.

Amazing. Once again, the vandalism was creative, but why?

And how could it have been done so fast? Elena glanced at Papa who frowned at the scene before them, then turned back to the wet wad. It hadn't seemed necessary for staff to watch the spring while no guests were in residence. They would have to rethink that decision.

Papa shook his head and stepped back, taking her with him. "Cut the tent loose and find a place to dry it out. If it's not ready for occupants by tonight, the family scheduled to use it will stay in the house."

They watched for a while, then headed back to greet the second group. Her initial relief at everyone's safety now gave way to anger building inside her like steam in an engine.

"This makes me mad." She jabbed her umbrella in the direction they'd come, catching the edge of Papa's umbrella and knocking it out of his hand. "I'm sorry. Let me get it."

"No, no. I'll get it." He released her long enough to retrieve it and come back. "This *is* frustrating. I don't like having someone sneak around our property, especially with the intent to cause mischief."

"It seems to me no one, other than that odious Mr. Higgins, has anything to gain," she said, as they resumed walking. "But, the last time I talked to him, he had no idea what was going on."

"I can hardly bear to think of him talking to you the way he did." Papa spoke through clenched teeth. "I'd hoped the two of you would never come in contact."

"God gave me the strength to deal with him; however, I'm sure he'll be back."

"I'm afraid you're right."

Elena delivered their welcome to the second group, and she and Papa went back to the house where the morning post waited for them on the hall table. She and her father each picked up a stack and took it to the study.

After opening several reservation requests, Papa said, "I

believe your idea to take the guests into Brighton has already had an effect. Several have mentioned they would like to go."

"Mr. Atwood is good with the advertising. I see it in the ones I'm opening, too. I don't want to take credit, though. God is providing ideas, and I give him the glory. He knows what we need."

Papa harrumphed. "What if it's not God's will for us to keep the estate? I certainly don't deserve to after what I did."

"Of course he means for us to keep it. He is a forgiving God."

"I hope for your sake you're right."

The message on the next piece of paper Elena pulled out of its envelope chilled her. It read: "Accidents can happen on the road."

She gasped, and Papa immediately came around behind her chair to read over her shoulder. She handed him the note and rubbed her arms. "Is he planning to ambush the guests on the road now?"

He went back to his chair. "That's what the message implies." He laid the note on the desk, took off his glasses and rubbed his eyes. "All these notes are bullying tactics. ""Do what I want or else.'" He dropped his hands and gazed at her. "Whoever is sending them feels threatened by what's going on here. So far, we've ignored him. The question is, do we continue?"

Papa wasn't going to tell her what to do, even after telling her at first, she was wasting her time. It was another welcome example of his support. It made her happy but didn't bring an easy answer.

"Oakwood has always been a safe haven for me, so the things we've had to deal with are disconcerting to say the least. I don't like being bullied, though, and I think we've been right to ignore it so far."

She got up and paced from one corner of the desk to the other, hands behind her back. "It's a fearful thing to think someone else could get hurt, and it would be my fault because I didn't heed the warning. However, I believe God is with us. We need to trust him."

She stopped, put both hands on the desk and leaned toward Papa. "We need to pray."

"You think it will help, don't you?"

"Yes."

He got up, closed the door and the two of them sat together on the loveseat.

"Heavenly Father, thank you for the opportunity to make this resort available to families who might not have been able to afford a holiday otherwise. I believe you mean to help us out in our financial situation, and I thank you for that. I want to ask now for your watch over the guests and the staff as we finish out the summer. Please show us what to do, and we'll give you all the praise. Amen."

Papa gazed at her with misty eyes. "You are so like your mother. She was always stronger in the faith than I." He took her hands in his and gave them a squeeze. "I know you pray for me. Promise you won't give up."

"I promise." She pulled her hands free and hugged him around the neck. "I love you, Papa."

Thursday dawned clear and bright after several days of rain. A perfect day for an outing. The wagon had been fitted with bench seats, and the five families who paid the extra money to go to Brighton settled in. Elena smiled and waved as the merry group left.

The Smiths went along to celebrate Noah's recovery. The many doctor visits had been expensive, but to see the little boy running around again made the cost worth it. And the Smiths planned to leave Saturday. Another reason to smile.

She entered the house in time to see Mrs. Turner coming down the stairs. Daniel followed with her luggage and went out the front door. She'd been so glad to see Noah out of the house, which meant his brothers would be out from under foot, that she'd forgotten what it would mean for his caretaker.

Mrs. Turner smiled as she approached. "Good morning, Miss Bishop. I imagine this is a happy day for you. I know it is for your father."

"I am relieved to see the boy well, and I won't miss hearing Mr. Smith yell, ""That's enough"", when I least expect it. I don't know how Mrs. Smith does it."

"I'm sure I don't know, either." The kind lady clasped her hands in front of her. "I want to thank you for the opportunity to help. It was good to feel needed."

Warmth for this special woman filled her. "I believe God sent you to us in our hour of need. Not only for Noah, but for the good influence you've had on my father."

"I'm glad I could be His handmaiden. I'll miss you all, but I should be going."

"Where will you go?" Did Papa know Mrs. Turner was leaving? She'd had such a good effect on him. Would he fall back to his old ways when she was gone?

"Back to my nephew's. With Noah in his family's care, it wouldn't be proper for me to stay. And my nephew's wife is always happy to have extra help."

Mrs. Turner started for the front door and Elena joined her. "I suppose she enjoys your companionship, as well. I'm wondering though,... have you spoken with Papa?"

"We said our goodbyes last night." Elena squinted as they passed through the front door into the sunshine and walked toward the waiting carriage.

Elena waited for Mrs. Tuner to be seated, then said, "I'll miss your company. I hope your nephew will consider coming to stay with us again." Maybe she'd misjudged the affection she suspected between Mrs. Turner and her father.

"We'll see. Goodbye, Miss Bishop."

Elena lifted her hand in farewell as the carriage set off.

When it reached the end of the drive she turned back to the house. As she approached the door, movement at the corner of the house caught her attention. Had a man ducked out of sight?

She made her way to the end of the house and peered around the corner. Nothing unusual. It could have been her imagination. Not surprising with all the strange things going on, but she'd be sure to tell Papa.

CHAPTER TWENTY-TWO

*J*ustin's heart twinged when he found Elena sitting on a window seat in the study. Her arms wrapped around her legs, which she'd drawn up under her skirt, and her chin rested on her knees. She gazed out on the front lawn with a troubled expression. Had something else happened between the tent in the spring incident and his arrival home?

He stood in the doorway, unsure what to do about the emotions churning inside him. Why did he have the impulse to gather her in his arms and promise everything would be okay, when she'd made it clear she didn't want his help? Where did this need for her to turn to him for rescue and direction come from?

This was more than the easy friendship he'd felt for her over the years. He shook his head to clear his thoughts. Now wasn't the time to entertain those kinds of ideas. The most important thing was for Elena to see reason before Richard got home. He cleared his throat to get her attention and came across the room.

She turned and smiled when she saw him and her right cheek dimpled. So adorable. Suddenly, his hands were sweaty, and he couldn't think of a thing to say.

She swung her feet to the floor and patted the seat next to her. "How was your visit? I trust your aunt and cousin are well."

He wiped his hands on his pants as he sat and cleared his throat again. "It was a good visit. Mother enjoyed herself."

"And you didn't?"

"It was tolerable, but I would rather have stayed here. Lilian has a friend she feels would be a perfect match for me, so I had to make polite conversation with her on more than one occasion."

"You didn't care for her."

"She's an interesting young lady. She has an automobile."

Elena's gaze drifted to the fern on its stand next to him. "How nice."

Is she disappointed? He liked the idea that she might not want to share his attention with another woman.

"I didn't drive it, though."

Wide gray eyes came back to his. "Why not?"

"She offered, but she wasn't supposed to let anyone else operate it." He stretched out his legs and crossed one ankle over the other. "I'm not in a hurry to own an automobile, at any rate. A horse is more manageable."

She gave him a wistful smile. "I think I would have enjoyed giving it a try."

"I imagine you would." He tucked a few strands of silky hair behind her ear, his hand lingering a little longer than necessary.

Her cheeks turned pink, and he reluctantly drew back. "How did things go while I was gone? Any more accidents?"

Her smile disappeared, and her chin raised a fraction. "Nothing we couldn't handle, so if the real reason for your visit is to try to talk me into closing the resort, you've wasted your time."

She stood and started for the door. He jumped up and caught her hand, causing her to turn to him in surprise. "Seeing you is the reason for my coming." He gave her a broad smile. "Getting you to see the advantages of closing the resort sooner rather than later is an opportunity I can't pass up."

"You don't know what to do with me, do you? All these years I've let you talk me out of things, or into them. It must be hard, knowing you no longer have such sway over my thinking."

He stared. Did she read his mind? He clenched his teeth to reassure himself his mouth wasn't hanging open. "You're right. It's frustrating when you won't do as I suggest."

"Suggest? Don't you mean demand?"

The invisible band around his head tightened. "Let me ask you this. Have I ever led you on the wrong path?"

"No. The path you choose is generally without risk. However, sometimes we need to take risks to protect what we care about."

"And what do you need to protect, Elena?" Now he was getting somewhere.

"You know I can't discuss it. Suffice it to say the resort will carry on whether you, or Richard, like it or not."

He still held her hand so she turned and led him to the door. "As a matter of fact, a wagon full of happy guests left not too long ago for a visit to Brighton."

Before they reached the door, Wilson appeared on the threshold wearing a serious expression. Elena froze and squeezed his hand in a death grip. Justin turned to her in surprise. The tense set of her jaw and shoulders, not to mention the circulation being cut off in his fingers, shouted her belief that Wilson had bad news.

"I'm sorry to interrupt, but I've had word that a fallen tree is blocking the road to Brighton. I've dispatched men to take care of it. The families want to wait in the wagon, so they may continue once it's cleared away."

"Will it take long?"

"It's only a temporary set-back. More of a nuisance than anything."

"Thank you for handling it, Wilson."

Elena relaxed beside him, and the blood flow returned to his hand. She closed her eyes and took a deep breath, then slowly let it out. When they opened, pink colored her cheeks and her eyes widened. She dropped his hand and stepped away.

Squire Bishop and his daughter were hard on a man's ego. Was he that forgettable?

"Elena, what is going on?"

She took another step back and avoided eye contact. "We've had some bad luck with the tents, but I was hoping it wouldn't be a problem on the road."

He closed the distance between them and gripped her shoulders. She met his eyes, startled. "I hope you don't think I have anything to do with the bad luck you're having. I would like to see this resort come to an end, but I would never endanger lives or resort to vandalism."

Her eyes widened. "The thought never entered my mind. I think I know you better than that."

He let go of her shoulders and ran his hand through his hair. "Good." He went back across the room and sat on the loveseat. She followed but didn't sit until he patted the seat beside him. With a sigh, she lowered herself to the upholstered seat.

"All right, Elena. I want you to tell me what's going on. Have you made any progress finding out who could be responsible?"

Her shoulders slumped and she dropped her gaze to her hands clasped in her lap. "I have my suspicions but can't prove anything." She sighed again then raised misty eyes to his, deepening his desire—no, his need—to make everything right for her. "I can't discuss the reasons, but this resort must continue to the end of the summer, and it must be profitable."

Profitable? He gazed out the window with a frown. Had they come into some financial trouble? In his mind's eye, he saw the round man Squire Bishop was having words with in the drive.

He turned to Elena, who had returned to studying her hands. "Is someone blackmailing you?"

Her head jerked up and she gasped. Justin nodded. This made sense now. "On the day you fell in the spring, I came across your father and a man arguing outside the front door. I offered assistance, but your father said he'd handle it."

His heart ached to think of all she'd already been through and now had this to deal with. He reached for her hand and clasped it in both of his. "If you pay that man, he will only come back for more until he finally owns your estate. Has anyone informed the authorities?"

"It's not quite what you think, but you can be sure we've sent notice to the authorities about the mishaps we've been having."

He closed his eyes and rubbed his forehead. She wasn't going to tell him what sort of trouble they were in, at least not today, but it was time to accept the fact that the resort would continue. However, if he helped, there was a chance he could eliminate the mishaps and bring a quiet dignity to the proceedings. And hope-fully a ticket to America.

He held her gaze. "I'm going to help make sure no more acci-dents happen. With or without your permission, I'll do my best to prevent more tents in the spring or tied in a knot. And no more trees in the road."

She gave him a watery smile. "If you can accomplish that I would be most grateful."

Time to admit it, Justin. You'll do anything you can for her.

CHAPTER TWENTY-THREE

*A*s Elena watched Justin leave, her emotions couldn't decide where to settle. She hadn't told him why they were in financial trouble, but now he knew they were. She'd unintentionally betrayed Papa's confidence and would have to apologize.

She wandered over to the desk, dropped into the chair behind it and started organizing the mess her father left. It was a huge relief to know Justin would be helping now rather than obstructing. So why this jittery, butterflies in the stomach feeling?

Shuffling papers into their appropriate stacks wasn't helping so she gave it up, relaxed into the chair and pushed with her toes to swivel back and forth. The cause of her unrest might as well be faced. The friendly, teasing friendship the two of them had in the past had changed. They'd admitted as much that day in the gazebo.

Studying her hand revealed no physical reason why it should tingle at his touch. And her heart, she pressed her hand against the rapid beating in her chest. Why did thinking about him cause it to speed up?

She left the chair and went to gaze at the picture of her mother over the mantle. Her parents had fallen in love in their youth and married young. By all accounts, her mother never regretted it and her father's behavior after her death testified to his grief.

There was no point dwelling on it. Even if her heart was beginning to think of Justin as more than a friend, it would only lead to heartache. He'd been clear about his desire to leave, so why entertain such feelings.

The sun shone brightly the next morning, so Elena enjoyed tea on the terrace. She lifted a prayer of thanks for weather that allowed another wagonload of guests to venture out.

Closing her eyes, she took a deep breath of the new day's fresh air.

Firm footsteps on the flagstones drew her attention to Papa, who strode across the terrace toward her. Her smile faded and the cheerful greeting she'd been about to give died in her throat.

He pulled out a chair and sat, his back rigid, fingers drumming on the arms of the chair.

"What has happened?"

He turned stormy eyes to hers. "Justin came over early this morning to suggest we check the wagon wheels before we take any guests out. I was hard pressed to believe someone would be willing to cause harm to so many people. He insisted, and it's a good thing. One of the wheels had been loosened just enough to take the wagon half way to Brighton before it fell off, spilling the families out onto the road."

With trembling hands, Elena set her teacup and saucer on the table. What kind of person was capable of such action?

"All the wheels are tight and the families are off on their anticipated trip." He deflated into his chair, took a shuddering breath and rubbed his eyes. His hands dropped to his lap and he focused on her. "We have to find out who is responsible for this."

Papa's words had the same effect as a huge black cloud covering the sun. The chill drove away the warmth of a moment ago.

She frowned, her hands clenched into fists in her lap. "I hate to think it, let alone say it, but I'm wondering if the person is someone on our staff. It would certainly give him opportunity."

"That possibility has occurred to me, as well." He resumed drumming his fingers on the arms of the chair. "I can't think who would have a motive, though. We'll have to keep our eyes and ears open."

She swallowed the lump rising in her throat. It made her heart ache to think of any of their people being disloyal, let alone willing to cause physical harm.

Elena spent the day walking over the estate. She observed staff interaction with the guests at the recreation tent. Strolled to the spring and sat in the shade for a while. Went by the stables and talked to the men working there. She crisscrossed tent city, stopping to chat with guests and watching for anything amiss, and ate lunch and supper on the terrace with the guests.

Later that evening, Elena sat on a bench in the garden, trying to sort through all she had observed that day. The staff was friendly and helpful, and over all appeared to enjoy their job. The guests appeared to be satisfied that their week in the country was everything they'd expected. A heavy sigh escaped. That was a minor miracle considering all that had gone on.

She stood and ambled along the paths that separated the fragrant, colorful beds of roses, lilies, Canterbury bells, and other flowers she loved. The evening shadows prevented her from seeing the beauty around her clearly, but that didn't matter. As she strolled, hands behind her back, she mentally scanned the faces of the men and women who had been with her family all of her life. Not a single one stood out in her mind as someone who would be capable of the acts that had been committed.

The hedge at the back of the garden loomed in front of her, and she stopped there to gaze at the tents spread out in the park beyond. It was a peaceful scene, but experience had taught her how deceptive it could be.

She turned and headed for the house. They could make sure the wheels on the wagons were tight, but they had no control over what they might meet on the road. The summer was half gone, and as Papa had predicted, it didn't appear as though they would make enough money to pay his debt.

Her shoulders slumped, and she slowed to a stop, head down. Tears ran from the corners of her eyes to the tip of her nose and dripped to the ground. She'd been so sure this would work. Why would God give her this idea and then let her fail?

She dug in her skirt pocket for a handkerchief and pulled out a folded flyer, along with the square of fine cotton. One of the guests had given it to her after his trip to Brighton. He'd been enthused about whatever it was.

She dried her eyes and unfolded it. Not enough daylight remained to see what it advertised, so she hurried to the drawing room and found Papa already there, a book open in his lap, his glasses perched on his head. His melancholy expression pulled her up short.

"Are you enjoying your book, Papa?"

He started and turned toward her. "What? Oh, yes. Quite good."

Elena rested her hand on his shoulder. She had a pretty good idea what was on his mind right now. "Are you missing Mrs. Turner?"

"Can't get anything past you, can I?"

"Why don't you invite her to come back? We could say it was to keep me company." She smiled and sat on the edge of a chair close to him.

"That wouldn't be fair to Mrs. Turner. I very much enjoyed the time we spent together while she was here, but I don't want to mislead her into thinking I can offer her something more. We both know the resort is not going to make enough to save us in the end."

"We're not giving up yet." She waved the flyer in her hand. "One of the guests gave me this." After smoothing the paper under the lamp on the table next to her, another idea bloomed.

A picture of a tethered helium balloon with happy people standing in the basket under it filled most of the page. The text informed the reader that for a small fee one could experience the sensation of flying and see a spectacular view of the city and coast. The balloon was anchored by a rope long enough to let it float high above the ground for a short period of time. Then it was lowered safely down again.

Elena relaxed into the chair. Instead of going to Brighton, they could bring something of Brighton to them. All she'd need to do is go to the city and talk to the man who owned the balloon. And their estate would be saved.

"Elena, what are you thinking?"

CHAPTER TWENTY-FOUR

*J*ustin finished his inspection of the tents, stables and grounds early the next morning, then went to the terrace hoping to see Elena. He found her there in traveling clothes, with a cup of tea.

She smiled as he approached. "Good morning. Is everything in proper order?" She motioned to one of the seats at the table, inviting him to join her.

"I saw nothing out of place." He sat across from her. Nodding at her outfit, he asked, "Are you going somewhere? I'd be happy to accompany you."

Her eyes widened for an instant, but her smile stayed in place, although it seemed a little forced. "I'm sure you'd be bored. Thank you for the offer, though."

That was a red flag if ever he'd seen one. Wherever Elena was going she didn't want him to interfere, which meant she knew he wouldn't approve——which meant he had better accompany her. Maybe he could head off a disaster.

"I can't imagine being bored in your company, and as I have nothing planned for today, I must insist on escorting you." He smiled and settled into his chair.

Now the smile disappeared. "You insist? What if I don't want you to come?"

He laughed. "That's exactly why I think I should. I want to help you," *and myself,* "by making sure whatever you have in mind won't make trouble."

"I have my father's approval. I don't need yours."

He held his hands up in surrender. "Ok. How about I just go along for the ride? Maybe give you a second opinion on whatever it is?"

"I don't need a second opinion, either. You can come, but you had better not try to interfere."

"Right, then. Where are we going and when do you want to leave?" He straightened in his chair.

"We're going to Brighton, and I mean it Justin," she pointed a finger at him, "no interfering."

Footsteps approached from behind him. Luke. "Excuse me, Miss Elena."

They turned to see Luke standing a discreet distance away. "Your carriage is ready."

"Thank you, Luke. Lord Justin will be joining us."

"Very good, Miss."

Once on the road, Justin settled back in his seat and took in the fragrant summer vegetation on either side of them. The dark greens of the hedgerows and leaves of the horse chestnuts, oaks and other trees in the wooded areas contrasted with the vibrant pinks, purples and yellows of foxglove, yarrow and the thistle-like heads of common knapweed. He'd need to jot down details to use in a scene such as this in one of his books. Of course, in America, he'd likely find different—

A sharp elbow jab in the arm snapped him out of his daydream. He rubbed his arm and stared at Elena's exasperated expression. "What was that for?"

"You weren't listening to a word I was saying."

"I'm sorry. You have my full attention now."

She gave him a small smile. "I suppose you were off on your jaunt across the ocean."

"Something like that." He chuckled. She knew him well.

For a moment her expression turned wistful, then she was back to business. "Since you're coming with me we'll be able to cover more area in less time. You can go to the Palace Pier and see what activities our guests might enjoy that could be duplicated at Oakwood.

I need to speak with our attorney, Mr. Atwood, then I'll join you."

Might she be planning something risky between now and her visit to Mr. Atwood? It would probably be best to agree and then keep an eye on her from a distance.

"I see your point. I'll look forward to you joining me, though, as you'll have a better idea than I will what you can do at Oakwood."

She gave him a shining smile, and was that relief in her eyes?

"I'm sure you'll do fine." She patted his hand where it rested on his leg.

When they got to Brighton, Elena instructed Luke to let him out close to the pier. He climbed down and joined the tourists milling about the boardwalk.

Luke turned the carriage around and headed toward the business district. If they weren't back within thirty minutes, he'd try to find them.

The crowd swept him into the current and he found himself passing carnival style booths on either side of the pier. Some offered games of chance or souvenirs, while others tempted passers-by to indulge in fish and chips, cotton candy or toffee apples. The delicious smells made his mouth water, so he bought some cotton candy and sauntered on to the music pavilion at the end of the pier. He'd attended some concerts here and they also had dances. The guests should enjoy that.

Mission accomplished, he hurried back to the stony beach,

crowded with tourists in their colorful bathing costumes. Behind the beach lay shops, hotels and restaurants and the streets beyond held numerous boarding houses.

Justin took in the scene in a matter of moments. Elena and the carriage were nowhere in sight. A peculiar moment of panic filled him. He hadn't taken long, so maybe she wasn't finished, or maybe she never went to see her attorney at all. He raced down the street, brushing past meandering tourists.

As he tried to navigate through the crowd, a boy shoved a flyer into his hand. "Gas balloon rides!"

About to pitch it in the gutter, Justin hesitated. Gas balloon ride? He studied the paper. It offered the opportunity to rise above the trees in a tethered helium balloon for a spectacular view of Brighton.

His stomach knotted as he realized exactly where she'd gone.

CHAPTER TWENTY-FIVE

*E*xcitement pushed away Elena's twinges of guilt. She'd keep her word to Justin and ask Mr. Atwood for advice regarding Mr. Higgins. But not until she'd investigated the balloon ride.

"I want to go to Queen's Park, Luke."

To see the gas balloon? I'm not sure that's a good idea."

She sighed. If it wasn't her father or Justin, it was the staff trying to protect her. She supposed she should count herself fortunate that so many people cared about her well being. She straightened her shoulders. "I appreciate your concern, Luke. However, I am quite determined to go."

"As you wish, Miss."

Luke maneuvered the carriage through the streets leading to Queen's Park. Elena relaxed against the seat and tried not to imagine the horrified expression on her father's face if he knew what she had planned. She'd been able to avoid giving him much information when they'd discussed it the night before, but it didn't change the fact that he'd forbid it.

The city gave way to houses as they headed east. Her father had come a long way in the last couple of months. Surely, he was ready to put the past behind him. But what if bringing a balloon to the estate set him back, or made him worse?

She chewed on her bottom lip. As her mind drifted the scene changed and the picture of her beautiful, fun-loving mother over the mantel in the study occupied her thoughts. Her parents had had many friends, several of whom joined them in their love of ballooning. One awful day they had started out on an adventure—and only her father returned.

He refused to ever get into a balloon again. Eventually, as her father would not be consoled, their friends drifted away.

Elena had grown up quickly. She'd taken over the running of the estate with the help of Justin's kind mother and Oakwood's staff. And they'd been doing all right until her father had lost it all to the loathsome Phineas Higgins.

She blinked away tears and realized they were almost to Queen's Park. The sight of the huge balloon towering above the ground made her gasp. The fabric of the balloon had patterns of red, gold and blue. The sun reflecting off the gold made the balloon appear to glow.

A young man, perhaps in his twenties, headed toward a buggy and tossed his black suit jacket on the seat. He turned at the sound of their carriage approaching.

His green eyes twinkled when he noticed Elena seated behind Luke, and his handlebar moustache did nothing to hide his dimples when he smiled. Suddenly the lace collar of her rose silk blouse felt a little too snug and her pearl grey jacket too warm. She couldn't have refused him a smile if she'd wanted to.

When they stopped he took off his flat straw hat. "Good morning. Are you here for a ride in my balloon?"

Excitement filled her like frothy bubbles popping in a bubble bath. She felt sure this man wouldn't tell her to be careful or say she had better not do this or that. As a matter of fact, she could imagine him getting in all sorts of trouble as a child—and possibly as a man.

She gripped the side of the carriage, ready to bound out. "Yes. I'd like very much to ride in your balloon. Will you take me up now?"

He pulled a watch out of his vest pocket, popped open the lid, then snapped it shut with a sigh. "I'm sorry. My partner has already gone to town to meet a business associate at the Palace Hotel for lunch. I'm to be there in ten minutes. Would you consider coming back in an hour?"

The bubbles vanished leaving her with the ache of disappointment. She didn't have an hour. She would have to meet Justin soon, and if she came back with him he would forbid her riding in the balloon. Which, of course, she would ignore. But he'd somehow dissuade this nice man from bringing his balloon to her estate.

"I can't come back today. How long will you be in Brighton?"

"Another week or so." He smiled, lifted her hand from the side of the carriage and pressed her fingers to his lips.

Then he climbed into his buggy and, with a jaunty wave, he left them.

Elena watched him leave, butterflies fluttering in her stomach. That was the most romantic-leave taking she'd ever experienced. No one had kissed her fingers until now. She put her hand on her forehead. She was a little dizzy with the rise and drop in her emotions.

Luke cleared his throat. "Shall we be going back to find Lord Justin?"

She turned her attention to the balloon. "Not yet. I think I'll give it a closer inspection first."

Luke sprang from the front seat and offered her his hand. "Do you think you should?" At her glare, he had the sense to say no more.

Elena strolled toward the balloon, straining her neck to see to the top. She leaned a little too far back and found herself headed for the ground. Luke caught her and settled her on her feet. She stood still a moment and huffed out a breath of irritation with herself. When would she learn to be more careful?

Starting forward again, Elena shooed away the ducks that had wandered over from a near-by pond. They quacked their annoyance as they waddled back the way they'd come.

The basket under the balloon was woven just like any other, but much bigger. It could probably hold four people comfortably.

She ran her hand across the smooth willow, then grasped the edge and pulled herself up on tiptoes to peek inside. If she couldn't get in the air today then she at least wanted to imagine what it would be like. To do that she must get inside.

The mild fishy-smelling breeze blew loose strands of hair in her face as she searched the area. She brushed it away from her eyes and focused on Luke. "There must be a way for a lady to get inside. The picture on the advertisement showed a lady and gentleman in the basket. How do you think that might be accomplished?"

"Miss, if your father finds out I let you—"

He drew a breath and she held up her hand palm out. "Don't bother telling me I shouldn't get in. The nice young man who owns the balloon felt bad that he couldn't take me up now, so I'm sure he wouldn't mind if I at least experienced what it's like to stand inside the basket."

Luke gave her a dubious look and blew out the breath he'd taken. He pointed across the top. "I imagine a person could climb those steps and jump in."

She raced around to the other side. The winch the balloon was tethered to sat on this side, as well as the stairs, that Luke could see with the advantage of being taller. She started up the steps using the woven side for balance.

The wind picked up, rustling leaves in the trees close to the pond. The basket shifted as the balloon strained against its tether and a thrill shot through her. She leaned against the side and closed her eyes, imagining the sensation of swaying high in the sky.

Seeing what birds could see. Leaving whatever worries she had on the ground.

The clatter of buggy wheels and horse hoofs pounding on the road sent her to the top step. She balanced there by pressing her thighs against the rim of the basket. Justin careened around the corner and her breath caught in her throat. She'd never seen him go so fast. He shouted and jerked the poor horse to a stop. Luke ran toward Justin as he jumped to the ground.

A sudden gust whipped against the balloon, tugging the basket to the left. Elena grabbed at a rope tied to a ring on the side, but it didn't stop her from somersaulting in to land on her back. She struggled to a sitting position, then smiled. It felt as if she truly was floating into the sky.

CHAPTER TWENTY-SIX

*W*hen Justin saw Elena standing knee high next to the basket, looking for all the world like she was going to get in, his mind flashed back to her going under the water in the spring. This was so much worse.

"Stop!"

He skidded his rented conveyance to a halt next to the Bishop's carriage and jumped out just in time to see Elena tumble in. He raced toward the balloon as it lifted off.

"Elena! Stop!"

Justin sprinted by Luke, who was also running toward the balloon. A rope dangled from the side of the basket closest to him. Justin made a mad dash, jumped, grabbed the end and rose off the ground. Luke rushed up behind him and leaped to catch his feet but was too late. The balloon was rising so fast that Luke quickly became unrecognizable.

Justin's heart pounded an uneven rhythm as he struggled to catch his breath. He was too high to let go and too petrified to climb the rope. Then he thought he heard a voice calling to him. It was hard to tell because the wind rushed in his ears. Maybe God had sent an angel to the rescue.

"Justin! Look up."

He lifted his head to see Elena's surprised face peering over the edge, and swallowed the bile rising in his throat. What if she leaned over too far and fell out?

"Get back in!"

"What are you doing down there?"

"Trying to keep from getting killed—"

"Climb up!"

He tilted his head back to see her again.

"You're strong enough. Just pluck up your courage and climb up here."

Of course he was strong enough to climb up. But was he strong enough to keep from looking down, or thinking about how high he was?

He focused on his white-knuckled hands. They already ached from holding onto the prickly rope. His attention shifted to Elena. She was his reason to let go with one hand and start his assent.

Fear would not beat him.

He swallowed hard and pulled, let go with his left hand and placed it higher on the rope. Hand over hand, higher and higher, keeping his focus straight ahead. His muscles screamed at him, but not as loudly as the voice in his head telling him he wouldn't make it. He would fall to his death and Elena would die because he wasn't there to help her. Finally, his head was level with the bottom of the basket. One more pull and the edge was in his hand. He grabbed hold with his other hand and pulled up until his head and shoulders were inside the basket. Elena clutched the back of his jacket with both hands and hauled him in the rest of the way.

Justin landed on his back with his eyes closed and lay still while the world spun around him. Elena's hand cupped the side of his face, and he opened his eyes to see her hovering over him, her lower lip trembling. A tear dropped from her brimming eyes onto his cheek. In that moment he knew with certainty he'd do anything in his power to make this woman happy.

When he reached up to caress her face she collapsed on his chest, shaking with sobs. He held her close and marveled at the sensation of everything inside him melting to liquid. So, this is how it felt to turn into mush.

He let her cry for a minute, then eased the two of them into a sitting position. Her nose was red, her eyes swollen and her hair loose and flying around. She was a beautiful mess.

Elena blushed under his gaze, made a vain attempt to straighten her hair, then gave it up and dropped her hands to her lap and stared at them. "I was afraid you'd fall and it would be all my fault. You've never been anything but a good friend to me, protecting me, saving me from myself, and look what I've gotten you into."

She raised her tear-filled eyes to his, and he pulled out his handkerchief and handed it to her in a daze. Nothing more than a "good friend" when he'd just discovered she was everything to him? His gaze locked on hers, waiting for her to say she meant more than friends. She remained silent, appearing as though she expected *him* to say something. Finally, he said, "I'm going to get us down."

Her gaze dropped to the middle of his chest. Whatever she expected that wasn't it, but she quickly recovered. He stood and assisted her to her feet. The basket swayed under them and he froze. Elena's face lit up as she rushed to the side. "Oh, it's wonderful! Come and see."

Small careful steps took him to the side, which was almost chest high to Elena, closer to waist high to him. He drew in a deep breath and looked down. The small dot on the ground had to be Luke and he was getting smaller by the second.

This was too much like the nightmares that plagued him after Elena's mother died in a ballooning accident. He'd be soaring high above the ground and peer over the side of the basket. He tumbled out every time, terrified of hitting the ground. Of course, he woke up safe and sound, but that didn't stop him from deciding a long time ago that he would never go near a balloon, much less ride in one.

He swallowed hard. *"This is not a dream, this is not a dream."* It didn't seem to be working. He broke into a cold sweat and stepped back as darkness closed in around him.

When he regained consciousness, he found his head in Elena's lap and the rest of him cramped into a space fine for standing in, but too small for reclining. Once again Elena's worried face hovered over his.

He closed his eyes. It was beyond humiliating to faint in front of a woman, especially after she'd just finished praising him for being her hero. Her opinion of his protective skills had to be fading fast.

CHAPTER TWENTY-SEVEN

*E*lena cradled Justin's head in her lap. Her poor friend was as white as the Cliffs of Dover. She gently brushed a curl off his forehead and ran her fingers through the silky waves around his face. She'd always suspected he had a fear of heights and today proved it. He was sure to be embarrassed when he came around.

Before long his eyes opened. He took in his situation and closed them again. Her heart ached for him. Men had so much pride, her father being just one example.

She shook his shoulder. "Justin. I know you feel bad, but you shouldn't. Everyone is afraid of something."

His eyes popped open. "That may be true, but I don't see everyone fainting over it. I've never seen you swoon about anything."

"You're right. I don't think I have. What I have done is fall down or come close to hitting the ground, and more times than not you've been there to catch me or help me up. I wasn't able to catch you, but I hope I can lift your spirits."

"In that case, may I ask a favor of you?"

"Of course you can." This man had risked the thing he feared most to help her. Just the thought brought a rush of loving gratitude.

"Do you think we can keep this incident between us? I'd hate for Richard to hear of it, or anyone else for that matter."

She held up her right hand. "I won't breathe a word."

His relieved smile was beautiful to see. "Thank you." He sat up and scooted over to join her in leaning against the side.

"How long was I out?"

"Not long."

"Good. Our situation is getting worse by the minute. I don't want to waste time lying around. Do you mind checking to see if we're in danger of running into anything?"

She hid a smile. What did he think they might run into over the south of England? With a mental headshake, she got to her feet and scanned the horizon. It felt good to stand again and for once, be the person depended upon.

It didn't seem they were getting any higher, though they were traveling on a steady path west. She shaded her eyes and searched for familiar landmarks. Brighton shrank into the distance.

When she lifted her head, crisp wind rushed past her and whipped the loose hair around her face. Only a few pins remained in her hair, so she pulled them out and let it stream behind her. Exhilaration hummed through her body. Flying through the air was every bit as wonderful as she'd imagined.

"What do you see?"

She glanced at Justin and it occurred to her that maybe she should be concerned. His tense shoulders and serious expression clearly showed his worry. After all, they couldn't steer the balloon. She'd heard her parents and their friends talk about it. The two of them were at the mercy of the wind. She had no idea what they could do.

The realization of their peril sank in and caused a knot to form in her stomach.

Elena squatted next to him so the wind wouldn't carry her

words away. "We're not going to hit anything, unless a bird flies into our path."

"Good." He appeared less anxious. "Are we still over Brighton? Perhaps the men who own the balloon will be able to get us down."

Hiding the truth wouldn't help, even though she hated to see his anxiety return.

After a fortifying breath, she gave him the bad news. "We're traveling at a good pace, which means Brighton is miles behind us. I'm pretty sure there's no way to steer a gas balloon or stop it. A hot air balloon will drop with the temperature. I assume a gas balloon works the same way." She gulped. "I hope we're still over England when that happens. Otherwise we'll go down in the Irish Sea."

She never wanted to experience sinking under ice-cold water again. A shudder ran through her body. She sat with a bump and stared at Justin's face. His color was better and his usual self-confidence had returned. As a matter of fact, he didn't appear to understand the gravity of their situation.

She clutched the front of his jacket. "If we go down in the sea we'll drown, and no one will find us and everyone's lives will be ruined, and it's all my fault, because I wanted to bring the balloon to Oakwood to make more money to save the estate. We have to do something."

Justin pried her fingers off his jacket. "You'll be the first to know when I figure out what that is, and if we do go into the sea we won't drown. I know how to swim." He pulled her close and put his arms around her. "Where's that faith you've been talking about this summer? Instead of getting in a panic we should pray."

Elena leaned into him with a sigh. Being the one depended upon hadn't lasted long, but she found she preferred it this way. "You're right. We should pray. And while you're at it, please ask God to help the men who own this balloon to understand that I didn't mean to steal it."

He led them in a short prayer asking for protection and a safe landing. He also asked for mercy concerning the theft of the balloon. The prayer encouraged her enough to stand and check out their surroundings again. The wind had dropped a little, so the shoreline wasn't moving as rapidly under them. Still, it was amazing how far they'd come in such a short time.

In a bit, Justin pulled himself up to stand beside her. His hands clenched the edge of the basket in a white-knuckled grip, his whole body stiff as a statue. Neither of them said anything, but gradually his muscles softened into a more relaxed stance. He even hauled in the rope, coiling it into a pile beside their feet with a thoughtful expression.

"I never could imagine why you wanted to pretend you were flying when we were children. Especially after your mother's accident. I wanted my feet planted firmly on the ground. But this..." He swept the air with one hand. "This really is an amazing sensation."

She hugged his arm and he gazed down at her, eyes bright with understanding. It warmed her to her toes. She'd be happy flying with Justin forever.

CHAPTER TWENTY-EIGHT

*P*hineas sealed the envelope with the terms for the arranged marriage and applied the postage with satisfaction. This time he'd signed his name with a flourish. There would be no mistaking who sent this missive.

The envelope lay on the desk in front of him while he checked to make sure everything was correct. Squire Bishop's name headed the address. The offer was one he didn't think a loving father would refuse. After all, if Phineas were a father, he'd make sure his daughter had a secure home and a husband.

Chuckling, he rubbed his hands together. If his terms were accepted, he and Elena would marry within a fortnight, eliminating the need to carry on with the resort nonsense. Not to mention ending the tedious business with the sabotage operations. The longer it went on the more he worried that Ronald might get carried away and do something that would lead to an investigation.

He pushed back from the desk and levered his round body out of the chair with a grunt. Struggling to put on his jacket left him short of breath. He leaned on the desk a few moments to recuperate, then left the office. *If this gets much worse I'll have to stop eating those second servings of cook's pies and cakes.*

Phineas stepped out the door of his tavern into the sunshine. The bright light hurt his perpetually bloodshot eyes. He intended to put his letter in the postmaster's hands himself. And he'd have a nice stroll while he was about it.

The beautiful old house at Oakwood filled his vision. A smug smile settled on his face as he imagined stopping to enjoy the water flowing in the fountain. He'd pick one of the red blooms growing in the beds around it and slip it into the breast pocket of his jacket. Then he'd walk right in the front door where one of the staff would take his hat and ask if there was anything they could do for him.

A commotion on the street and sidewalk around him interrupted his daydream. When he focused on his current surroundings, he saw men, women and children gazing into the sky. Some pointed. Almost all exclaimed in surprise and excitement.

Scanning the blue expanse above them, he spotted a hot air balloon floating into the distance. These fools act like they've never seen one before.

Phineas stepped off the curb to cross the street just as a carriage headed toward the hotel district, came tearing by. Dust and debris swirled in a trail behind it. Shouts filled the air as people scrambled to get out of the way. Phineas instinctively moved back, caught his heel on the curb, and landed in an undignified heap on the sidewalk with an oof. He was too stunned to vocalize the expletives on the tip of his tongue.

Using his walking stick for balance, he struggled to his feet. It took a moment to steady himself, then he shook his fist in the direction the carriage disappeared. "Lunatic."

With a shaky breath, he peered to the right and the left. Seeing no traffic close enough to run him down, he started forward again. Soon he'd be enjoying a peaceful life in the country.

CHAPTER TWENTY-NINE

*I*n spite of the danger, Elena was on the adventure of a lifetime and she wanted to soak in every detail. Never had the sky seemed so blue or the clouds on the horizon so white. The ground below displayed a patchwork of rich colors. Vibrant green meadows held sprinkles of blue, purple and pink wildflowers. Various shades and textures of green marked wooded areas. Fine straight lines ran through it all, indicating roads, and squiggly, curving lines of meandering streams made their own path.

Birds flew around them, from time to time, as if checking to see how the thing she and Justin traveled in could fly without feathers. She smiled at the thought. They couldn't understand the concept of an object being lighter than air.

She closed her eyes, drew in a breath and slowly released it, reveling in the feeling that for this moment in time, they'd left all cares behind them on the ground. Justin stood beside her, sharing in this adventure and understanding her as never before.

Elena let her gaze linger on Justin. Did the experience mean as much to him as it did to her? He watched the scene below, a faraway expression on his face. She squeezed his arm. He turned to her and blinked.

"Where are you and what are you thinking of?"

"I'm wondering about the countryside in America. Will it be like this or wild and uncivilized? I've heard a lot of different things."

Directing her attention over the side allowed her to hide the feelings that might show in her eyes. She'd forgotten he wanted to head off on an adventure that wouldn't include her.

She pushed down the lump in her throat and brought her eyes back to his. "The only way you'll know for sure is to go see for yourself."

"The possibility remains to be seen, and it's not looking good right now."

Sympathy for him surged through her. Clearly, this opportunity meant a lot to him. What could be standing in the way? Financial difficulties, perhaps?

She studied the horizon while puzzling through the situation in her mind. Richard went to America to marry an heiress. He had the means to get there, but did he have to marry a woman with money because they needed it, or did he really care for her? And what about this business of the resort causing a disturbance in the neighborhood?

Justin received her scrutiny through narrowed eyes. He'd said all along that he was following Richard's orders this summer. The picture finally came together. If things didn't appear the way Richard wanted them when he returned, Justin wouldn't go anywhere.

With a frown she stomped her foot. "He makes me mad."

Justin's eyes widened. "Who?"

"Richard, of course." She moved away from him a little and planted her hands on her hips. "If you don't have my resort all tidied away before he comes home, he won't give you the funds to go to America, will he?"

Justin hesitated, and leaned on the rim of the basket. "What makes you say that?"

She huffed. Typical. He'd try to cover for his brother. "For one thing, under normal circumstances you wouldn't care if my father and I had a resort on our estate as long as no one got hurt."

His eyes snapped back to hers. "People *have* gotten hurt. You might not be standing here right now if not for me."

"Of course you'd bring that up." She hurried on. "I'm grateful, but you were trying to stop the resort before we even had the tents up. Most of our troubles have come because someone is trying to sabotage us. Only when we'd been under way for a while did we start getting the threatening notes I told you about."

"Elena, please tell me what kind of trouble your father is in."

Her chest tightened. "I promised Papa I wouldn't tell."

He wrapped his arms around her in an embrace clearly meant to comfort. She buried her face against his chest and let the tears flow again. Justin had always been there for her. Maybe it was time to stop fighting him.

Elena got herself under control and dug for a handkerchief in the beaded handbag that had miraculously stayed looped around her wrist. Justin put two fingers under her chin and tilted her face up, then gently wiped her cheeks with the handkerchief she'd given back to him.

She drew in a shaky breath. "I suppose under the circumstances it would be all right to tell you." A sweeping gesture included the basket and air surrounding them. "How much more trouble do you suppose I can get into?"

"I don't think that's a wise question." He stuffed the damp handkerchief in his pocket while taking a step away from her.

How could she tell Justin what had happened without putting her father in a bad light? She cast about in her mind for different ways it might be said and came to the conclusion there was no good way.

She rested an arm on the side of the basket. He leaned against the side next to her and looked at her expectantly. "The truth is Papa gambled the estate away to a man named Phineas Higgins. If we come up with the amount Papa owes, and it is a considerable amount, by the end of the summer we can pay the debt and keep our home."

There. She'd said it. Her heart pounded harder as she waited for Justin to respond with disgust or words of judgment, but neither came. The love and concern never left his face.

"There aren't many weeks left in the summer season. How close are you?

"Not as close as we should be, I'm afraid." Nervous energy wouldn't allow her to stand still any longer. She pushed away from the side and watched her feet as she paced the few steps required to get from one side of the basket to the other.

"My plan was to get the owner of this balloon to bring it to Oakwood for the guests to enjoy without leaving the estate. I hoped we could work out some kind of arrangement in which we would share the profits and no longer risk running into trouble on the road."

From experience, she knew this wasn't an idea Justin would have considered good, regardless of the balloon's location. He wouldn't take that kind of risk. She squared her shoulders, stopped in the center and waited, fully expecting a lecture on the folly of such a plan.

He'd been standing with his hands in his pockets, watching her make the short trek back and forth. "It wasn't a bad idea. I can imagine your guests lining up for the opportunity to go up in a balloon. Assuming they had the money."

His affirmation of the plan surprised her, but her shoulders sagged at the mention of money. "I hadn't thought of that." Most of their guests were there because they couldn't afford to stay in Brighton. "It seemed like a good opportunity."

Stepping to the center, he put his hands on her shoulders. "It *wasn't* a bad idea".

"Thank you, but whatever kind of *idea* it was is a moot point now." She moved from under the warmth of his hands to peer over the side. "Of all the clumsy accidents I've had in my life this one has to be the most spectacular."

"I have to agree. But consider the bright side. Someday this will make a great story."

As she gazed at him the humor she'd seen was replaced with something else. She wasn't sure what she was seeing, but it made her heart beat faster.

His eyes drifted to her mouth and she swallowed hard. He cupped the side of her face with his right hand and leaned closer. Her eyes closed as his lips gently touched hers. The sensation filled her with wonder and she stepped closer. His kiss was sweet and tender. If she was honest with herself, she'd always imagined receiving her first kiss from Justin.

CHAPTER THIRTY

*K*issing her had been a risk.

But Elena's smile sent warmth coursing through him. And relief. He hugged her and laughed with joy. Exhilaration made him feel he could fly without the balloon.

Now more than ever, he wanted to be the one to keep her safe from the world and bring the happy shine to her eyes. Never in his life did he think it would take flying high above the earth with her to make him realize it.

Suddenly a cold gust sent them speeding along in a new direction. They went to the side and looked over to see nothing but the Irish Sea under them.

Elena stiffened beside him. "What are we going to do?" Her was voice thin and quivering.

"We'll be okay. I predict we'll be over land again before dark." He wrapped his arm around her shoulders and gave her a squeeze.

"We'd better be. If gas cools like air, we'll go down with the sun." She rubbed her arms against the chillier air.

He couldn't believe they'd passed beyond England's southern coast already. He pulled out his pocket watch. Four o'clock. His stomach grumbled as if to confirm the time.

The sun was sliding down in the west and if he wasn't mistaken they were flying a little lower as well. He decided not to point that out. "I think I have a bit of good news.

"Can you tell what direction we're going?"

With her back to the wind, her long golden-brown hair blew around both sides of her face, hiding the little crease that appeared in her brow when concentrating. She pulled her hair back with both hands and held it while checking the sun's position compared to their heading. She turned to him, puzzled. "Northwest."

"Right, and the sea isn't terribly wide between England and—"

"Ireland. We're headed for Ireland. It's not very big. If we pass over it, we'll have the Atlantic Ocean under us."

Justin reached out to smooth the worry lines from her forehead. "We aren't even there yet and, anyway, I have an idea."

Hope sparked back to life in her eyes. Her faith in his ability to save them, made him feel like he could do anything. And this time he couldn't afford to disappoint her. If his idea didn't work they'd be in trouble. If they got out far enough over the ocean, he didn't like their chances of being found.

"This is what I hope to do." He stepped to the side and looked down. Even though they'd lost some altitude, they were still higher than he'd like.

Elena stood beside him and looped her arm through his. "What? Don't keep me in suspense."

He glanced at her then back down, trying to will the basket to descend, if only a little more. "When we get over land I want to snag on a tree, or maybe the mast of a boat in a harbor. If people see us they'll help us down. If not, we'll have to manage ourselves."

"That sounds like a good idea, but how?"

He picked up the end of the rope he'd coiled earlier and tied it into a bulky knot. "I'm going to throw it out so it'll drag along the ground. It ought to catch on something."

"Yes. I see what you mean."

They watched for a while in silence, then Elena let out a shaky breath. "I feel awful about making your mother and my father worry. I've been trying, all afternoon, not to think about what Papa will assume when he hears we went off in a balloon." She gazed at him with tear-filled eyes. "He's been doing so much better this summer, but if he believes I've been killed I'm afraid it'll destroy him."

He nodded then pulled her into a hug. "I've been thinking about him, too. As soon as we have the opportunity we'll send both of them a wire. They may still worry, but at least they'll know we're all right."

When Justin spotted Ireland through the twilight, he picked up the heavy coil of rope and got ready to heave it over the side at the opportune moment. He'd grown concerned they might not make it before dark.

The spot of land grew larger until he could see a sandy beach. A little way up to the right was a small harbor with fishing boats bobbing on the waves. A village sat close to it. Light shining from the windows made a welcoming sight. He wanted to cheer, but they weren't out of the basket yet. Best not to get ahead of himself.

"Look at all those trees on the other side of the beach!"

She turned to him with a smile, "You're hoping the rope will catch on one of those."

"Yes. And since they grow up the hill, we'll have a better chance. The ground will get closer without us having to get lower." He narrowed his eyes, straining to identify the trees. "It looks like there's everything from oaks to hawthorns in there. Their branches should support us if we end up in one of them."

As soon as they got close to the beach, Justin heaved the rope over. It landed in the water with a splash, changing their momentum immediately.

He and Elena leaned over to watch the end of the rope drag across the sand, bouncing and bumping over rocks and boulders as it went. A thick growth of tall grasses made a band of green and brown between the beach and the trees, but it didn't have much effect on their forward progress.

Justin gripped the edge. Even though the balloon had started to descend, they were still above the treetops. Surely, they wouldn't pass over without the rope getting caught in something.

They sailed over the first of the trees without the slightest tug. His stomach clenched. Elena stood wide-eyed, clenching the wicker rim. Two steps took him to the ring holding the rope. "Dear God. Please help this to work."

He reached over, grabbed the rope and swung it back and forth. It swirled through the leaves, snapping small twigs in the upper branches. They slowed a little.

The land rose up under them, bringing the rope in contact with larger branches. Encouraged, Justin swung harder.

The thrashing rope caused a large family of roosting black birds to fly up and away with raucous cries of protest. Elena shrieked and they both jumped to the center to avoid wings and sharp beaks.

Justin's breathing had just returned to normal when the basket jerked to a stop, throwing the two of them against the side.

Elena gasped and held on tight.

"Justin. You did it!"

CHAPTER THIRTY-ONE

"*Ha*! That wasn't me. That was God."

They both hung on to the rim as the wind pushed the balloon, tipping the basket to the side. Elena was thrilled they'd stopped, but she didn't like the idea of being dumped out of the basket like dirty water from a tub.

Her stomach knotted. Light was fading fast, but she could still see a long way lay between them and where the end of the rope lodged in the trees below them.

The wind let up and the balloon straightened. She took a shaky breath and turned to Justin. "How are we supposed to get down?"

"We'll have to use the rope."

"Oh, of course." She should have realized he could just pull on the rope to lower the basket to the trees.

"I should have known you wouldn't be afraid," he said with a chuckle.

"What's there to be afraid of? I can even help pull on the rope if you think it'll help."

"Exactly what is it you think I'm going to do?"

She hesitated while unease settled in her stomach. "You'll have to tell me, Justin. I can see from your expression we aren't thinking the same thing."

He pointed over the side. "Do you see where the rope disappears into the trees?" She nodded. "I'm counting on the knotted end being wedged in branches strong enough to hold our weight." Indicating the rope's length, he said, "I'll slide down and find a secure place to stand. Then you'll come down and I'll be there to make sure you have a safe landing."

She gulped and stepped away from the side.

"I'm afraid we'll have to depend on your tree climbing skill, or I should say descending, to get to the ground."

"Flying safe and secure in the basket of a balloon is one thing. Sliding along a rope at this height to end in the top of a tree is quite another. Why, the last time I was in a tree I had to have help getting down. I'd somehow managed to forget how to do it." She took another step back.

A nervous laugh slipped out. "If I don't fall out of the basket, I'll fall out of the tree."

Hysteria foamed and bubbled inside her tense body. How could he think she was capable of this? He knew how clumsy she was.

He closed the distance between them and clasped her hands against his chest. "I know you can do it, just as you knew I could climb up the rope at the beginning of this adventure. God helps us do the things we can't do on our own."

"We can do this, Elena." His eyes shone with faith and confidence.

She straightened her spine as they went to the side.

Justin shook out his handkerchief. "Watch how I do this. Be sure to keep your handkerchief between the rope and your hands. Otherwise you might get rope burn."

She wiped her sweaty hands on her skirt and opened the neck of her handbag to pull out a handkerchief. A deep breath in and released fortified her. "Let's go."

Justin took another moment to pray for safety, then went over the rim. The basket swayed and bounced as he settled onto the rope. He wrapped his ankles around it, squeezed it between his knees and held it in his hands. He looked up at her. "I'm going to back down slowly. There's no need to be in a hurry."

Poor Justin's face was white as could be, but he didn't hesitate. If he could do this with his fear of heights, then she could, too. God would take care of them.

He reached the trees and disappeared into the leaves sooner than she thought he would. "Okay, Elena. I'm waiting for you."

She pulled the hem of the back of her skirt up between her legs and tucked it into the front of her waistband, so her legs wouldn't get tangled. There was nothing lady-like about it, but it couldn't be helped.

Without giving herself time to think, she swung one leg over the side and wrapped it around the rope, then held tight to the rim while she lowered her other leg. First one hand then the other grabbed the rope. She tried to adjust her handkerchief under her hands, but it fluttered out of her grasp and floated toward the trees. A lump rose in her throat.

"Are you okay, Elena? Have you started down?"

She hugged the rope. His voice sounded so far away.

"Elena. Can you answer me?" If he decided to climb up to see for himself the rope would jump all over the place.

"I'm okay."

Justin had looked like an inchworm going along the rope. She tried to follow his example but only managed to wiggle around until she got the right rhythm. Then she made progress. An eternity later, she inched through the tree's leaves and into Justin's waiting arm. She clung to him with all her might. He hugged her tight while holding the trunk of the tree with his other arm.

"Here's some good news," he said in her ear. "Since the tree is on a hill we're not as high as I thought we'd be."

She loosened her grip to peer down and saw he was right. Not only that, but the branches were fairly close together. They made their way to the lowest level without too much difficulty. Once they reached the bottom branch, Justin jumped into the thick undergrowth, then assisted her.

As soon as her feet hit the ground, she remembered her state of dress. Mortified, she jerked her skirt out of the waistband and shook it out.

Justin had made sure she was steady then crunched off through the undergrowth behind her. She took a quick glance to see if he was going to tease her, but he was paying no attention. As a matter of fact, he'd already disappeared from sight in the dim forest.

CHAPTER THIRTY-TWO

*A*s soon as Elena was on the ground, Justin blew out a big sigh of relief. She was safe, but this was far from over.

He waded through knee-high plant life, snapping twigs and crunching dried leaves. Justin wanted to keep his back to Elena long enough for her to right her skirt. She would be embarrassed in the extreme if she thought he noticed. But it had been smart thinking on her part, to make pantaloons out of her skirt.

Crunching, shuffling noises came toward him and stopped at his side. "What are you looking for?"

"I hope we'll find a trail that will lead us out of the woods. There must be deer about. It would be narrow, but cleared, not as likely to trip us up."

"It's hard to see anything in the dark." She shot a quick glance his way, then turned her eyes back to the ground.

"We don't have to have a trail. As long as we keep going downhill we'll come to the beach."

"What will we do then?"

"We'll worry about that when we get there." He tucked her hand in the crook of his elbow and started down. "Watch your step."

They crunched along, sending small animals scurrying through the undergrowth. He untangled Elena's foot twice when she got caught in a vine and kept her on her feet when she tripped over roots.

It was no wonder she'd had so many accidents in her lifetime. If there was anything to trip over or run into, she found it. He wondered briefly if there was a scientific explanation for it or if she was just plain unlucky.

After thirty minutes of picking their way through the undergrowth they stepped from the trees, waded through the tall grass and came to a stop on the sandy beach. He shook out the cramped muscles in his arms and legs, then stretched his back. Getting Elena safely down the hill had made him tenser than he realized.

Elena sank to the sand and he joined her. "My legs won't hold me up another minute. I've longed for adventure, but apparently there is a limit to how much my body can take in one day."

"The day isn't over yet. We have to walk to that fishing village we saw as we came in."

They sat for a few minutes, watching the gentle waves roll up on the shore. The ruckus they'd caused in the woods earlier had calmed down, and Justin became aware of peace settling around them like a comforting blanket.

The mild temperature, and the rhythmic sound of waves washing onto the beach soothed his frayed nerves. Elena sat next to him, snuggled under his arm. He couldn't remember any time in his life he'd been happier.

"We should get going." He heard the regret in her voice.

He stood and pulled her to her feet, causing her to wince. "What is it?"

"It's nothing. My hands sting a little."

Turning them palms up he saw they were red, but thankfully not burned. He kissed each palm and after he'd secured her arm through his, they began the trek toward the village.

"The houses appeared closer from the air. How much farther do you suppose it is?"

"Not much, I hope." The soft sand made the going slow and it kept getting in his shoes. He should take them off before the grit between his feet and the leather gave him blisters. Elena hadn't said a word about her feet being bothered, so he didn't want to complain.

It suddenly dawned on him that it would be easier to walk if they were closer to the water. He steered her toward the shore and found that the damp sand, did indeed, make the going quicker.

Elena stopped and stared out over the sea. The rising moon cast a silvery path across the water and stars glittered in the dark sky above them.

She breathed out a sigh. "It's beautiful. Mesmerizing." She glanced up at him then turned her gaze back to the sea. "I wish I had time to sit and enjoy it. God's creation is wondrous."

"I couldn't agree more."

The next thing he knew she had tugged her hand out of the crook of his arm and plopped onto the sand. "What are you doing? We can't stop now."

"I know, but I'm not going to be this close to the water and not get my feet wet." She rapidly unbuttoned her shoes. Once off, she discreetly removed her stockings and stuffed them into her shoes. He watched, surprised.

She stood, wiggled her toes in the sand and smiled. "It feels heavenly. So much better than the rocky beaches we have at home." She turned to him. "You should take your shoes off and see what I mean."

He stared at her a moment. Why not? My feet hurt, anyway. He sat and removed his shoes and socks. When he stood he dug his toes under the sand and scooped some up on top of his foot, then shuffled along. He watched the cool, silky-smooth sand sliding over his feet, then turned to Elena with a grin. "This is delightful."

She laughed, caught the hand that wasn't holding his shoes and tugged him toward the shoreline. They strolled along the edge, letting the warm water lap over their feet. He didn't mind that the hems of his pant legs were getting soaked, or that this had been the most terrifying day of his life. It was all worth it to be here now, with Elena.

"I see boats." The regret in her voice was clear and he stifled a groan.

He saw them, too. Two piers stretched out into the water with several boats tied along each. Some had tall masts and others had smoke stacks. It was too dark to see the color of the hulls.

When they headed back onto the dry sand, Elena gave a yelp and started hopping around. "Something is biting me." She took off running down the beach. He'd barely had time to start after her when she stepped in a hole and fell face first to the ground.

He ran to her side and knelt down, helped her roll over then sit up. She gave a cry of pain when she moved her right foot. Tears streamed down her cheeks. "Oh, Justin, I've done it now."

Her toes peeked out from under the sodden hem of her skirt. He gingerly lifted the edge to get a closer look and winced. Her foot was already swelling from the ankle down. His gut twisted. This shouldn't have happened. He was supposed to keep her safe.

A shout sounded and they saw two men, with flaming torches, standing at the top of the sand dune Elena had fallen beside. Justin stood and watched the men approach slowly. They came to a stop about eight feet away and stared at them with a mix of fear and suspicion.

One was tall and wiry, the other shorter and beefy. Both had red hair that bristled under their caps, and bushy beards. They wore overalls with shirtsleeves rolled up to the elbows, and heavy boots.

Justin wasn't sure what to make of their manner, but hoped they'd be willing to help. "Gentlemen, it's good of you to come see about our predicament. I'm afraid my friend has twisted her ankle and we are in need of assistance."

He glanced at Elena. Even though her pain was obvious, she

had stopped crying and regarded the men with a hopeful expression.

"I'm Justin Ramsey, by the way." He paused, waiting for them to introduce themselves. They looked at him and Elena and then at each other.

Finally, the taller man asked, "How did you get here?"

Understanding dawned. Of course, they would be wondering how the two of them came to be on the beach with no apparent means of transportation. He'd heard that fishermen were a superstitious lot.

Elena piped up from where she sat in the sand. "We came in a balloon." She pointed the direction they'd come from. "It got stuck in the trees back that way."

The men glanced at each other, frowned and turned back to Justin. The tall man spoke again. "We didn't see a balloon and I'm thinking that's a pretty big thing to miss."

"I know it's hard to believe, but it's true. We arrived just as it was getting dark. I'd be happy to show you where it is, but it would be nice if we could get the young lady inside first. Her ankle needs attention."

The men approached cautiously and held their torches lower, so they could see Elena's offending appendage. They both breathed a sigh that sounded like relief to Justin's ears. What were they expecting? A mermaid tail?

CHAPTER THIRTY-THREE

*E*lena couldn't understand the men's reluctance. It was almost as if they were afraid of Justin and her, or maybe protective to the extreme of this shoreline. Was it so hard to believe that they could have arrived in a balloon?

Her ankle and foot throbbed. The pain would make it easy to let her tears flow and might make the men more sympathetic. When they came around to see for themselves, their expressions went from suspicious to concern and they both released a breath.

The taller man spoke, "Something will have to be done for that. We should take her to your cottage, Hugh. Branna will take good care of her."

"I agree. We'll leave it to you to carry your wife, Mr. Ramsey. Owen and I are used to catching fish, not rescuing young women."

The men headed back the way they'd come without watching to see if she and Justin followed. Elena stared at their retreating backs a moment, then turned to Justin, who also seemed perplexed. He shook his head and crouched next to her. "You heard the men. I'm to carry you. Are you ready?"

She was more than ready to get off the sand and get help for her ankle. And she didn't mind being carried in his arms, but it would be the second time this summer he had to transport her in such a manner. "Maybe if I lean on you I could hop on my good foot."

He gave a short laugh. "And maybe you'll cooperate without an argument." Justin quickly tied the laces of his boots together and hung them around his neck. He handed Elena her shoes, then scooped her in his arms and started up the hill.

A red-hot stab of pain shot through her foot and ankle when it lifted from the ground and bumped into her other foot. A cry escaped before she could stop it.

"I'm sorry, Elena. I'll try to be careful."

Remorse filled his voice, as if he blamed himself for her injury. She wrapped one arm around his neck and cradled her shoes to her chest with the other. "It's not your fault," was all she could say before she buried her face against his shoulder, biting her lip to keep from making another sound.

Elena lifted her head when they came to a stop. Hugh threw open the door of a cottage and called, "Branna. We'll be needing your help." He led the way into a warm room which served as both kitchen and living area. The tantalizing aroma of fresh bread and mutton stew greeted them.

A plump woman, with hair dark as midnight and a kind face, dropped her mending on the table and hurried over. A boy of about twelve years followed. "What'd you find, Da, a mermaid?"

Hugh threw a quick look at Owen then said to his son, "Don't be daft, boy." He pointed at Elena's swollen ankle. "Just a regular young woman who stepped in a hole."

Elena would have laughed if she didn't hurt so much.

Branna winced in sympathy when she saw Elena's swollen, discolored foot. She directed Justin toward a small sofa. "Put her on the settee, sir. I'll see what I can do."

The settee wasn't long enough for her to lie on, but it had a high back that curved around both ends. Justin placed her so she could lean against the end facing the kitchen, and gently laid her

152

legs on the seat. She couldn't help a small gasp of pain when her foot came to rest.

Branna patted her shoulder and smoothed her hair away from her forehead. "There, there, dear. We'll get you fixed up." She turned to her husband. "Hugh, put the kettle on. Tea is the first thing we'll need."

Hugh huffed, then said, "Tea isn't the answer for everything, Branna."

She frowned and Hugh went to the stove.

She turned to the boy, who was on his way to being the spitting image of his father. "Kevin, I want you to go down to Dingle's pond and get me a bowlful of comfrey." The young man had been staring at Elena since they'd come in the door. His face fell on hearing his mother's directive. There was no argument, though. He picked up a large wooden bowl and left.

Owen was next on Branna's list. She pointed at the bucket sitting by the door. "Take that to the icehouse. I want it full of ice chips." He didn't appear happy, but he picked up the bucket and headed out the door, grumbling as he went.

While Branna went to help with the tea, Elena leaned forward to see just how bad her foot appeared and gasped again. How could it have gotten so big? It had to be twice its normal size.

Justin tried to ease her back against the curve of the sofa. "I know it's not a pretty sight, but the swelling will come down. You should try to relax."

She groaned. "I can't relax. That isn't natural." She stared in morbid fascination, gritting her teeth against the pain that throbbed with every heartbeat. What if her foot got so big it exploded?

Suddenly, Justin's face was between her and her foot, effectively blocking her view. She blinked a couple of times to bring him in focus. He knelt beside the sofa and said something. She frowned. "I beg your pardon. What were you saying?"

"Mrs. Murphy has some tea for you."

"Oh!" She turned to see the motherly woman standing at her side, holding a steaming mug. "I'm sorry."

"Don't you worry, Mrs. Ramsey, I understand." She handed her the mug and Elena took a sip of the strong tea. Without milk or sugar, it took all her concentration not to make a face. "I'll be right back with a pillow to put under your foot. It helps to have it lifted up."

As soon as she left, Elena turned to Justin. "Mrs. Ramsey?"

"I'm afraid I haven't straightened them out on that yet. They seem to assume a man and a woman in our current situation would be married."

She closed her eyes and let her head fall back. Remorse filled her. There didn't seem to be an end to the ways she could ruin his life. He had escaped death, but now he would be obligated to marry her instead of going to America.

A thump sounded next to her. She opened her eyes to see Justin settling onto a chair he'd carried over from the dining table, his expression serious. "Elena, I'm–"

"Justin, I'm sorry." She didn't want him apologizing first for something that wasn't his fault. "I've compromised you and, being a man of honor, I'm sure you feel it your duty to marry me."

Tears clogged her throat. She swallowed them down and went on. "I would never force you to do that. I want you to go to America and live the life you've dreamed of."

He smiled, took the mug and set it on the floor. Then he reached for her hands and clasped them in his. "I believe the compromising usually works the other way around. However, in this case I can see we're both to blame. After all, no one made me climb up that rope and join you in the balloon's basket. I could have let you go sailing off alone."

He wasn't mad at her. She sighed as a tear rolled down her cheek. How could she not have known before today how dear he was to her? Now that she knew, it made her more determined to ensure he got to live the life he wanted.

Branna approached with a pillow. "Your foot will be more comfortable resting on this." She gently eased Elena's foot onto the pillow as the door opened.

Owen clomped in with the bucket followed by a raw-boned woman with a dour face. Branna straightened. "Good. Set it on the table."

She turned her back on the couple and Elena saw annoyance flicker across Branna's face. "I'm going to put this oilcloth under your foot, as well, so the pillow won't get wet."

Elena clenched her teeth against the pain each time her foot was moved. She no longer wanted to see it. If it was getting bigger, she didn't want to know.

Owen set down the bucket and he and the woman, who had remained focused on her from the moment they entered the cottage, came across the room to the sofa.

Justin stood, but Branna motioned him back in his seat. "Those kinds of manners aren't necessary right now." She turned and acknowledged the woman. "Hello, Maeve, you're here to help I assume."

"That's right, Branna. My husband thought I might be needed." Maeve spoke, but never took her eyes off Elena. Branna opened her mouth, then closed it and went to the table. Maeve, in the meantime, gave Elena's feet and legs a thorough inspection.

Elena glanced at Justin. He mouthed the word "mermaid" and chuckled.

Maeve turned her small, eyes on Justin, taking him in from his head to his feet and back. "You think it's funny that your wife's been injured?"

His eyes widened. "No, not at all. I appreciate the help, but there's something I should clear up."

"Give back her tea."

Justin's mouth fell open for the few moments he stared at her. Then he picked up the mug and put it in Elena's hands.

Elena took a sip to hide her smile. Justin's reaction to this woman's appalling lack of manners was too funny. Maeve's eyes were on her face now. "Where did you say you came from?"

"We started out from Brighton around lunch time and arrived down the beach about an hour ago."

The woman frowned and pursed her lips. Elena could see why Branna had appeared annoyed, earlier. Maeve wasn't a pleasant person.

"Excuse me." Branna stepped between Maeve and Elena, holding a bundle of cheesecloth which she settled gently on Elena's swollen foot. It was filled with ice chips and after the initial shock of cold, it soothed.

Kevin banged in through the door with a bowl full of green plants and thunked it on the table. Branna hurried over, leaving Elena and Justin to Maeve's interrogation.

Maeve crossed her arms over her chest and looked down her nose at them. "Owen says you came in a balloon. I find that hard to believe."

In all her life, Elena had never encountered someone so rude. She hardly knew how to respond. Thank goodness, Justin didn't have the same problem. "Madam, I assure you we did indeed arrive in a gas balloon. I will be happy to show your husband where it is as soon as my friend is settled comfortably."

"You saying you two aren't married?" Maeve's surprised expression quickly settled into a scowl. She pointed a finger at Justin, "You're out about the countryside alone with a lady who is not your wife? Maybe that's accepted where you come from."

All conversation in the room stopped. Maeve resumed her haughty posture. "Or maybe she isn't a lady, or even human."

Elena's face and neck flushed, and the heat kept going until her whole body burned. She pressed her lips tight against the words that wanted to pour out. Words she knew wouldn't honor God.

Kevin ran to the sofa and Maeve moved to stand in front of him. He slipped around her and scanned Elena from her feet to her face. Maeve grabbed him by the arm and dragged him away, protesting. "She looks like a real girl to me."

"You can't tell for sure. Either way, you don't need to be getting close to the likes of her."

Justin came to his feet. "Now see here. I'll not allow Miss Bishop's reputation to be slurred." He stood straight and tall and made eye contact with each person in the room. Elena almost cried as he came to her rescue again.

Maeve's eyes widened and she took another step back, hauling Kevin with her.

Justin's stern face and tone of voice earned him everyone's undivided attention. "I've tried several times to clear up the misunderstanding that Miss Bishop is my wife. I hope you will now do me the courtesy of listening."

Justin told the entire story of their friendship and their adventure. He paused and rested his hand on her shoulder before continuing. "I'm sure our families are worried sick about us. We thank God you found us and brought us here."

Branna wiped her eyes with her apron and Hugh coughed a little before saying, "We were glad to help." He jabbed Owen with his elbow. "Weren't we?"

Owen's face was contrite. "Yes Ma'am. Just seemed mighty peculiar is all."

To Elena's relief, even Maeve's face had softened.

Kevin grinned. "I told you she was a regular girl."

CHAPTER THIRTY-FOUR

S quire Bishop remained calm and strong for the sake of Lady Ramsey, as they traveled to Brighton. He had sent her a message as soon as Luke returned to Oakwood with the news about Elena and Justin. She sent a message straight back telling him she and her driver would pick him up shortly.

"I'm sure they'll be fine," Lady Ramsey said for the hundredth time. She tapped her fan in the palm of her gloved hand as she'd been doing for most of the ride.

"I'm sure you're right." He tapped the fingers of his right hand on the cushioned seat to the same rhythm as Lady Ramsey's fan. It was all he could do not to yell at the driver to go faster. The man was already going as fast as safety allowed.

Luke sat in front so he could identify the balloon's owner in case they needed to search for him. He turned to Squire Bishop. "It would probably be best to go straight to Queen's Park. The man who owns the balloon will have returned from his meeting by now."

"Good thinking, Luke. It's a place to start."

"I'm sure they'll be fine," said Lady Ramsey.

Their carriage slowed to turn into the entrance at Queen's Park just as a buggy barreled out. "That's him." Luke pointed at the back of the buggy racing up the road.

The squire leaned forward. "Turn around, man. Follow him."

The driver brought the carriage around and urged the two horses to pick up the pace. They soon gained on the buggy raising a cloud of dust in front of them. The squire cupped his hands around his mouth. "You there, in the buggy. Stop!"

The man continued without pause, even though his hat flew off and rolled along the side of the road. As they drew closer, Squire Bishop called again. "I say, you in the buggy, please stop."

Now the driver of the buggy looked over his shoulder then slowed to a stop. He hopped out and ran back, finger pointing at Luke. "You!" His wind-blown, auburn hair stuck out all around his frantic face. "What did you do with my balloon?!"

"I didn't do anything. It was my mistress. Here's her father to talk to you."

Squire Bishop climbed out of the carriage and stood with his arms at his sides, hoping to show a non-aggressive stance. The wild-eyed young man turned on him. "What have you done with it? The balloon's owner will have my neck if it's been stolen or damaged."

Lady Ramsey spoke from her seat in the carriage. "Oh, dear, I'm sure they'll be fine."

The young man's eyes darted to Lady Ramsey then back to the squire. "What's she talking about? Who'll be fine? Where's my balloon?"

The squire sorely hoped he'd laugh about this someday. Only Elena could have gotten into this situation. He drew in a breath and strived for as much calm as he could muster. "It seems my daughter was investigating your balloon when she fell in and the tether broke away from its anchor." He nodded his head toward Lady Ramsey. "This fine lady's son arrived just as the balloon lifted off. He managed to grab the rope but was carried off with it."

The squire folded his arms across his chest. "Now, how do you intend to get them back."

The young man's eyes bugged out and he sputtered, "Me! Wh..Wh..Wha..?" He stopped and took a breath. "Your daughter is responsible. What are you going to do about it?" It was clear by the panicked look in his eyes that the squire had the upper hand and he knew it.

Lady Ramsey's commanding voice startled them. "Do you or do you not know how to operate the balloon?"

They all turned to stare but the squire smiled in relief. His friend and neighbor had snapped out of it. His focus returned to the agitated young man, as he answered Lady Ramsey. "Yes, ma'am. I was hoping to buy a balloon of my own after a couple more years of working for Mr. Waddle." His head drooped. "Now I'll be sent to jail until I can pay for this one."

The squire grunted with disgust. "Are you giving up so easily? Think of something!"

"What about you, Squire Bishop? You were in the Aeronautics Club."

He regarded Lady Ramsey. She met his eyes with confidence. He had vowed never to have anything to do with ballooning again. But this was different, wasn't it? Today he would make a new vow. Self-pity would no longer rule his life.

Decision made, he climbed into the carriage. "Take us back to the launch site. I'll see if I can determine wind speed and direction."

The young man jumped out of the way, as the driver brought the horses around and started back toward the park. Then he climbed into his buggy and followed.

Minutes later, the squire stood in the space the balloon had occupied earlier in the day. He licked his index finger and held it over his head. The wind blew to the west. Ireland, then, if they were lucky. Wind speed was trickier. It was fitful here on the ground, coming in gusts one minute, and a gentle breeze the next.

Once they were high enough to catch the air stream, their speed could pick up considerably.

"Judging by the wind direction, I'd guess they're half way to Ireland by now."

"If you charter a steamer you might get there by sundown."

Squire Bishop turned to find the wild-haired young man behind him. "What's your name, son?"

"Robbie Denton, sir." He met the squire's eyes. "I want to help, but can we leave Mr. Waddle out of it? Maybe we can get the balloon back in one piece and he won't have to know it was gone."

"The only things I'm concerned about bringing back in one piece are my daughter and Lord Ramsey. The balloon is up to you. If you can retrieve it without help from Mr. Waddle, that's your concern."

Robbie backed up a step, face flushed. "I'm sorry. I didn't mean to imply your daughter and her friend aren't important. They are, of course, the only real reason to search. I know a man who charters boats. If you'll follow me I'll take you to him."

"Now we're getting somewhere. Lead on, Robbie Denton." Squire Bishop's knot of frustration loosened a little as he climbed into the carriage. Having a plan of action always made him feel better. He'd have gone mad sitting around waiting for bad news to be delivered or for everything to straighten itself out.

They followed Mr. Denton to the marina. In no time they were chugging through choppy waters on a small steamboat called the *Albatross*. The squire gripped the varnished rail at the bow, gazing alternately at the sky and toward the horizon. A short burly man came up beside him and clapped him on the shoulder. "Don't you worry, Squire Bishop. The Albatross will get you to Ireland before morning."

He turned to the man, who had introduced himself as Captain Miller, and narrowed his eyes. "I was given to believe we could get there no later than sundown this evening."

The captain smiled, causing lines to spring up all over his

tanned leathery face. "Maybe if the sea was calm and the engine was running proper-like. As it is, we got both those things against us."

The squire's hands curled into fists. "Did Denton know this when he hired you?"

"Sure, but since I'm his uncle, he likes to send customers my way."

The squire turned back to the horizon and squeezed his eyes shut. He had an overwhelming desire to throw something into the sea right now. Maybe if he *imagined* Denton going in, he wouldn't act on it.

They'd churned along in the water for about two hours when the squire felt a shudder run through the boat. Lady Ramsey stood with him at the bow, one hand on the rail, the other holding down her green hat. The long feathers clustered on the sides twisted and flapped in the wind. She grabbed his arm. "What was that?"

He shook his head, but as the boat slowed its forward momentum, it wasn't hard to guess the cause. His heart and his hopes both sank, and the anxious breath he'd been holding mentally released.

Sometime later, the squire drummed his fingers on the arms of the deck chair while he and Lady Ramsey waited for the captain to tell them if the engine could be fixed. It was beyond frustrating to be dead in the water while their children were in who knew what kind of trouble. "As soon as we get back we'll charter another boat. One fit enough to get us to Ireland."

"Oh my." Lady Ramsey stood, wobbled to the side and lost her lunch. The pitching, rolling boat had turned the poor lady's face the same shade of green as her hat. She took unsteady steps as he assisted her back to her seat. "I'm sorry you had to witness that. I'll try not to let it happen again."

"I'm afraid a promise along those lines will be hard to keep. Rough waters can make even the strongest man weak if he doesn't have sea legs." The knots tying and untying themselves in his stomach got worse. So many things were out of his control.

He leaned back in the chair and closed his eyes. Elena would say they should pray about this situation. He considered it. Did he have enough faith to ask for help? A quiet voice in his heart said, "Try it."

He turned to Lady Ramsey. She rested against the back of her seat with a handkerchief pressed to her mouth. He cleared his throat and she turned watery eyes toward him. "I think now would be a good time to pray, if you don't mind." She nodded, so he sent a prayer to God for the first time since before his beloved wife died.

He said amen then noticed the captain walking toward them. He didn't have the face of a happy man. "Squire Bishop, Lady Ramsey, I got the engine to turn over, but I'm afraid she won't be able to take us on to Ireland. We're hoping she'll get us back to Brighton."

The news didn't surprise the squire. The surprise came in the peace he felt about it. God would take care of Elena and Justin.

Now if only he could feel the same peace about what might be going on at Oakwood.

CHAPTER THIRTY-FIVE

*A*merica and the man his grandmother wanted him to find would have to wait. Justin gazed at Elena's relaxed features. Branna's ministrations must have relieved Elena's pain enough to allow her to sleep. He tenderly brushed strands of hair from her forehead. Before he went anywhere, including India, he would do what he could to help Elena and her father.

Her father. He straightened in his chair and glanced around the room for Hugh. They needed to get a telegram to Squire Bishop and his mother.

He spied the fisherman at the table, a mug of steaming tea in his hand and a Bible open in front of him. Branna sat near, mending. Owen and Maeve had gone home when they saw there was nothing to worry about and Kevin was in bed.

Justin approached the table and Hugh looked up with a smile. "Is there something we can do for you, Mr. Ramsey?"

Branna jumped to her feet. "Can I get you more stew? More tea?"

Justin shook his head and smiled. "Is there a telegraph office near? We need to get word to our families."

Hugh rolled his eyes and quirked his mouth to one side. "I'm afraid our village is too small. I've been to the county seat more than once about it and they keep telling me the same thing."

Hugh's voice rose as he talked and Branna jumped in. "Now Hugh, this isn't the time for politics."

He gave his wife a nod. "You're right." He turned to Justin, his eyes full of sympathy. "In the morning I'll take you to Cork. Once there you'll have no trouble finding a boat to take the two of you to England."

"I'll make up a pallet for you in Kevin's room. Not what you're used to, I'm sure, but the best we can do."

Justin swallowed his disappointment over the telegraph office and forced a smile. "Thank you. You've been more than kind. I'd like to stay out here, though. She might wake up during the night."

"I'll be keeping an eye on her. You and Hugh need to get some rest. Tomorrow will be a long day. I'll need to change the comfrey poultice in a few hours."

Justin resumed his seat next to Elena while Branna gathered blankets for his bed. He hated to wait. The longer they were away and their families had no word, the worse it became. They'd surely worry, not to mention he hadn't yet thought of a way to prevent Elena's reputation from being completely ruined. He wouldn't force her to marry him and then wait while he spent the required time in India.

Justin breathed a sigh of relief when he saw the glow of dawn's first light. This had to have been the longest night in history. He'd spent most of it lying on his back, staring at the window. Rustling sounds came from the bed and Justin turned to see Kevin studying him.

"I have to get up now, Mr. Ramsey. You can have my bed if you want."

"Thank you, Kevin, but I'm anxious to get a start on the day."
A real bed could wait. Right now, Elena was his priority.

He got to his feet, stretched out his stiff muscles and got
dressed. Elena already held a mug of tea when he reached her side.
Her smile on sight of him turned to a grimace when Branna
changed the ice bag on her ankle.

He cringed inwardly at the sight of her swollen, discolored
foot. If only he could have prevented the accident. The chair still
sat by the sofa so he slid into it. "How's the ankle? Has the
swelling gone down at all?"

"A little." She gave a shaky laugh. "It's not a pretty sight,
though. All black and purple. And I have little red spots on both
feet and legs up to my knees. They're driving me mad with their
itching."

Branna handed Justin a mug. "Little bugs in the sand, poor
dear. I've got something to help relieve the itch."

She stepped away from them and came back with a bowl full of
gray paste and handed it to Justin. "This may irritate at first, but
you'll soon find it soothing." She dipped her fingers into the goop
and spread it on Elena's uninjured foot. Then she scooped up some
more and lifted the hem of Elena's dress just high enough to apply
it while protecting her modesty.

Elena breathed a sigh of relief. "It's helping already.
Thank you."

Branna returned her smile. "You're welcome. Now about the
ankle. I don't think it's broken, but you'll want to have a doctor
look at it. It'll be quite a while before you can put any weight
on it."

Justin turned grateful eyes on Branna. "The sooner we get her
home the better. We're in your debt. May we pay you for the help
you've provided?"

"No payment is necessary. It's the least we could do. We'd
keep her here until she's fit, but I know her father will want
her home."

After breakfast, Justin picked up Elena and followed Hugh to his fishing boat. Kevin brought up the rear carrying a pile of blankets and pillows. Hugh took his passengers up the coast to Cork and went with Justin to the telegraph office, while Kevin kept Elena company.

Justin sent a message saying they had landed safely in Ireland and were on their way home. No need to mention Elena's injury. That conversation could wait.

He came back to the boat in possession of two tickets for the next steamer out and a wicker chair on wheels. Elena glanced at the chair, then let her head drop back against the pillow. "What are you going to do with that? Isn't it a boardwalk chair?"

Kevin stood with a grin. "I know. Miss Bishop is going to ride in it. Right, Mr. Ramsey?"

"Right, Kevin. Elena, I think you'll be more comfortable in this chair than with me carrying you. This way your foot won't be swinging about and the way the chair curves up in front should protect you in case someone bumps into the chair."

"That's a good idea. I'm glad you thought of it."

Justin hated seeing the pain and exhaustion in her pale face. He didn't even want to see her ankle. Her appearance had been better after her near drowning.

"We're on a bit of a tight schedule. The ferry taking passengers out to board the steamer leaves soon."

Hugh held the chair steady while Justin set Elena on the seat and Kevin stacked a couple of pillows under her feet. Elena reached for Justin's hand and he clasped it. "How long will it take us to cross?"

"All day, I'm afraid. Counting rail time, I don't imagine we'll get to Brighton until tomorrow morning."

Hugh and Kevin walked with them to the ferry. Elena's voice wavered as Justin pushed her along the board planks. "Too bad we can't fly home. It wouldn't take as long."

The thought of getting back in the balloon's basket made

Justin's knees weak. Traveling by boat and then rail sounded a lot safer to him. Not to mention the higher likelihood of arriving at their destination.

When they reached the ferry, they said their goodbyes to Hugh and Kevin, and Justin pushed the chair up the gangplank for the short trip to the ship. Soon he and Elena settled in their chosen seats for the long day. Visions of what could happen when they got home tried to crowd into his mind, but he firmly shut them out. Other than doing what he could to keep Elena comfortable, today they would simply ride to their next destination. Nothing could go wrong while they were on the ship.

CHAPTER THIRTY-SIX

*E*lena huddled in her chair on the deck and watched the horizon rise and fall. If the balloon ride had been exhilarating, this was its opposite. Miserable had to be the most accurate word for travel by steamer. In the balloon she had fresh, cool wind in her face and a panoramic view. Plodding along on the water with its constant rolling motion made her queasy.

Justin, on the other hand, seemed to love this mode of transportation. He'd been at the rail for a big part of the day. She switched her focus to where he stood, arms folded along the top of the rail. The wind ruffled his dark hair and lifted his coat tails. Sea spray glistened on his face.

Suddenly he called out, "Dolphins!" Parents hurried their children to the rail, eager to show them the large mammals leaping up and diving back into the water beside the ship. She caught glimpses when the crowd shifted. Children squealed and adults ooed and ahhed over the animals. They were entertaining, but all she wanted was to put her feet on dry land. Or foot, as the case may be.

The dolphins moved on and the people drifted away from the

rail, looking for something else to amuse them. Justin sauntered back and sat in the chair next to her. He reached for her hand and closed his warm fingers around it. "It's been a long day, hasn't it?"

"Yes. It's given me plenty of time to think about the balloon. How much do you suppose it cost? It's bad enough we have Papa's gambling debt but replacing the balloon will be impossible. We'll end up in debtor's prison."

She shifted toward him and grimaced. Every little movement caused the throbbing in her foot and ankle to worsen. He gripped her hand tighter. "There's no point worrying about that now, and for the record there's no way I'd let you go to prison."

"For now, I'll see if I can get more ice."

When he let go of her hand she caught it before he could leave. "Don't go. It doesn't help that much."

He sank back to his chair, his face full of concern. "It won't hurt." He ran his hand through his wind-blown hair. "I have to do something."

"You did." Elena gestured to the makeshift prop for her foot. "And you've gotten ice twice already."

"At least let me get you some soup or tea."

His eyes pleaded with her to let him do something. "Tea would be good."

"Be right back." He kissed her forehead and hurried off to the dining room.

She rested her head against the back of the seat and closed her eyes. Tea should stay down. She didn't want to risk anything else. Some of the more seasoned passengers had suggested she keep her eye on the horizon as it should keep her stomach settled. It didn't. She found it hard to keep her eyes on something that kept moving.

Soup sounded good at lunchtime. Thinking the fresh air should be good for her she elected to stay on the deck. Justin ended up eating his meal and most of hers.

Footsteps thudded against the wooden deck. She opened her eyes and turned her head to see Justin striding toward her.

"I may have the answer." He rolled the wheeled chair next to her and proceeded to lift her into it, being careful not to bump her foot. As he got her settled, he said, "Several people in the dining room told me it's much better to have a full stomach when on the sea. They say it has never failed to guard against sea sickness."

Before she could utter a word one way or another, Justin propelled her along the deck. Her face burned with embarrassment as people turned to stare or hurried to step out of their way.

Justin stopped in front of a doorway leading to the inside of the ship. Clearly the chair would not fit. She could imagine his consternation. He liked to have things planned out, be in control, but he'd been flying by the seat of his pants from the moment he'd grabbed hold of the balloon's rope.

She sat in that position for only a few seconds before he backed up and turned the chair to fit snug against the wall. "I'm sorry, but I'll have to carry you." He came around and slid one arm behind her back, one arm under her knees and lifted her out.

Elena hid her smile as she put her arm around his neck. He appeared more determined than sorry.

They traveled the narrow hallway with Justin moving sideways so he wouldn't bump her foot against the wall. It was an awkward way to go, but it didn't seem to bother him in the least. They reached the dining room without incident and stepped through the doorway. Many passengers already sat at the tables, enjoying their supper. Justin attempted to pull a chair away from a table with his foot but it didn't budge. He tried the one beside it with similar results. "Huh, I guess you'll have to fit down between the chair back and the table top."

Justin settled her sideways on one chair while laying her feet gently on the seat beside it. Just as he was sliding his arm out from under her legs a group of little boys, maybe eight or nine years old, ran in, pushing and shoving each other. One of the boys bumped into Justin, nearly causing him to push her feet to the floor. The boy shouted out, "Sorry, mister," and kept going.

Elena sucked in a breath.

"Are you all right?"

"I'm fine. Go on. I'm okay."

When Justin returned, so did her appetite. "The soup is good. I'm glad you got it."

"I thought so, too. I figured if you didn't want it I could always finish it for you again."

"I'm sure you could. While you were gone, I inspected the chairs I could see from here, and I believe they're all fastened to the floor. The table doesn't move either. Why do you suppose the furniture is bolted down?"

"I would guess it's in case of a storm. They wouldn't want the tables and chairs sliding around while the ship rocked on the waves. Someone could get hurt. Or if the ship capsized everything would fall to the ceiling along with the people. That wouldn't be good either."

Justin continued to enjoy his meal but Elena's appetite vanished and her heart rate increased. The idea of a big storm or worse, the ship turning over, terrified her. She tapped the tabletop with her index finger while she considered the possibilities. The sky had been overcast the entire day but didn't appear threatening. There hadn't been strong gusts of wind like they experienced at home before the weather turned bad. The temperature hadn't dropped. No one appeared concerned. But still…

"Do you think it might happen today?"

"Do I think *what* might happen today?" Justin glanced at her then continued eating.

"Storms. Capsizing. Catastrophe!"

"Catastrophe?" He smiled and took her hand in his. "No, nothing along those lines. I'll tell you something I've learned in these last couple of days, Elena. If God can take us safely across the sea in a balloon, he can certainly take us back across on a ship. I wouldn't have worried about the ship anyway, but having experienced the balloon first, I don't think I'll worry about any mode of transportation again."

Chill bumps raced up her arms at his statement of faith. How she loved this man God had placed in her life.

"Let's go back to the deck. It shouldn't be much longer." He carried her out the door, and the noisy cries of seagulls greeted them. "That's a sure sign we're getting close."

He turned to the place they'd left the boardwalk chair. It was gone. Vanished. When they looked down the deck toward the bow of the ship they spotted the boys, who'd bumped into Justin earlier, pushing it around the front end of the ship.

Elena sucked in a breath. "Oh, no!"

Justin groaned and set her in a chair by the wall.

"Why would they do that?"

"Because they're boys. I'll be back."

Elena watched him run up the deck and disappear around the corner. In a few minutes a woman screamed, then more screams erupted. She strained to see what could be going on. Next the low rumble of a wheeled chair rolling over the wooden deck met her ears, followed closely by more screaming and yelling coming from the opposite direction.

The rumbling got louder.

Soon, the boardwalk chair careened around the corner at the other end of the ship. Two boys with wide grins pushed, running as fast as they could. The sturdy shoes they wore with their knickers, and jacket pounded against the wooden deck. A boy rode in the chair, whooping and hollering. He appeared to be the youngest of the three. They had to be brothers because they all had curly, sandy brown hair and teacup handle ears. Justin appeared close on their heels. Passengers scattered to one side or the other, leaving a clear path in the middle.

They barreled down the deck toward her. At the last possible second, the chair turned aside. With a loud crack, it plowed into the railing. The boy inside flew forward and hit his head on a post. He picked himself up and staggered in a circle before taking off after the two who'd been pushing.

Justin surveyed the wreckage, hands on hips. If he hadn't seen the whole unfortunate incident, he would have trouble believing it. A small crowd gathered to see and comment on the damage.

"Well, that's done for."

"You might be able to fix it if–"

"Clearly you aren't looking at the same rubble as the rest of us."

"Someone might have been killed. You never should have brought that contraption aboard." A man with a bulbous nose jabbed a finger his direction.

All heads turned toward Justin. Faces that initially showed curiosity turned to blame.

Justin heard Richard's voice in his head, regaling him of all the unfortunate things that happened because of Elena. He didn't see how she could be held responsible for this, but he doubted Richard would see it that way.

He gestured toward the broken chair and spoke in a calm voice. "This contraption was for the singular purpose of transport for my injured friend. If anyone was hurt I'll be more than willing to help, but I'll not be held responsible for rowdy boys stealing the chair and running wild about the ship."

A voice called out, "All right then, who's responsible for the disturbance?"

Half the people in the crowd pointed at Justin. He held back an exasperated sigh as they made way for two of the ship's employees to reach him and the debris. "We've been chasing after the mayhem all around the ship." The winded men stared at the splintered wicker and three wheels sticking out at odd angles.

The taller one asked, "What is it, or was it, to be more specific?"

"It was a chair on wheels. My friend sprained her ankle so I purchased it from a tourist business on the boardwalk in Cork. I thought riding in a chair would be less awkward than being carried everywhere. We're traveling to Brighton to meet her father." Justin could actually feel a shift in the attitude of those around him.

"The poor dear. Now what will you do?" asked a lady to his right.

"I'd like to know where those boys' parents are. My children would never behave in such a manner," said a lady to his left.

"Quite right." The man who'd condemned him for bringing the contraption on board changed his focus. "Their parents are to blame for this. Round them up and see what they have to say."

Justin was glad the man no longer held him to blame, but it didn't help the situation. He'd still have to carry Elena, making it more likely for her foot to get bumped.

Elena! He needed to make sure she was all right. He left the group and the ship's staff to work out what to do and found her right on the other side of the deck. He didn't realize he'd run full circle. She had her hands tightly clasped in her lap and her face appeared paler than it had been all day.

He hurried to her side. "Are you all right? Is your stomach feeling worse?"

Her eyes widened at his question. "Yes, for a whole different reason. What's going to happen? Are you in trouble?"

Before he could answer another member of the crew, wearing a grim expression, approached the group at the rail. This man appeared older, and judging by his uniform, was of a higher rank. He worked his way through the knot of people and spoke with the two crewmen already there. The people stepped back, scanning the deck.

"There he is." A man wearing a flat straw boater hat pointed at them.

The crewman strode toward them followed by the first two. Justin tensed and stood to meet him.

The man offered his hand. "I'm Captain Clark."

"Justin Ramsey." He saw nothing in the captain's face or demeanor to give him pause as he shook his hand. That soon changed.

"I'm afraid we have a situation on the aft deck."

CHAPTER THIRTY-SEVEN

After supper, Phineas settled into the cutout of the oval faro gaming table in the tavern's main room and waited for Mr. Brown to arrive. The old man was almost as pathetic as Squire Bishop. He complained about undeserving children, drank freely and laid his bets in the same order every game. Phineas smiled as he shuffled and reshuffled the cards. Soon there wouldn't be nearly as much to go around to those undeserving children.

He gazed around the room. A good number of regulars occupied many of the tables. Those he didn't recognize gave him pause, especially if they came alone and didn't try to join in conversation with anyone. He picked out two men tonight who had started coming to the tavern around the same time as Mr. Brown. One sat a table to his left and one to his right. Nothing about them stood out as remarkable or unusual, but he didn't trust them.

On two different occasions he'd been accused of cheating at faro, once by a player at the table and once by someone sitting at another table watching. Neither accusation was proven. To be on the safe side, he sat at the faro table with his back to the wall. He didn't like the idea of anyone looking over his shoulder whether he was cheating or not.

Phineas took out his pocket watch and flipped it open. Seven o'clock on the dot. Mr. Brown arrived right on time. The man must have slept in his clothes. Wrinkles and creases covered the expensive fabric of his suit. With the exception of a fringe of gray around the edges, the man's bald head gleamed in the light. His step was a little unsteady as he approached the table. Phineas allowed himself a smile.

He stood and offered Mr. Brown his hand. "Good evening. Would you like to wait for other players to join us or go ahead?"

"I don't want to wait all night on the chance someone else will decide to play. Let's get started." He pulled out a chair and sat directly across from Phineas.

Phineas loaded the cards into the dealer's box. The "layout," a board with the suit of spades pasted on it in numerical order, lay between the two of them. Mr. Brown pulled his wallet out of an inside jacket pocket, removed some bills and slapped a one-pound note on the ace.

The first card in the dealer's box was always discarded leaving fifty-one cards in play. Phineas drew the next two cards. He placed the first one, the "banker's card," to the right of the dealing box. The next card, the "player's card", sat to the left of the box. The banker won all bets matching the "banker's card." Bets placed on the "player's card" earned an even money payout. If the bet placed matched neither card it remained on the table. The player could withdraw it or move it to another card.

Seeing the bet on the ace made Phineas smile. Mr. Brown would be predictable as usual. That made it easier to manipulate the game. The fact that he was easily distracted helped, too. The noisy conversation in the room, people coming and going and the music all vied for his attention. If he wasn't looking around he was filling Phineas' ear with stories about his sorry family.

Neither of the first two cards was an ace. He slid the one-pound note to the queen without comment.

The game continued with Mr. Brown winning some and losing

some. Every time he lost he bet a higher amount the next time around. It was all Phineas could do to keep from rubbing his hands together in anticipation. It wouldn't be much longer before the man was out of cash and ready to bargain with something more substantial.

Mr. Brown might be easily distracted, but Phineas focused on his goal, yet aware of everything going on around him. The man at the table to his right got up and left. *Good.* Phineas glanced at the other man he'd been keeping an eye on. He didn't seem to be interested in the game, but one never knew.

"One more game, Higgins," slurred Mr. Brown. "Any chance you could spot me another ale? You know I'm good for it."

Phineas signaled a server, who went to get another mug.

The ale appeared in front of Mr. Brown and he gulped half of it down. "It's a little warm in here don't you think? Mind if I take off my jacket?"

Without waiting for a reply, he got unsteadily to his feet and swayed a few times before getting hold of the table. He leaned toward Phineas as though to share a confidence. "I think you may have a problem with your floor. It doesn't seem quite even. A person could lose his balance."

"Thank you for letting me know. I'll check into it. Do you need help with your jacket?" It never did any good to rush people when they got to this point, but Phineas was impatient. What valuable item was Mr. Brown willing to part with on the chance that he might earn all his money back?

"No, no, I'm fine." With slow and deliberate movements, he removed his jacket and hung it over the back of his chair. Then he carefully lowered himself to the seat.

Phineas had curled his fingers into a fist in his lap to keep from drumming them on the table top. "Are you comfortable?"

"Yes. Play on, man."

Phineas made a show of shuffling the cards and put them in the box. Even after all the years he'd been "earning" extra income, he still had a giddy excitement in his middle when the big win was imminent. "Please place your bet."

Mr. Brown opened the wallet he'd left lying on the table when he took off his jacket. A befuddled expression crossed his face. "I don't seem to have any money left." He peered at Phineas. "I've played out." The corners of his mouth turned down and his lower lip trembled. "I've got to have something to go home with."

"I understand. I'd feel the same if it were me." Phineas leaned forward. It was his turn to share a confidence. "Money is not the only thing you can bet. Others have laid jewelry, deeds to property, even ownership of their horse. I don't do this for everyone, but I'll make you a special offer. If you have something you can wager and you have the winning card, I'll double your return. Depending on what it is, you could win back everything you've lost over the last few weeks."

The worry lines on Mr. Brown's face eased away as understanding dawned. The older man leaned back, tapping the fingers of both hands on the table. He maintained eye contact with Phineas, which made him jittery.

The finger tapping stopped.

Glancing right, then left, he focused on Phineas again. "You aren't cheating me, are you, Mr. Higgins? That sounds like a very generous offer."

Phineas shook his head and smiled. "I assure you my offer is sincere. If you have the winning card I will double your return."

A line of sweat ran between Phineas' shoulder blades. He was confident he'd played the man correctly, but when it came to this moment his nerves didn't always agree with him.

Mr. Brown heaved a sigh and pulled his jacket off the back of the chair. He fumbled around, reaching into every pocket until he withdrew a folded sheet of yellowed paper. After laying it on the table, he shook out his jacket and carefully rehung it on the chair.

"I've been thinking for some time now that I might sell this piece of property." He waved it in the air between them. "This is the deed to my mother-in-law's house in Shoreham. Its value should be worth what I've lost to this point. The only reason I haven't sold it before now is that my mother-in-law would have to move in with us."

Phineas followed the paper with his eyes. "That is acceptable if you're sure you want to take the chance."

Mr. Brown slumped and studied his hands, now lying still on the table. In a soft voice, he said, "If I lose now and then my wife nags me for a while. If I came home empty-handed, she'll make my life a living hell." He raised his eyes to Phineas. "I have to take the chance."

Satisfaction settled over Phineas as he continued to hold the expression of a concerned host.

"I'd like to examine the deed if you don't mind." He took the paper held out to him and scanned over the document. It appeared authentic. Laying the deed to the side, he moved a bag of chips from his side of the table to Mr. Brown's. "You may use these to place your bets. The first one to have the matching card wins the game."

Phineas gathered the cards together and shuffled them thoroughly before putting them back in the box.

Mr. Brown laid his chip on the ace. Phineas drew the banker's card and laid it on the right side of the box. A jack. Mr. Brown stared intently at the spot to the left of the box waiting for the second card to appear. A nine filled the spot.

Phineas paused. "Do you wish to change your bet?"

"No, keep going." He loosened his tie and opened his collar.

A five and a ten came up next, followed by six and a king, eight and a four and seven and a two. Mr. Brown moved the chip to the queen. The next two rounds were also no wins. He moved the chip back to the ace.

Phineas drew a slow breath and pulled an ace from its reserved spot at the top of the box and laid it in the banker's spot. The card laid on the player's spot was a queen.

Mr. Brown stared at it, disbelief clear on his face. Then he looked at Phineas with desperation. "Just one more chance. Will you give me one more chance?"

"No. You agreed to these terms and we'll stick with them." Phineas picked up the deed, folded it in half and slid it into his inside jacket pocket. "When will it be convenient for you to meet at my lawyer's office to have the deed transferred to my name?"

"Never!" Mr. Brown got unsteadily to his feet. "When is this sort of thing ever convenient?" He tried to pull his jacket off the back of the chair, but only succeeded in tipping the chair to the side on two legs.

Phineas jumped up and hustled around the table to rescue the chair at the same moment the jacket slipped free. He attempted to get hold of the jacket. "Let me help you put it on."

"No." Mr. Brown jerked it away. He tried to line up his arm with the opening to the sleeve and kept missing. "I'm sure I can't afford any more offers from you."

"I assure you there's no charge for my help."

The man who'd sat alone at the table to their left approached. Phineas stiffened, then relaxed when the man addressed Mr. Brown. "I wonder if you'd allow me to help? I'm thinking some fresh air is what you need."

Mr. Brown turned an unfocused gaze on the stranger and after taking several moments to consider his offer he handed the jacket to him. The two of them made their way out the door and into the night.

Phineas stood watching the door for a few minutes. When neither of them returned he gathered up the faro cards, put them in the dealer's box, picked up the sack of chips and headed for his office. He wanted to examine the deed at his leisure.

CHAPTER THIRTY-EIGHT

*R*ichard Ramsey smiled fondly at his new bride as they stood by the rail of the ship. One of her hands gripped the crook of his arm while the other held her hat against the brisk breeze. What a delight she'd turned out to be. He imagined they'd have as happy a marriage as his parents.

"We should be in England tomorrow, Melissa. You must be ready to get back on dry land."

"I'm looking forward to renewing my acquaintance with your mother. My parents will be more than happy to leave the ship. I hope it won't take them long to recover."

"The crossing is miserable for many people. I'm glad you have sea legs."

"I am too. My parents felt just as bad when we made the trip last year. I was surprised when they said they wanted to come with me. I don't think their departure will be any time soon."

He patted her hand where it rested on his arm and gazed out over the ocean. He hoped they wouldn't want to stay more than a month. They were nice people, but her father was a bit pushy. He didn't need anyone trying to tell him how to run his business.

Elena. Her name came unbidden to his mind. He hoped that

wasn't a bad sign. Justin had better have everything under control at home. The last thing he wanted was to have to straighten out any chaos Elena may have left in her wake.

"Melissa, do you remember Miss Bishop? She lives on the estate next to ours."

Melissa laughed. "Of course I do. How could I forget the person who threw eggnog in my lap? I know it was an accident, but she wouldn't stop apologizing. She's a sweet young lady. Why do you ask?"

"I'm hoping an acquaintance between the two of you will improve her tendency to be clumsy. All manner of accidents befalls her."

"Maybe it would be better if I kept my distance."

The twinkle in her eye told him she jested. "You make a good point, but as my wife you may not be able to. My brother is keeping watch until we get home. We're ahead of schedule, so I should probably wire him before we get on the train. Give him a forewarning."

He relayed this information with a smile, but he wasn't at all certain what they'd find.

Squire Bishop strolled through the garden, enjoying the laughter and pleasant banter of their campers. This idea of Elena's worked well for the families and for them. Unfortunately, there still wouldn't be enough money to pay off his debt at summer's end. Only a few weeks to go.

When he reached the back of the garden, he leaned his forearms on the gate and let his gaze drift over the activity in the park. Thankfully, there'd been no accidents or odd occurrences in the last two days. Whoever was responsible hadn't discouraged families from coming. A sure sign of God's blessing on their endeavor, Elena would say.

He tilted his head back to watch the darkening sky. Elena's balloon idea might have brought in the last of the money needed, or maybe not. At this point all he wanted was to have her home safe and sound. Wherever he and Elena ended up going would be home as long as she was there. Time to stop putting it off and make a plan for their future.

He turned and headed up the path, letting his eyes linger on the house, the terrace and garden. The Bishop family had lived here for generations and now, because of his weakness, it would go to Phineas Higgins. He'd spend the rest of his life regretting that mistake.

When he reached the terrace, Rosie came running out, leaving the door open behind her. Screaming, yelling and crashing noises drifted out. "Sir, you have to come to the kitchen. Mrs. Harris has gone bonkers."

"Slow down, Rosie. What about Mrs. Harris?"

She took a couple of breaths then started again. "Mrs. Harris is yelling about rats and throwing the pots about. Wilson can't get her to calm down. Please come talk to her."

He hurried to the kitchen in time to see a pot fly across the room and crash on top of a pile of cooking ware. Wilson worked his way toward Mrs. Harris, ready to dodge if a pot came his way. "There now, Mrs. Harris. Let's have a cup of tea and a talk."

Wilson sounded as if he was trying to calm a skittish horse, but his cook was having none of it. She picked up a large knife from the table beside her and hurled it. It struck the wall above the pots point first and stuck there. She picked up another knife.

The squire had trouble comprehending the sight before him. Mrs. Harris, generally an even-tempered woman, was throwing knives. He was tempted to use Mr. Smith's favorite two words, "That's enough." Instead he said, "Mrs. Harris! What is the meaning of this?"

She stared at him several moments before she appeared to

recognize him. "Rats, Squire Bishop, in my kitchen. I can't abide rats."

"Are you sure? You've never had rats in here before, have you?"

Mrs. Harris squared her shoulders. She appeared as dignified as a wild-eyed woman wielding a knife could look. "We have never, but I seen one right over there." She pointed at the wall with the knife.

Rosie and the two kitchen maids, who'd been watching from behind him, gasped and fled down the hall.

The squire strode to the wall and searched through the pile of pots. This was an extreme reaction to seeing a rat, in his opinion. He saw no sign of a rodent. Maybe she *had* gone bonkers, as Rosie suggested.

"I think you scared him away." He joined her at the worktable. "Why don't you put that knife down, and we'll let Wilson and the men search the kitchen and set some traps? He'll let you know when it's safe to return."

Behind her, he saw a rat peek out from under the stove. "Come, Mrs. Harris, let's leave it to Wilson." He urged her on, motioning with his hand toward the door.

"Right, Sir, Wilson will take care of it." She laid the knife on the table. The rat chose that moment to dart out, running over her foot in the process.

She let out a screech shrill enough to make a banshee proud and ran to the table the staff used for meals. In no time she scrambled on top and yelled, "Kill it! Kill it!"

Wilson grabbed a broom and slapped at the rat as it dashed to the other side of the kitchen and disappeared behind a cabinet full of crockery. Another rat appeared from the pantry and ran under the stove. Wilson let that one go and peered in the pantry. His knees sagged and he held onto the doorframe to steady himself. Before he even turned around the squire could guess what he'd found.

"Close the door Wilson and get your men."

The door closed with a slam and his white-faced servant hustled out.

That left him with Mrs. Harris, who stood trembling on the table. He went to the table and lifted his hand to assist her to a chair and then to the floor. "Let me help you down. I'll walk you to your quarters. There won't be any rats there."

Her gaze had been darting from the cabinet to the stove and other obvious hiding places. Now she gave him her full attention. "How do you know? This house might be infested."

With the kind of summer they'd had, he wouldn't be surprised. "If that's true, surely one would have been spotted elsewhere by now. Please, come down. You're making me nervous."

She scanned the room one more time, then accepted his hand. They moved quickly from the kitchen to her quarters and stopped at the door.

"This isn't far from the kitchen. There could be rats in here, too."

"I'll be happy to check." He entered the small sitting room almost afraid of what he might see. But the room was clear as was the bedroom. He came back to the door. "I didn't see any. I think it's safe."

She narrowed her eyes. "Did you look under things?"

This sounded like the kind of conversations he'd have with Elena when she was a child and he'd been sent to make sure no monsters lurked in her room. "I assure you I looked everywhere."

She relaxed somewhat, but still entered the room with caution. "I won't work in that kitchen until all of the vermin are gone."

"I understand. I have confidence Wilson and the men will take care of it in no time."

Mrs. Harris closed the door and the squire hurried back to the kitchen. They'd better clean them out fast. A lot of people needed to be fed.

He opened the kitchen door to a chaotic sight. He'd never seen so many rats in one place. Every man on staff, including Old Bill, carried food out the back door or chased rats with brooms. Some got swept out, others got clobbered. And, he noted, women weren't the only ones afraid of rats, as evidenced by the yelping and hollering going on. He rolled up his sleeves and waded in.

CHAPTER THIRTY-NINE

*J*ustin's stomach clenched. "What's the problem, Captain?"

"I'm afraid we have a little boy with a large lump on his head lying unconscious on the deck at the aft end of the ship. The doctor is seeing to him, of course, but I wonder if you can tell me who he is and what happened."

"I can tell you what happened, but not who he is. The boy was riding in the rolling chair he and two others took while we were in the dining room. I gave chase and when the chair hit the post the boy flew forward, hitting his head. He got up and ran."

"Hmm. We'll check the passenger manifest. Meanwhile I'll have the crew asking around. Other than his injury, there are a few words I'd like to have with his parents when we find them."

"Good luck. I hope the boy recovers."

The captain moved off and Justin sank into the chair beside Elena. She leaned her head on his shoulder. "Thanks to me, ever since you've been home, one thing after another has gone wrong. And now you'll probably be stuck with me, not to mention stuck in England. Richard won't be happy about any of this." She paused to wipe her nose with her handkerchief. "I'm sorry."

He put his arm around her shoulders and squeezed. "I wouldn't consider you and I together as me being stuck. I'll admit I've had more excitement in the last few weeks than I've had in the last two years, but it's good for me. It builds character, as my mother would say." He kissed the top of her head. "I can't imagine being without you."

"Thank you. I feel the same way." She gave him a teary smile.

"As for Richard, he won't be home for another month. We ought to have everything running smoothly by then."

When the ship finally came to port, Justin carried Elena to the train station where he got two tickets to Brighton. In an hour they were on their way again.

Justin helped Elena stretch out on the seat in their compartment, being careful as he propped her foot on a pillow. She moaned a little anyway. Her ankle still appeared red and swollen, and heat radiated from it. "I'll see if I can get ice."

She nodded and closed her eyes. As soon as he left, she struggled to sit and scrubbed her legs with her skirt between her hands and her skin. The itching drove her crazy. It was tempting to claw away at the skin with her fingernails, but of course she wouldn't. Surely the doctor in Brighton will have something to help.

Before she'd gotten much relief, Justin came in with ice chips tied up in a napkin. She froze. Scratching wasn't ladylike, but now that she'd started, the itching intensified to a level that wouldn't be denied. She rested her forehead on her bent knees and clenched her jaw and fists until her eyes watered.

Justin settled the ice on her foot then rested a hand on her shoulder. "I wish I could do something about the flea bites. If it wouldn't be completely inappropriate I'd help you scratch."

She imagined the two of them madly scratching away at her legs and smiled. She lifted her head and found him kneeling beside her, his face even with hers, and caught her breath. His beautiful compassion-filled eyes warmed her to the center of her heart. They remained in that position a moment, two moments.

Justin slid his hand from her shoulder to the back of her neck and stroked her jaw with his thumb. Every part of her shivered with anticipation. He leaned toward her and she reached to draw him closer. When her fingers touched his face, he stopped and leaned back, letting his hand fall away. "If I want to remain a gentleman I can't stay here." He picked up her hand and kissed the palm, somehow managing to convey his feelings through that less-intimate touch. "I'll be nearby." He got to his feet and left, closing the door firmly behind him.

She swallowed her disappointment. They'd be accused of impropriety anyway. Two nights away from home together would brand them sinners in the eyes of the world. She flopped back on the seat. At least they would have the satisfaction of knowing the truth, whether anyone else believed them or not.

The rhythmic clack of the wheels on the rails lulled her into a fitful sleep. Every time the train stopped at a station, it jolted her awake. The seat on the other side of the compartment remained empty for the first few stops. After the train jerked forward again, she dozed off. Next time she awoke to the sound of scuffling and a man's angry voice outside the door.

"This is my compartment, I tell you. I always use this one. You'll have to find another."

The door opened a crack then slammed shut. "That may be the case, sir, but tonight it's not available. My friend has been injured, and I'll not have her bothered."

"Is your friend occupying both seats?"

"Well, no."

"Then I demand you let me in. I'll certainly not *bother* your friend."

A third voice joined them. "Is there a problem, gentlemen?"

"Yes conductor. This man won't allow me access to the compartment even though there's only one person in there."

"The occupant is a woman," Justin said, "and I don't feel it's appropriate for this stranger to sit in there looking at her."

Elena agreed with Justin. He was the sweetest most protective man she knew.

"Humph. I have a daughter. I know how to treat a lady."

"I'm sorry, sir. This is a public compartment. You can't stop other passengers from sitting with you."

The door opened, admitting a stout middle-aged man carrying a bag and an umbrella. Justin came in right behind him. The man put his bag on the rack over the seat and sat holding his umbrella between his knees.

Justin gave her an apologetic look then sat on the opposite end of the seat and watched the unwanted passenger. The man made a point of staring out the window or at the floor. She took in his shiny shoes, neat three piece suit and bushy mustache which twitched every three to four seconds.

No one spoke so she closed her eyes, willing sleep to come, but she couldn't relax knowing the stranger sat just a few feet away. Then a steady thumping began. She opened one eye to see the man bouncing his umbrella up and down on the carpeted floor. He didn't appear to realize he was doing it. She checked Justin's reaction. He scowled at the man, arms crossed over his chest, both feet flat on the floor. The tense atmosphere made it hard to breathe.

They listened to the thumping all the way to the next stop where the man jumped up, grabbed his bag and left.

"Thank goodness." Justin stood and stretched, raising his hands up and out to the sides. He smiled at her from his side of the compartment. "I think I should stay here in case anyone else feels the need to join us. Do you mind?"

"I'll feel much better if you stay."

"Good." He slouched into the seat, and stretched his legs out in front of him.

As soon as they started again, Elena relaxed into sleep. It seemed as though the train made a million stops. Sometimes another person or two sat beside Justin, sometimes he sat alone. By the time they reached Brighton, the sun had come up.

"Almost home." Justin lifted her in his arms.

"My appearance is disgraceful. I don't know if anyone will recognize me." The wind had blown her hair into complete disarray while they were in the balloon, leaving it to straggle around her face and shoulders. Her clothes were dirty and wrinkled, and she needed a bath. Now that she thought about it, she *hoped* no one would recognize her.

"Yes, well, we're both in need of help in that area. Visiting the doctor is our first stop, though. That and sending a message to your father and my mother saying we're on our way."

A porter found a cab for them and they settled in for the ride to the doctor's office.

"I hope there haven't been any problems while we've been away. I can't wait for some peace and quiet."

Justin patted her hand. "I'm sure everything's fine."

CHAPTER FORTY

"*M*rs. Harris, I promise you all the rats are out of the kitchen as well as every service area connected to it." Squire Bishop faced the cook at sunrise in the drive outside the house. After battling all night, adrenalin was the only thing keeping him going. He rubbed his gritty eyes with his thumb and forefinger.

Mrs. Harris fixed him with a steely gaze and a determined set to her chin. "That may be, but there was a rat in my room. If one took refuge in there I shudder to think how many others are hiding about the place."

"All of the staff is searching as we speak."

"As well they should." She paused, her features softening. "I've served your family for many years, and I'm sorry to leave you at a time like this. It's been one thing after another this summer, and I know the rats aren't your doing, but I have my limits."

"I understand. As soon as I can, I'm sending a man to Brighton for supplies. We need to replace what we threw out. If you'll write a list of the things we should get, you may ride along. Will you help me with that?"

Mrs. Harris pulled a handkerchief from the small purse she'd been clutching and dabbed her eyes. "Yes, sir, it's the least I can do."

He went inside and sent the first maid he saw to fetch paper and pen and deliver it to Mrs. Harris. Then he headed for his room. His dirty rumpled clothes needed to go.

Richard filled his lungs with air and released it with a smile. He didn't mind traveling, but there was nothing like being in England. He watched the activity on the docks, from the rail of the ship, as they waited to go ashore. Brawny stevedores and longshoremen, with their shirtsleeves rolled up to their bulging biceps, loaded or unloaded cargo from ships tied to piers as far as he could see. Coal, steel, iron and more went off to Asia, Europe and the United States. Shipments of everything—from tea, sugar, butter and cows —to pianos, raw cotton and wool arrived in England.

A large group of people stood on the dock with expectant faces raised to scan those standing at the rail. The men wore black or brown three-piece suits, and the ladies in their multi- colored outfits looked like flowers scattered in a planting bed. Melissa stepped beside him wearing a deep blue skirt and jacket that matched her sparkling eyes. He held out his elbow and she slid her hand around it. "You ready?"

"Yes."

Two women standing beside him suddenly jumped up and down, squealing and pointing. "There he is! There's Papa." They waved wildly and called to him. He hadn't spotted them and it was far too noisy for him to hear them. That sort of scene played out up and down the rail and on the dock as people saw the loved ones they'd come for.

When the gangplank was secured, the passengers surged toward it, eager to leave the ship behind. He turned, with Melissa, and spied his pale in-laws seated on deck chairs nearby and maneuvered through the streaming people to their side. "As soon as we reach the dock, I'll hire a cab and wagon to take us to the train station. London isn't too terribly far from Brighton. I estimate we'll be home by early afternoon."

"Glad to hear it, Ramsey." His father-in-law stood and assisted his wife to her feet. "I don't remember the crossing to America being this tedious."

"I'll be grateful to arrive at your lovely home." His mother-in-law dabbed at her upper lip with her handkerchief.

"Good. Let's go." Richard hadn't dealt with much sickness in his life, so it was hard to understand how Melissa's parents felt. In his mind, sickness equated weakness.

He got everyone off the ship and settled in a private rail compartment for the next leg of the journey. They couldn't get there too soon for him, either. His home and his land drew him back. He anticipated sharing it with Melissa.

One concern lurked at the back of his mind and the familiar nagging headache that came with it. Even though Justin had assured him Elena would be no problem, his experience told him it wouldn't be that easy. He wouldn't be surprised if everything was topsy-turvy when they got there. Just a few more hours and he'd know.

Phineas came straight from breakfast to his office and settled into his high-backed swivel desk chair. He took the deed he'd "won" from Mr. Brown out of the middle drawer and spread it flat against the blotter to examine it with a magnifying glass. The legal language, the signatures and the seal marking it as authentic all appeared to be in order. Even his contact, who specialized in forgery, had declared it authentic.

He laid down the glass and leaned back in his chair, causing the spring to groan as it tilted. The property was some distance away, and he didn't want to leave right now to inspect it, or verify it was actually there, as the case may be. With his elbows propped on the arms of the chair, he tapped his fingertips together while contemplating the best course of action.

That's it. He sat forward abruptly, his chair squawking a protest. Ronald could go for him. It was time to recall his nephew from Oakwood anyway. As he reached into a side drawer for a piece of stationary, the office door flew open, slamming against the wall behind it with a resounding bang.

Phineas rocked back in his chair with a yelp, banging his knees on the bottom of the center desk drawer. The chair just as quickly sent him forward again giving him an excellent view of his nephew standing in the doorway, laughing.

"You should see yourself, Uncle Phineas. Did ya think the bobbies was after ya?"

"Ronald, get in here and sit down!" He reached for the gun he kept in the top drawer, then thought better of it. No one would work for him as cheaply as his nephew, and he'd have his sister to answer to.

The young man closed the door and sauntered to the desk, where he slouched into the seat opposite Phineas. He wasn't laughing anymore, but the smug smile on his face made Phineas think about his gun again.

He rubbed his sore knees as he studied Ronald. The boy was a bit of a wild card. Phineas was half-afraid to know the reason behind the self-satisfied smirk.

"Well, aren't you going to ask why I'm here?"

"As a matter of fact, I had decided to send for you. I didn't expect you to appear at my door this morning, but since you're sitting before me, I'll tell you what I need."

Phineas watched the smile disappear from Ronald's face. The young man needed to remember who was in charge.

Ronald straightened his back and leaned toward Phineas. "I'm not doing anything else until you pay me for the Oakwood job."

"You were supposed to stop their little "camp business." As far as I can tell, all you did was annoy them. I don't know that I can pay you for that."

The smile was back. "I'll guarantee that 'camp business' is done. If you ask me nice, I'll tell you how I did it."

Phineas spoke through clenched teeth. "If you want to see payment of any kind you will tell me what you've done."

Ronald leaned back hooked his thumbs under the lapels of his jacket. "I infested their kitchen with rats. They hauled out all the food, the entire staff is searching the house and the cook quit. They have a lot of people to feed, and I don't suppose those people will stay where they can't eat." He brushed his palms together twice. "Problem solved."

"Huh." Phineas relaxed and regarded his nephew with reluctant admiration. Bishop ought to be even more motivated to accept his offer now.

"I have some business at the estate today. Come back tomorrow morning. I'll pay you and tell you about a property I want you to investigate."

After Ronald left, Phineas opened the left bottom desk drawer and pulled out a container of whiskey and a shot glass. He uncorked the bottle, filled the glass, and lifted it in a silent toast to himself. The amber liquid burned its way down in one gulp. After returning the items to the drawer, he stood and headed for the door, anticipation putting a spring in his step. He'd hire a carriage to take him to Oakwood by early afternoon. By this time tomorrow, the estate would be his.

CHAPTER FORTY-ONE

*D*r. Townsend finished wrapping a herringbone strapping around Elena's ankle and eased her leg down on the examination table. "You're a lucky young lady, Miss Bishop."

Elena smiled, as the lanky doctor sat in his desk chair, pulled his handkerchief from the breast pocket of his black suit coat and polished his spectacles. "The lady who helped you in Ireland did the right thing with the resources she had available."

He adjusted the spectacles on his nose and regarded her with brown eyes. The elderly man wore his gray hair parted in the middle and had a trim mustache the same color. He'd been their physician for as long as she could remember. "I'm grateful. The family who took us in made an excellent example of the Good Samaritan from the Bible story."

"It's good to know there are still people like that in the world."

He turned and pulled a leather-bound book from the bottom right drawer. Elena could see her name on the cover. "What's that?"

The doctor's eyes twinkled. "I use this book to record all the occasions I've had to treat you. This is the first time you've had a sprain." He wrote the information in small, neat script, and chuckled. "Considering the number of times I've seen you, I'd say that's pretty amazing."

"Yes, well—don't forget the bug bites." Elena gave in to the urge to scratch. The red spots on her feet and legs still itched terribly.

Dr. Townsend held his pen in the air. "Ah, yes. That's new, too." He recorded it and laid the open book on the desk to let the ink dry.

"For the next two weeks, I want you to rest as much as possible, but for those times you must be up, I'm going to give you a pair of crutches. And," he held up one finger, "a prescription for ointment for those bites." He pointed his finger at her. "They'll heal faster if you stop scratching them."

Elena's face grew hot, and she gripped her hands together. "I'll do my best."

He slapped his knees. "Good. I'll be back in a minute."

In a few moments, the doctor came through the door holding a pair of crutches, with Justin close behind. They helped her from the table, and she had a quick lesson on how to navigate with sticks under her arms. The doctor walked them to the door and handed her the prescription. "Remember, stay off your feet as much as possible."

"I'll do what I can to make sure of that."

"I believe you will, Lord Ramsay." The doctor smiled and clapped him on the shoulder.

Elena maneuvered to the waiting taxi with some difficulty. Justin helped her up to the seat and followed her in. Dr. Townsend closed the door behind them and spoke through the open window. "Be careful, Miss Bishop, and be safe."

"Thank you."

As the taxi moved forward, she sighed and looked at Justin. "Those are the words he always says to me on departure."

"I can't imagine why."

"Very funny." She bumped him with her elbow.

The visit to the apothecary didn't take long, and at last they were on their way home. When they reached the edge of Brighton they came upon a wagon filled with foodstuffs of every kind. It moved at a fast pace considering the load, stirring up a cloud of dust behind it. As they pulled around to pass, Elena was stunned to see Luke holding the reins and wearing a grim expression.

She turned to Justin. "Did you see that? They must be replacing all the food in the kitchen. They can't possibly have eaten everything in the last two days. What do you suppose happened? If there's no food at home, what are the people eating? Poor Papa! What are we going to do? Maybe we should stop Luke and ask him what's going on."

Justin gripped both her hands. "If we stop Luke it will take him that much longer to get back, and it appears he has no time to waste. I don't know what's going on, but we can't panic. We can do nothing from here." He put an arm around her shoulders and held her tight. "Try to relax. Take deep breaths."

She leaned into him. "You're right. There's nothing we can do but pray. Dear Lord, please help Papa."

Elena dozed on and off in spite of the rough road. She alternated between worrying about what Papa was going to say, longing for a bath and her bed, and what was going on at home. All the while Luke stayed not far behind them.

At last they came to the stone wall surrounding Oakwood and turned in at the gate. The majestic oaks lining the drive offered shade as they approached the house. Luke turned off on the service drive and disappeared around the back of the house. As they got closer, Elena saw a carriage standing by the entrance and her father in conversation with a man outside the front door. Her muscles went rigid when she recognized him.

Justin leaned around her to peer out the carriage window. "What's he doing here?"

Elena lowered her voice even though they were too far away

for the men to hear them. "He shouldn't be here. The summer isn't over yet."

"I don't think your father's enjoying their conversation."

Neither would Phineas, by the time she'd had five minutes with him.

Richard's in-laws breathed an audible sigh of relief when the estate came into view. The telegram he'd sent from the ship should assure everything would be in readiness when they arrived.

He counted on Justin being there. The fact that nothing appeared out of place calmed his fears for the most part, but he knew better than to completely let down his guard.

As they approached the front entrance, the hair on the back of his neck stood up. The door should remain closed until they arrived, at which time the staff would come out and stand in line to greet them. Instead, the door stood open, and no less than three footmen, one after another, ran from the house holding what appeared to be rat traps. Richard, his bride and her parents watched as the men ran across the lawn and disappeared into the woods surrounding the property.

A shriek from inside the house riveted their attention on the doorway. A faint, "Oh, my," came from Mrs. Worthington.

The carriage stopped, and Richard threw open the door, sending it into the side of the vehicle with a bang, jumped to the ground and marched toward the house. Before he got to the door, his butler appeared calm as usual. Not a wrinkle could be seen on his black suit, his shoes shone and there wasn't a gray hair out of place.

"Good day, sir. Welcome home."

This brought Richard up short. Another shriek and running footsteps sounded from inside, yet Grashel didn't bat an eyelash. Richard eyed the doorway, then his butler and returned his gaze to the doorway. Finally, he stared at Grashel and pointed toward the house. "What's going on here?"

His butler glanced at the carriage and Richard turned to see Melissa and the Worthingtons standing on the drive. They probably wondered if it might be a better idea to climb back inside or proceed to the house.

He turned his attention back to his butler.

Grashel lowered his voice. "I'm afraid this is not the best time for guests. We seem to have a rodent invasion."

"Rodent?" Richard's hands turned clammy.

"Yes, sir." He leaned toward him and whispered. "Rats."

Richard's stomach twisted. He hated rats but couldn't let a boyhood fear control him. Still, he was glad he had his back to his guests. They would have been alarmed at the look of disgust on his face.

"Where is Mother?"

"In the garden, sir. She says she'll remain there until the crisis is over."

Judging by what he'd seen so far, the crisis wouldn't be over for some time. The best course of action would be to get his mother, and then go to Oakwood until matters were settled here. He only hoped he wouldn't find chaos there.

CHAPTER FORTY-TWO

*R*ichard took the quickest route through the house. Some of the sofas and chairs lay on their sides. Furniture and other items usually standing on the perimeter of the room stood in the middle. House staff scurried around with brooms or containers for captured quarry. He could only imagine what the rest of his family home looked like, and how long it would take to put it back to rights.

He stepped onto the back terrace—and away from the turmoil —with relief. It didn't take long to find his mother sitting under an arbor in her favorite corner of the garden. She relaxed on a bench with a book, as if the chaos inside occurred on an everyday basis.

Amazing, but even more amazing was his brother's absence. He took a calming breath.

"Mother, where is Justin? Why isn't he handling this?"

She looked up with surprise. "You're home. We weren't expecting you for another month."

He came to a stop in front of her. "It seems we've arrived at an inopportune time."

"You could say that." His mother closed her book and patted

the seat beside her. "Where is your bride? I want to hear about your trip. You haven't even given me a proper greeting."

"I apologize. Hello, Mother. It's good to see you, but we don't have time for conversation. Melissa and her parents are waiting in the carriage."

She stood and slid her hand around his elbow. "I'm looking forward to seeing them. Of course, they won't want to come in the house."

He didn't want to face the bedlam inside, so he escorted her around the outside. The walk would take a while, so he used the opportunity to ask about his brother again. "Where is Justin? I would have expected him to be here at a time like this."

"He and Elena are traveling home. I expect we'll see them soon. He has no idea what's going on here."

Hmm, maybe he took Elena to visit a relative or friend. Maybe this wasn't her fault.

"I've decided to go to Oakwood until our home is back in order. I hope Squire Bishop is up to taking us in."

His mother slowed her pace and stopped. He turned to her. "What's wrong? Has something happened to the squire?"

"No, well yes. You'll find he's a different man. The man he was before he lost his wife."

"That's good news. Going there shouldn't be a problem, then."

"Except that he's been busy. I'm not sure now is a good time. It might be best to go back to Brighton. Melissa and her parents would likely enjoy a holiday there. In a few weeks, things will be back to normal here and you can return."

Richard studied his mother, trying to see past the pleasant expression on her face. She was hiding something, and his suspicions about Elena came flooding back. He knew without looking that more of his hair had turned gray, and he hadn't seen the cause of it yet.

He rubbed at the tension in the back of his neck, then resumed walking. "We've been traveling for these past seven days. I hate to ask them to bear another long carriage ride."

His mother hurried to catch up and he gave her a side-glance. "Besides, I might as well have all the bad news in one day."

She didn't answer, but her tight-lipped expression told him he wouldn't like what he'd learn.

Elena and Justin's carriage pulled up in front of the house. Turning his back on Mr. Higgins, her father rushed to open the door and peered inside. "Elena, are you all right?"

"I'm fine Papa or will be in a few days."

"What do you mean? What's wrong?"

Justin leaned past her. "Excuse me, sir."

Papa stepped away to let Justin descend. She handed him her crutches, which he leaned against the side of the carriage and reached in for her. He backed out with her in his arms.

As soon as she had her crutches adjusted, Papa kissed her on the forehead. "I'm glad to have you back. You, too, Justin. I'm looking forward to hearing what has transpired these last few days, starting with your injury, Elena. What happened? Please don't tell me you fell out of the balloon."

"Nothing that dramatic. I stepped in a hole and sprained my ankle."

Phineas thumped his walking stick on the ground. "Squire Bishop, I demand you tell me what's going on here."

Elena, Justin and her father pivoted to glare at Mr. Higgins.

Anger made Elena want to give him a good poke with one of her crutches. "How dare you come to our home and speak to my father like that? You have no business here."

Mr. Higgins puffed out his chest and struck the ground with his walking stick. "Oh, but I do. Your father and I were just discussing the letter I sent to offer a way out of your troubles."

"Forget it, Higgins. Your proposal is out of the question."

"Don't be hasty Bishop. Perhaps your daughter would like to know the details. She may be amenable to saving a place in her home."

Elena couldn't imagine agreeing to anything he might offer, but curiosity demanded she ask. She gave Mr. Higgins her attention. "What are you suggesting?"

"I propose we marry, thereby allowing you to remain in your home."

She almost choked on the bitter taste of bile rising to the back of her mouth.

"That privilege belongs to me." Justin stepped closer and put his arm around her shoulders.

His declaration thrilled her. But how could she do it? She wanted him to have the life he'd told her about at the beginning of the summer.

Before anyone could respond, the clattering of horses' hooves and carriage wheels sounded behind them. They turned to see Richard jump to the ground as soon as the vehicle stopped.

His long strides closed the distance before Elena could grasp that he truly stood in front of them. Could he possibly have picked a worse time? What happened to that one more month he'd spoken of?

Beside her Justin blew out a long breath.

Richard sized up her crutches and her and Justin's disheveled appearance with a frown. "Other than the fact that you haven't held up your end of the agreement, what is going on here?"

Mr. Higgins harrumphed. "That's what I'd like to know."

"Who are you?" Richard demanded.

"I have business with Squire Bishop and his daughter and have had nothing but interruptions. You and your lot need to wait your turn." Mr. Higgins turned his contemptuous gaze to Justin. "It would be to your advantage to forget some foolish sentiment you think you feel for this man. He doesn't appear able to provide for you and your father."

If Richard looked surprised at Mr. Higgins's earlier remark to him, he appeared dumbfounded now. "What's this, Justin? You're proposing to marry Miss Bishop?"

"I am." Justin's firm tone implied he expected no arguments. "In light of the fact we've spent the last two nights together, it is the honorable thing to do."

Richard stared at Justin, apparently stunned into silence.

A quick glance her father's direction showed he wore a grim expression.

"It doesn't matter to me if she's a used woman. Reputation isn't a big concern—"

Justin sprang at him, grabbed him by the lapels and jerked him close. "You will never refer to Miss Bishop as a used woman. We were in the same location, not the same bed." He released him and came back to her side but continued to glare at him with clenched fists.

Elena let go of the breath she'd been holding. She'd been sure Justin was going to strike Mr. Higgins. Perhaps a distraction would help. "Mr. Higgins, this is our neighbor, Lord Ramsey, the Earl of Kinley."

Making a show of straightening his jacket, Mr. Higgins shifted his focus from Justin to Richard. He took off his hat and made a small bow. "I am Phineas Higgins, soon to be your new neighbor."

"What's he talking about, Bishop?" Richard turned from Mr. Higgins to Papa.

"I'll tell you what I'm talking about." Mr. Higgins thumped his stick on the ground again. "Squire Bishop here made a wager at my establishment in Brighton, and he can't pay."

A knot formed in Elena's middle. Of course, Mr. Higgins would reveal their situation to Richard.

"The summer isn't over yet, Higgins," Papa growled at him.

Mr. Higgins sneered. "Your little camp resort never would have made enough money to pay your debt. Why prolong the misery? Send everyone home and prepare to leave."

"What resort camp?" Richard stepped forward. He focused first on Papa and then on her. "What is he talking about?" He leveled a gaze at Justin. "Did you know about this?"

Elena's thoughts and emotions swirled. What could she say or do to help this mess?

Justin faced his brother. "I did."

Wilson came down the walk, turned and spoke quietly to Papa.

"I have to ask you to excuse me. My attention is needed inside. I'll return when I can. Elena, you should come in and sit down."

"Now wait a minute. Are we being left to stand in your drive?"

Papa turned to Richard. "I'm afraid my home isn't conducive to entertaining at this time." He turned and headed for the house. "Please come again in a few days."

Richard's eyes widened. Elena had a feeling he wasn't used to being left in the dark or outside someone's home.

Mr. Higgins cackled. "I imagine it would be hard to host neighbors with rats running over your feet."

Elena gasped and Justin's posture stiffened beside her. Rats? What was he talking about?

Papa stopped on the fieldstone walk and strode toward Higgins. "What do you know about this?"

The color drained from the man's face, and he backed toward his carriage. "Oh, you know how word gets around. The servants talk."

Richard scowled and followed Mr. Higgins's hurried backward steps. "My staff has been too busy trying to rid our home of rodents to spend time talking to anyone about it. If I find out you're responsible, you'll answer to me."

Mr. Higgins bumped into his carriage, turned and scrambled in. "I had nothing to do with rats at anyone's house, and you can't prove I did."

Then he stood and addressed Papa. "You better read that letter again and see how much I'm offering. Don't be hasty in turning it down."

Papa came to stand beside Richard. "We're through talking, Higgins. Time to go."

Wisely, the man picked up the reins and directed his horse up the drive.

CHAPTER FORTY-THREE

*E*lena and the others stood speechless for several long moments. Finally, Papa turned and walked to the front door, speaking as he went. "If you want to come in, I'll find someone to make sure you have something to sit on." When he reached the threshold, he faced them. "I have nothing in the way of refreshment to offer, but at least you won't be standing in the drive. Now again, please excuse me."

Lady Ramsey came to Elena's side and gave her a quick hug. "My dear, why didn't you tell me you wanted to raise money to save your home? We would have helped you."

"Thank you, but as you can imagine, Papa is mortified. He's not begging anyone for help and forbade me to speak of it."

"Oh, men and their pride. That loathsome man probably cheated your father."

Richard spoke up. "Men have pride for a reason, Mother. It motivates us to take care of our own mistakes. I'm going to guess this rodent infestation is somehow Higgins' way of sabotaging the squire's efforts."

Elena closed her eyes with a shudder. She'd wondered about sabotage. The odd things happening over the last month, and even the wagon accidents all pointed to it. And now this. She'd like to grab Mr. Higgins by the lapels herself and shake him until his teeth rattled. He'd put lives in danger because of his greed and desire for revenge.

Justin put his arm around her shoulders. "You should go in and elevate your foot."

She suddenly realized how weary she was. "I'll sit for a while, but there's too much work to be done to rest for very long."

Lady Ramsey patted her arm. "I agree with Justin. Getting off your feet is the best thing for you right now. I'll be glad to stay and do what I can to help."

Justin squeezed her shoulders. "I will, too, of course."

"I can't ask you to do that, either of you. It sounds like you have trouble at Kinley."

"Quite right—"

"I don't mean to interrupt, Richard," said Lady Ramsey, "but Mrs. Worthington, Melissa and I would like to help. I have no idea what's happening here, but these are our neighbors and they need assistance. We want to do what we can."

The Worthingtons and Melissa joined the group around her. Melissa patted her hand where it gripped the handle of the crutch. "I hope we can be friends, and this will give us a chance to get to know each other better."

"I don't know what to say." Elena blinked at the moisture in her eyes.

"Say yes," said Justin. "Sometimes you just need to accept help."

Overwhelmed and grateful, Elena said, "All right. Let's see what can be done."

Richard excused himself to help sort things out at Kinley. Although his voice sounded resigned, he didn't appear angry. That was a relief. Elena wouldn't want him to be upset with his in-laws and new wife on her account.

Justin and Elena led the way into the house and stopped inside the front door. As promised a sofa and some chairs sat in the entry hall. The rooms leading off the hallway appeared to be in a complete state of disarray. She sank onto the sofa and turned so she could stretch her legs out. Justin plumped the throw pillow and set it behind her.

She could only assume the whole house looked like this. When the staff did a thorough cleaning they basically turned each room inside out. It was done a few rooms at a time, though. Not all at once.

Her helpers' expressions revealed every emotion from *What have I gotten myself into?* to *Let's get to it.*

"You can change your mind," Elena said. "This is worse than I imagined."

"I'll admit it took me by surprise." Mr. Worthington took off his jacket and rolled up his sleeves. "But I'm not afraid of work. How about you, Dear?" He turned to his wife, who hadn't spoken from the time they arrived.

Elena took notice of her now and was alarmed by the woman's pale face. Mrs. Worthington swayed a bit, as if she could hardly remain on her feet.

"Please have a seat, Mrs. Worthington. You don't look well. Justin, see if you can get her a cup of tea."

Mr. Worthington helped his wife to a chair while Justin hurried toward the kitchen.

"I'll find your father, Elena, and see what I can do to help." Lady Ramsey followed Justin.

Melissa knelt by her mother's chair. "Are you still feeling seasick?"

Mrs. Worthington patted Melissa's hand where it rested on the arm of the chair. "I'll be fine. I just need some rest. Go see what you can do." She made shooing motions toward her husband. "You too, Franklin."

They hesitated then took the same direction as Justin and Lady Ramsey.

"I'm sorry to hear about your seasickness. My stomach doesn't do well with travel by ship, either. I wish we had a room available for you to use. You won't get a proper rest sitting in a chair."

"Thank you for understanding, and don't apologize for things out of your control. I'm happy to stay right here. I don't think I could handle any more traveling about, even in a carriage." She rested her head against the chair back and closed her eyes.

What was taking Justin so long? Elena fidgeted, folding and unfolding her hands. Surely, he'd come back soon and tell her the reason for the condition of the house. Suddenly a shriek sounded from above, followed by running footsteps. Elena started and stared at the ceiling.

Whump! "Got him!"

One of the maids cried, "I saw it move. Hit it again, hit it again!"

Whump. whump, whump! "He's dead now, Mary. He won't be moving again until I carry him out."

"Thank you, Daniel. Please hurry. I can't bear to see it."

Elena smiled to herself. Daniel had been admiring Mary from afar, but now he was her hero. She'd enjoy seeing where this took them.

Justin arrived with a mug for her and Mrs. Worthington, who no longer appeared relaxed.

Elena's heart went out to her. "Are you sure this is where you want to be?"

Mrs. Worthington thanked Justin for the mug then turned to Elena. "Believe it or not, things might be in worse shape at the Kinley estate. I think this is the better choice." She gave them a weak smile and settled back to sip her tea.

"What happened, Justin?"

He sat on the edge of a chair across from her, his brow drawn into a scowl and his lips pressed together in a thin line. "Rats."

"Rats?" she repeated faintly. What Mr. Higgins said was true?

Her body went cold. She wrapped both hands around the mug to warm them.

"The saboteur released dozens of rats into the kitchen and now they're finding them all over the house. Your father and the rest of the men have been working to get rid of them since last night, so they feel most of them have been captured or killed." He dragged his hand through his hair. "Apparently the rodents that escaped or were tossed out went straight to Kinley, and you know how Richard feels about rats."

"Oh, no. You should go help him."

"I will, but I'm needed here right now. There's more bad news —Mrs. Harris left. Luke took her to town when he went in to get that wagon full of supplies we saw on our way here."

"I'll be back in a little while." He stood and squeezed her shoulder.

A stone settled in Elena's stomach. If the rats were in the kitchen first, they would have thrown out all the food. They had a lot of hungry people to feed, and even though they had more food now, Mrs. Harris wasn't there to take charge.

She slumped against the pillow and stared at the floor as tears burned her eyes. Poor Papa. He'd had to deal with mayhem for these last ten weeks, because she'd insisted on having a summer resort. Now the people would leave and Papa would have gone through it all for nothing. They didn't and wouldn't have the money they needed, so they might as well leave as well. Unless...

Elena straightened her spine. She could still save them. Maybe God's plan was for her to save their estate by taking Mr. Higgins' offer. She'd just make sure Papa could stay here as well. And the staff. The idea of it came close to making her gag, but she had to think of Papa and the rest of her Oakwood family first.

Tears, that wouldn't obey her orders to stop, ran down her cheeks. She'd send a letter in the morning.

CHAPTER FORTY-FOUR

*J*ustin went to the kitchen first. To his way of thinking the most important job right now was feeding all the guests. He stepped in the door and found the large room had already been scrubbed top to bottom. Foodstuffs lay in a big pile on the staff dining table, and four ladies, including his mother and Melissa, bustled around making short work of getting breakfast ready. He didn't know about Melissa, but he could honestly say in all the times he'd stopped in their kitchen for a cookie or a chat with their cook, he'd never seen his mother there. However, a person didn't have to know how to cook to fill bowls and put things on a plate.

He went in search of Elena's father. That day, Justin saw Squire Bishop's true character, and admired and respected him for it. By evening, they both had worked alongside the staff in almost every room in the house, no matter how heavy or unpleasant the job.

The most impressive thing about the day was the way the squire handled the guests. Unfortunately, many of the rats had found the tents. Every guest wanted to leave with their money refunded. Squire Bishop was apologetic and polite in spite of the abuse some of the guests dealt out.

Justin wanted to be that kind of man.

When he saw the way things were going he approached the squire. "I'm going to Kinley and send a couple of men with wagons and our carriage to help take the people to Brighton."

Squire Bishop clapped his hand on Justin's shoulder. "I appreciate all the help you've been here. Thanks to you we've gotten many of the bedrooms done, but I know your brother will be glad to have your help there."

"I didn't do more than you or the other men, but it's probably time for me to go home. I'd like to tell Elena goodbye first."

"Last I knew she was in her bed asleep. Come tomorrow to see her and let us know your progress."

Fifteen minutes later, Justin went in his front door expecting to see the same disarray they'd seen on arrival at Oakwood.

He greeted Grashel in the entry hall. "I'm surprised to see how orderly these rooms are. Richard said you had a rat problem here, but nothing seems out of place."

"We've done a lot of work today, but not all of the rooms appear as the ones you see here."

Justin turned toward the kitchen, hoping to find Richard there. "I need you to send two wagons, the carriage and drivers to Oakwood. All of their guests are leaving."

Justin hadn't eaten dinner and his stomach let him know it. He hastened his steps. Hopefully their kitchen was up and running. When he entered the big room the delicious smell of beef stew and freshly baked bread wafted over him, making his mouth water.

Bags, boxes and crates still sat on one of the work tables, but otherwise the scene was business as usual. Mrs. Stevens bustled between stove, oven and work table, making sure everything ran smoothly.

She caught sight of him and hurried over to give him a hug. "I'm glad you're home safe and sound. We worried that balloon you floated off in might take you across the sea."

He gave her a smile and a hug in return. "I'm fine, Mrs.

217

Stevens, just hungry. It's a relief to see you have the kitchen under control."

"We've had a day of it all right, and several more to come. I've never seen anything like it in my life." She took a handkerchief from her apron pocket and dabbed at the perspiration on her forehead.

"Your brother's in the servant's hall having a bite. He'll be happy to see you."

One of the kitchen maids approached with a tray holding a bowl, bread and a pot of tea. "Follow me, Sir."

Richard sat at the table making quick work of his stew. Justin sat and dug in, stifling the urge to laugh at his brother's appearance. His sleeves were rolled up, the top two buttons of his shirt were undone, his hair stood out as though he'd been tugging at it and Justin felt sure he saw a smudge of dirt on his forehead. If only he had the equipment to take a photograph. He doubted he'd ever see him like this again.

Richard poured tea in his cup and stirred in some cream. "Have they made accommodations ready for Mother, Melissa and her parents?"

Justin swallowed a savory spoonful before answering. "They'll be comfortable tonight. I'm impressed with what's been done here."

"We have the advantage of more staff to do the work, but the disadvantage of more to clean. The staff has done wonders with many of the rooms but there is still much to do. When I sent men in for supplies to restock the kitchen I told them to buy every rat trap they could get their hands on. We have at least one in every room of the house."

Richard didn't engage him in further conversation, which he was thankful for. He didn't want to stop eating to talk. As soon as he'd emptied his bowl, Richard spoke.

"I hardly know what to ask first." He raked his hand through his hair, standing it on end.

That explains his hair.

"When did Bishop lose his estate to…what's the man's name?"

"Phineas Higgins."

"Right. I don't believe all this resort business was going on before I left."

Justin drew a deep breath and let it out. Elena hadn't wanted him to say anything, but since Higgins already announced it to everyone within hearing distance that morning, there was no secret to keep. "He lost the wager before you left, but they didn't start receiving guests until after. I told her the resort would result in noise and other possible problems, but she believed God gave her the idea to raise money to pay the debt. It seems they have until the end of August to come up with the money."

"When did she tell you the reason for doing this?"

"Not until we were in the balloon headed for Ireland."

"A balloon headed…why?"

"Why Ireland?"

"No. Why a balloon? Well, yes, why Ireland? What on earth were you thinking to go anywhere near something like that with Elena? Frankly, I'm surprised you survived."

Justin squeezed his eyes shut and shuddered. It would be a while before his stomach stopped churning every time he remembered the burning sensation of the rope in his hands, as he dangled above a landscape rapidly growing smaller beneath him. He broke out in a cold sweat just thinking about it.

He drew a deep breath and replayed the entire adventure. When he finished, Richard burst into laughter. "I wish I'd been there to see it."

Laughing at him? Justin suddenly wanted to shake his brother. "Don't you care that Elena and I almost died?"

"Simmer down. You have to admit it must have been quite a spectacle. If it had been captured on film, people would have flocked to the theater to see it."

Richard was right—it was a fantastic story. And the sound of his laughter made Justin smile. It didn't happen often and for him to be able to laugh at a time like this might mean he wouldn't be so quick to ship him off to India.

His brother wiped his eyes, his smile still in place. "You managed to land in Ireland and secured passage for the two of you back to England. How long did your adventure last?"

"Two and a half days. We got to Oakwood right before you did. Elena sprained her ankle soon after we landed, but we saw the doctor as soon as we got to Brighton this morning."

"I see." Richard sobered. "And how do the resort guests feel about the activity?"

Justin swallowed hard, as if it was his disappointment rather than Elena's. "They're all leaving. I sent vehicles and drivers over to help get them to Brighton."

"What will the Bishops do?"

"I don't know. Squire Bishop didn't think they'd earn enough anyway but wanted to support Elena. Mr. Higgins offered to keep her at the house if she'd marry him. Needless to say, her father isn't happy with that idea, and neither am I."

Richard propped his elbow on the table and leaned his chin on his palm. "The rats didn't happen by accident and Higgins' behavior leads me to believe he's responsible."

"Agreed" Justin leaned back and stretched his legs out under the table, crossing them at the ankle and laced his hands behind his neck. He told Richard about all the sabotage attempts. "Their attorney is involved, but his angle is trying to prove Higgins cheated to win the wager. Proving he's involved in the activities at Oakwood will be hard."

"He could have hired someone to get a job there and cause problems. That person would have perfect opportunity if he worked on the estate. We need to find out if someone new is working there and if the problems started after that."

"Good idea." Justin straightened in his chair, glad for a plan of action. He stood, then sank back to the chair like a balloon losing air.

"Whoever released all those rats most likely hurried to Brighton to brag about it to Higgins. He wouldn't wait around for us to figure it out."

"Probably not, but it's something to check into. We'll go over first thing tomorrow."

The men stood and walked toward the door. Richard crossed the threshold then turned back to Justin. "I also meant to speak of our agreement."

Justin froze. His heart not daring to beat.

"I'm sure you can agree; peace and tranquility are not what I found when I arrived home. We'll help the Bishops get to the bottom of this and then I'll write to Uncle George."

He stared at Richard. His heart restarted with painful beats against his chest and he sucked in a lungful of air. "But, what about Elena?"

His brother laid his hand on Justin's shoulder. "Under the circumstances, marriage is the honorable thing to do. As soon as you're established, you can call for her to join you." Richard gave his shoulder a squeeze, then turned and left.

Justin slumped against the door jam. He'd known his brother was capable of making this decision, but had allowed himself to believe, with all things considered, he wouldn't.

How would he tell Elena?

CHAPTER FORTY-FIVE

*T*he next day, Phineas paced from one side of his stuffy office to the other. He'd shed his jacket and loosened his collar, hoping it would help him think. So far he hadn't come up with one decent idea. If only he hadn't mentioned the rats.

He rapped his knuckles on his head. How could he have been so stupid? What if they connected him and Ronald? And now he wondered about the property he'd won from Mr. Brown. Was that real or a set up? Maybe he shouldn't have sent Ronald to inspect it so soon.Squire Bishop and his neighbor, the earl, hadn't responded well to his threats. He should have taken that possibility into account.

Loud knocking at the door interrupted him mid-step. He called a weak "Come in," and two burly men marched into the room, pushing Ronald ahead of them. The pale, wild-eyed boy barely resembled the smug young man who'd sat across the desk from him yesterday.

Ever the gambler, Phineas made sure his facial expressions gave no clue to his thoughts. Frowning, he glowered at the two big men. "What's the meaning of this? Why have you brought him in here?"

They both wore cheap suits, the jackets of which strained across broad shoulders and around large biceps. Their bowler hats remained on their heads. The man with a scar on his cheek spoke. "We caught him snooping about a property in Shoreham. Says you're his uncle and you own the place. Trouble is, the man in charge there don't agree."

"Tell them, Uncle Phineas. Tell them you have the deed."

"Right, Ronald. I'll do better than that. I'll show them." Phineas went to his desk, pulled the deed out of the drawer and smoothed it on the desktop. All while the idea that he'd been the one played this time settled on his chest, making it hard to breathe. But he could bluff better than most, so if this deed turned out to be a fake, he'd still make them believe it to be real.

Both men crowded close to the desk to see the deed. The man who'd spoken before stabbed his finger down on the deed. "I don't see your name anywhere."

The three of them straightened and Phineas looked Scar Face in the eye. "You're right. The previous owner and I haven't made it official yet. I may have been premature in sending my nephew over. It won't happen again."

The big men glanced at each other. The silent one shrugged and Scar Face turned back to Phineas. "Since you have a deed in your possession, we won't take you to the station, but you should be prepared to bring it in as proof, if they don't take our word for it. In the meantime, stay away from the property."

"You can be sure of that, gentlemen." Phineas herded them to the door and opened it. "Tell the barkeep I said to give you both a mug on the house."

"We'll do that. Good day, Higgins."

Phineas gently closed the door then spun to face Ronald. The boy had wisely put distance between them. If Phineas had been warm before, now he wouldn't be surprised if steam rolled off his body. Fear made him angry. Ronald made him angry. He strode to his desk and pointed at the door. "Out!"

Ronald scrambled across the room and through the door, slamming it behind him.

Phineas dropped into his chair, propped his elbows on the desk and rested his face in his hands. *What am I going to do?*

Elena would never again take her own bed for granted. However, her agenda today did not include lying around. The first order of business was writing the letter to Mr. Higgins. The idea of agreeing to his proposal made her skin crawl, but she'd do what she had to in order to save her family home. Hopefully, he'd agree to her stipulations. Best to get it done before she changed her mind.

Scooting to the edge of the mattress she swung her feet over the edge and cried out as hot pain blazed up her leg. Carefully, Elena eased her feet back up and pulled the blanket over her legs. How could she have forgotten her ankle?

After ringing the bell for assistance, her mind turned to the puzzle of who could have brought the rats. She reviewed the staff's faces in her mind, trying to think of someone out of place. She named them one after the other, until she came to one she didn't recognize. *Who was he?*

Justin arrived at Oakwood with Richard just as Squire Bishop and Wilson stepped into the study.

Squire Bishop waved them in. "Please join us, gentlemen. We've been trying to sort out who our saboteur was."

Justin and the other three settled in the chairs and on the love seat occupying the end of the room near the windows.

His brother crossed one leg over the other. "That is exactly what Justin and I have been talking about. It seems likely to be someone working here, someone with easy access to the property.

Are you quite sure of the loyalty of your staff, or have you hired anyone new?"

Wilson stiffened. "None of my staff would be responsible for what's gone on here. I'd vouch for each of them myself."

The squire nodded. "I concur. We've been family here for many years. How about at your place? Have you hired anyone new? Your estate is close enough to give someone access to my property."

"No. One of our stable hands left, but he wasn't replaced."

"I know who it is." Justin and the others turned at the sound of Elena's voice. She hobbled over to them on her crutches. Justin jumped up so she could have his seat, which she sank into with a grateful smile.

The squire took her crutches and set them aside. "Who do you think it was?"

"At the beginning of the summer, Ollie was found with a head injury. We hired a young man who said his grandmother lives in the village. He's probably the one who hurt Ollie, so there'd be a job opening to fill."

Justin brought a footstool over and gently set Elena's foot on it. "Do you know his name?"

Wilson snapped his fingers. "I do. He called himself Ronny Smith, a nondescript fellow, appeared harmless." Wilson deflated in his chair. "I was in a hurry to fill the post and didn't check for references. If I had, none of this would have happened."

He stood and faced Squire Bishop. "An apology won't right this, but I'll understand if you want to relieve me of my position."

The squire motioned for him to be seated. "I won't hear of it, man. Anyone can make a mistake, no matter where it leads. I need you here."

"Thank you, sir." He returned to the chair he'd vacated and sat, shoulders hunched.

Justin spoke up. "You've provided us with a name, Wilson, so our next step is clear." Everyone gave him their attention. "We need to go to the village and make inquiries about a woman with the last name of Smith, or see if anyone has heard of Ronny Smith."

Squire Bishop got to his feet. "Exactly what I was thinking. If the young man gave us his real name, we should be able to track him down."

"That's a big *if*." Richard also stood. "I wouldn't if I were about to engage in criminal activity."

Justin took a step toward his brother. "It's something to try, though. I'll be glad to start right now."

"No." Squire Bishop headed for the door. "I'll go. It's my job and I've neglected it far too long." He paused at the doorway. "Someone should alert the authorities in Brighton and Mr. Atwood about this Smith fellow."

As soon as he disappeared, Elena said, "I'll go to Brighton. I'm not any use here with this ankle, but I can deliver a message."

Justin knelt beside her. "Your ankle is exactly why you should stay here. You need to stay off it. I can go to Brighton."

"I'm sure Richard could use your help at Kinley."

The last thing Justin wanted to do was go home and clean house. The staff could manage. Direct involvement in helping Elena and Squire Bishop was more important.

Richard came to stand beside them. "Miss Bishop, I agree with Justin regarding staying home to rest your ankle, but you are the best one to give a first-hand account in Brighton. You should go with her, Justin.

"Wilson, continue directing the staff in setting the house to rights. I'm going back to Kinley. The Worthingtons, my mother and my wife should be able to take up residence there by this afternoon. Please keep me informed of progress here."

As soon as Richard and Wilson left, Justin sat in the chair closest to Elena.

"Why are you sitting down? We should go right away."

"I have something to tell you first."

Her brow wrinkled. "Oh, no. What's wrong? I suppose Richard said you can't go to America."

Her perception always amazed him, but it was more than not going to America. Justin stared at the floor. The weight on his chest made it hard to breathe. He should have told her the whole story in the balloon. Now it felt as if he'd been keeping secrets after she'd told him everything. He shared about Richard's wish for him to enter the military and their agreement that Justin could go to America only if he managed to keep things in order while he was gone. "Last night he reminded me of our agreement, and said he'd write a letter to Uncle George once things are settled for you and your father."

Elena's eyes filled with tears and she reached her hand out to him. Instead of taking it, he knelt and wrapped his arms around her, holding her tight. "I don't want to leave you to go to India. I made that agreement based on my ego, when I should have taken time to think. I'm sorry, Elena."

Justin loosened his hold, so he could see her face. "I didn't even stop to wonder what God wanted me to do. I was already set on my own agenda. You see, my maternal grandmother sent me a letter from her deathbed asking me to go to America, and search for a man in California. Someone my grandfather had business dealings with. She didn't give me details, but she did instruct me not to tell Richard, or anyone for that matter, what my real purpose would be for going."

"So, doing research to write a book is a cover story."

"No, I wanted to do that anyway, but adding this secret mission made it more exciting."

"God has a plan. It's hard to imagine India being part of it, but I've come to realize I don't know what He's thinking." She heaved a deep sigh. "I thought the resort was the answer to our problem, but it seems he has another way of saving the estate. My job is to be obedient to his will."

Elena gave him a sad smile. "Either way you would have left

me. I never wanted to get in the way of what you had your heart set on."

Justin cupped her face in his hands. "I would've taken you with me. What a grand adventure we'd have had."

"I love you, Justin. No matter what happens..."

Exhilaration filled him at her declaration. He touched his forehead to hers. "I love you, too." Then he kissed her. Not softly and gently, but with an intensity he hoped conveyed just how much.

CHAPTER FORTY-SIX

*E*lena and Justin wasted no time getting on the road to Brighton. Justin sat in front with Luke so she could sit sideways with her feet on a pillow. It was a strange way to ride. Even though the carriage was reasonably comfortable, when the wheels bounced over bumps in the road, or dipped into potholes, she had to hang on or get dumped off the seat.

Justin turned to her again. "Are you doing all right? It won't be much longer."

Elena had to smile. Apparently, he never got tired of hearing the same answer. "My ankle hurts, but it's worth it. I can't wait to talk to Mr. Atwood."

When they got in town, Elena had Luke stop at the first post box she saw and drop her letter in. She refused to let herself think about it beyond bringing her family salvation. Even if they found the saboteur, it didn't mean her father's debt would be erased.

They finally arrived at Mr. Atwood's office. Elena sat across from their attorney, her foot propped on an overturned dustbin with Justin seated beside her. She skipped the small talk and launched into the reason for their visit. "We have a clue about who our saboteur might be. We hired him early in the summer to fill in for an injured stable hand. He said his grandmother lived in the village, so Papa is there now trying to find her or see if anyone has heard of him. He says his name is Ronnie Smith."

"Smith. It's probably not his real name. Your father might turn up something, though."

He tapped his fingers against the ink blotter on his desktop, while staring at the wall behind them. "Higgins grew up in the village." Mr. Atwood directed his attention back to Elena and Justin. "There is doubtless a connection."

Excitement buzzed in Elena like bees in the flowerbed. "That's right. Mr. Higgins' mother could be the grandmother. I believe there was a daughter, too, who left some time ago. Oh." The excitement ebbed away. "His mother is deceased, so she can't be the grandmother."

Justin squeezed her hand, where it lay on the chair's armrest. "She might be. Most likely Smith isn't his real name, but the young man might have said his grandmother lives there because she used to. I would guess he counted on the village's connection to the estate getting him hired."

Mr. Atwood opened a desk drawer, pulled out a pad of paper and jotted down the information they'd given him. "I've been investigating since your father first came to see me, and found that Phineas does, indeed, have a sister who lives in the area. It's a good guess that her son would be around the age of the young man you hired. I suspect they are one and the same.

"Have you been to the authorities yet?"

Justin gave her an I-told-you-so look when she glanced at him. "We've come straight here, although Justin felt we should go to them first."

"That's all right." Mr. Atwood reached for the telephone. "I'll ring them up and see if a constable can join us here. I have some news to share with you as well."

Soon, Detective Taylor sat with them, his hat balanced on one knee. He pulled out his notepad and pencil. "All right then, what have we got?"

Elena didn't hesitate to speak. "We believe we have an idea who set the rats loose in our kitchen, which by the way, spread to the Kinley estate.

When she'd finished, Detective Taylor flipped the pad closed and tucked both it and the pencil into his inside jacket pocket. "This isn't the first time we've had complaints about Mr. Higgins. The bloke's been running on luck for a long time now. Could be it's about to run out."

"I've been doing some digging on my own, these past weeks, and I found out Higgins has a nephew named Ronald Baker," Mr. Atwood said. "After speaking with Miss Bishop and Mr. Ramsey, I'm reasonably sure he's the person responsible for the trouble at the estates. I have no doubt Ronnie Smith and Ronald Baker are the same person."

The detective pulled his pad back out and scribbled on it. "We'll keep an eye on him. A lot of people will be happy to see Higgins and his accomplice go to prison for a long time."

After he left, Mr. Atwood leaned back in his chair, his hands folded over his stomach. "I tried to duplicate your father's predicament to see if Mr. Higgins could be caught at his own game. An actor, who presented himself as Mr. Brown, frequented the tavern to gamble. Two other men came at different times of the evening and sat separately. They kept an eye on Higgins, but the way his faro table is situated it's hard to see if he's cheating. One of the men felt sure he was but couldn't prove it."

Elena slapped the arm of her chair with her left hand. "That man is mean and sneaky. There must be some way to catch him."

"You've described him well." Mr. Atwood sat forward and rested his arms on the desk.

"Mr. Brown ended up 'losing' a property in Shoreham. I'd given him a forged deed to use and of course Higgins was happy to take it. He didn't waste any time sending his nephew to look the place over. A friend of mine lives at the address I put on the deed and was watching for someone to come. When Ronald showed up, they called the authorities. He told them the property belonged to his uncle, Phineas Higgins, and he could prove it was his."

Mr. Atwood chuckled. "I can only imagine what Higgins thought when the men dragged Ronald into his office."

"It doubtless put a good scare in him." Justin turned to her with a grin. "As it is, he's probably been kicking himself ever since he implied he knew about the rats."

"I have no sympathy for Mr. Higgins. Who knows how many lives that man has ruined? I assume he showed the men the phony deed."

"Yes, but it appeared real to them. They warned him to stay away from the property and left."

"So you mean, after all that work, there's nothing to show for it? You can't prove he cheats and the deed appears real."

"I know it sounds frustrating, but one thing is clear. His nephew runs his errands and the authorities will be watching him.

"If Higgins tries to find Mr. Brown again he won't be able to. That should make him nervous, and nervous people make mistakes. I believe we're closing in."

Elena balled her hands into fists. "I'm glad we're closing in, but if we can't prove he cheats, Papa will still owe him our estate." *And I'll owe him my life.*

"Don't give up yet. I have one more trick up my sleeve."

CHAPTER FORTY-SEVEN

*O*n their return to Oakwood, Elena spotted her father going into the study, and hurried, as quickly as her crutches allowed, to join him. "What did you find out, Papa? Is there anyone named Smith in the village?"

He turned and smiled at her. "I had Wilson send one of the staff to get Lord Ramsey a little while ago. When he gets here, I'll tell you what I found out. In the meantime, let's make ourselves comfortable."

Justin had just helped Elena prop her foot on the stool, when Richard entered the room, followed by Rosie with the teacart.

The squire waited until everyone was served, then told them about his search. "I spoke to the village residents most likely to remember a boy named Ronnie Smith. Several remembered a Ronnie Baker, whose grandmother was Henrietta Higgins. When he got older he wanted to be called Ronald."

He continued talking while he helped himself to a strawberry tart and a lemon biscuit from the plate on the teacart. "I'm not surprised to see this connection to Phineas Higgins. In the future he may want to hire someone with more imagination when it comes to false names. What escapes me is why I didn't think of it before."

Elena grinned at the news she was hearing, and what she was about to share. "Justin and I learned the young man is Mr. Higgins's nephew and he does other errands for him, too." She went on to fill them in on the news Mr. Atwood had given them.

Justin turned to the squire. "I believe Higgins acquired Mr. Brown's property the same way he got yours. He cheated. We just have to figure out how."

Elena watched her father. Would he consider it, or would he continue to blame himself?

Richard leaned forward. "I think Justin's right. I've played faro a few times, and didn't see anything I could call cheating, but surely the dealer's box can be manipulated. The owner of the establishment wouldn't take the chance of his customers winning more than he does. I say we go to Brighton and have a look at the box."

The squire slapped the arm of his chair. "Agreed."

He set his teacup to the side. "And while we're at it, we should have Ronnie, or Ronald, brought 'round, so we can be sure he's the one we hired on here."

Elena jumped in. "Right. Let's leave first thing in the morning." Each of the men zeroed in on her with various levels of disapproval on their faces. A flush heated her cheeks.

Papa spoke first. "You won't be coming with us on this trip, Elena. A tavern is no place for a lady, and I don't want you anywhere near Higgins. At least I can protect you from that."

Disappointment brought her close to tears. She wanted to see this through to its conclusion. Not trusting herself to speak, she simply nodded.

She listened as the men decided on a time to leave in the morning and Papa told Wilson to send a man, as soon as possible, to let Mr. Atwood and the authorities know what they had planned. The three men left the room, but Justin knelt beside her chair and covered her hand with his.

"This must be hard, but I agree with your father. Who knows

how Higgins will respond? We don't want you exposed to anything unsavory."

Elena gazed into his eyes and laid her hand on his cheek. "I understand the objections, but as you say, it's hard to be left behind."

At supper, Papa shared that Richard had come for their house-guests around noon, since one of the wings at Kinley was ready for occupants. "Our staff has done a wonderful job here as well. A good part of the house is back in order."

He paused, and it surprised Elena to see tears gathering in his eyes. "Their loyalty through the summer and during this latest catastrophe is beyond compare."

"They're family." She reached over and gave her father's hand a squeeze.

Elena laid her napkin on the table next to her breakfast plate, while her father finished his tea. Pounding sounded at the front door and she jumped. "What in the world? That can't be Justin."

The two of them made their way toward the front of the house in time to see Wilson hurrying to the door. When he opened it, they saw Phineas Higgins standing on the porch, with his fist raised to begin another assault.

Several moments passed, as they stared at each other. Mr. Higgins recovered first and stepped over the threshold.

His bold action brought Papa to life. He strode forward. "What are you doing here? You have a lot of nerve after admitting to orchestrating the rat invasion."

Elena stayed put, leaning on her crutches several feet behind the confrontation.

"I admitted to no such thing and you can't prove I did."

He waved an envelope in the air between him and Papa. "I'm here at the invitation of your daughter." He nodded in her direction. "She has accepted my proposal with a few stipulations. I suggest we talk about them and set a date to finalize the deal."

She regretted eating breakfast. Now her churning stomach had something to bring back up.

"Is that right?" Papa turned to her with a frown, then swept his hand toward the study. "Perhaps we do have something to talk about."

A smug expression settled on Mr. Higgins' face as he strutted into the study. Elena closed her eyes. "Dear Father, I'm willing to follow your plan. Please give me the strength to do it."

She entered and found Papa standing behind the desk, reading the letter she'd sent yesterday. As soon as he finished, he laid it down and brought a wingback chair closer to the desk. While she settled into it, he brought a stool and lifted her foot onto it.

Mr. Higgins watched without comment, but his tapping toe gave away his impatience to proceed.

Once Papa was seated, he indicated a straight-back chair by the desk and Mr. Higgins made himself comfortable. Papa picked up the letter and put on his glasses. "I see there are three stipulations. Number one allows me to remain in the home and number two mandates keeping all the present staff." Papa peered over the top of his glasses at Mr. Higgins. "Is that acceptable to you?"

"I'm not happy about it but I can live with it." He shifted in his chair. "I want to set the date to wed for two days from now. That will give us time to get all the paperwork in order."

Elena's mouth went dry, making it hard to swallow. She coughed lightly to clear her throat. "You're forgetting number three, Mr. Higgins. This agreement is void if you are found guilty of a crime."

He focused his mean little eyes on her and gave her a nonchalant smile. "I don't foresee that being a problem, but I agree if it can be accomplished before the time and date set for the nuptials."

Wilson appeared in the doorway. "Excuse me, sir. Lord Ramsey and Mr. Ramsey are here."

The two men entered the room and came to an abrupt halt. Richard pointed at Mr. Higgins. "What's this? Why is he here?"

Justin crossed the room and stood beside her chair. He leaned down and spoke in her ear, "Are you all right?"

She shook her head. If this marriage actually happened she'd never be all right again.

"Why are you two always coming 'round?" Mr. Higgins sputtered. "I'm here by invitation. Squire Bishop and I are finalizing the agreement making Oakwood and Elena mine."

Both men gave her an incredulous look, then turned to Papa. Richard, always first to speak, asked, "Are you mad? What about our conversation yesterday?"

Papa took off his glasses and rubbed his temples. "We were discussing Elena's third stipulation. If Higgins is found guilty of a crime, any agreement made is null and void."

Justin slammed both hands on the desktop and leaned forward. Looking Papa in the eye, he said, "I love your daughter. There will be no agreement, ever."

"Stop! Don't sign anything." Mr. Atwood charged into the room, his ancient portmanteau swinging at his side in his haste. "Squire, there are further developments you need to know about before you make any agreement with this man."

Elena kept an eye on Mr. Higgins. His bravado was quickly turning into a full-blown case of nerves. He pulled out his handkerchief and dabbed at his neck and forehead and glanced at the door. "This conversation has nothing to do with me, so I'll take my leave."

When he stood, all the others did as well. Mr. Atwood gestured toward Mr. Higgins. "You are part of this discussion. I'll admit I'm surprised to see you here. We all planned to come see you at your tavern at noon today."

He took a step back. "Why?"

"Because we've heard the food is good, and we're having a meeting with you and the police." He turned and addressed the room at large. "What say we head to Brighton now? You take the lead, Mr. Higgins, since we're going to your establishment."

The man scurried from the room and they soon heard the sound of the front door closing.

"Mr. Brown has lodged a complaint and the authorities are finally ready to act. They'll be at the tavern at 1:00 to talk to Higgins and inspect his dealer's box. The plan is also to have Ronald, or as you know him, Ronnie, there. If he's backed into a corner, I don't think it'll take much to get him to tell all he knows about his Uncle Phineas."

Papa and Richard left to make arrangements for a carriage, and Mr. Atwood came to her chair. He winked. "This is the trick I had up my sleeve. Mr. Higgins luck is about to run out."

Justin clapped Mr. Atwood on the back. "Good work." Then he reached down and squeezed Elena's hand. "This is wonderful news."

"I hope so, but I have my doubts he'll be there. Then what?"

"Don't you worry, Miss Bishop, he can be convicted whether he's there or not."

She watched them leave and prayed for God's justice.

CHAPTER FORTY-EIGHT

One thing was for sure—Justin wouldn't let Elena marry Higgins.

If he had to kidnap her and elope, he'd do it. Richard could find someone else to send to the military.

Arriving at the tavern with Richard, the squire and Mr. Atwood, Justin noticed the tempting aroma of roasting meat. When this was over, maybe they could eat. Most of the tables were full, and everyone appeared satisfied.

The four of them scanned the room and saw nothing of Higgins, nor the police.

Mr. Atwood led them to a table. "We might as well wait for the show to start."

They hadn't been sitting long when Justin saw four constables come in herding a young man along in front. Mr. Atwood went to meet the group, while the rest of them stood and waited. As they approached, Justin tried to place the young man. He looked familiar, but Justin didn't think he could positively identify him.

When they came to a stop in front of the three men, the squire's eyes narrowed. "Hello, Ronnie. You left without notice. It's a good thing Ollie recovered from his head injury in time to take his job back. You remember Ollie, don't you?"

Ronnie's face had paled on seeing the squire and he backed up into the constable behind him. "I don't know what you're talking about."

Squire Bishop glanced around the room "Do you know where your uncle is? We've come to see him."

"If he's not down here, he's in his rooms upstairs."

"Lead on. We're right behind you."

Phineas knew he couldn't have gotten to the tavern much ahead of the others. He rushed up the stairs and unlocked his door. His heart raced as he ran to his desk, pulled his briefcase out of the bottom drawer and filled it with all papers, bank notes or IOUs that could implicate him in criminal activity.

In the bedroom he grabbed his valise and stuffed it with clothes and money. Now if he could just get downstairs and out the back door. He tried to slow down his breathing as he tip- toed to the door. The short gasps made him dizzy.

He reached for the doorknob and heard what sounded like hundreds of men pounding their way up the wooden staircase. Too late. The adrenaline fueling him evaporated, leaving him with limbs so weak he could barely drag himself to his desk. Phineas sat in the chair, opened the top right drawer, pulled out his gun and laid it in front of him.

When they reached the door, one of the constables knocked. No response, so Mr. Atwood told Ronald to go in and see if his uncle was there. Ronald hesitated, then slowly opened the door, peeked in and closed it. "I didn't see anyone. We should come another time."

"I'd like you to try again, and this time, go all the way in. He should be expecting us."

With a shuddering sigh, Ronald opened the door and stepped in.

Justin wondered what the boy was so afraid of. Maybe they shouldn't have made him go in.

They heard Mr. Higgins say, "Hello, Ronald. Do you have friends with you?"

"Not friends," Ronald's trembling voice answered,

The constables waved Justin and the other men away from the door.

"Let them in. It's not polite to leave people on the doorstep."

The door swung open. The constables rushed in and came to an abrupt stop. The rest of the men followed.

The sight that met Justin's eyes left him cold. Mr. Higgins sat at his desk with a gun to his temple.

One of the officers took a step forward. "Now then, Mr. Higgins, there's no need for that. Why don't you put the gun down, and we'll go to the station for a nice chat?"

Phineas gave an unpleasant laugh. "The only way I'm leaving is if you all stand back and let me walk out on my own." He paused and Justin could now say he'd seen a truly evil smile.

"Better yet, let me take Ronald. Then if you get too close, I'll shoot him."

Ronald slid toward the door and Justin moved in front of the opening. "Don't worry. We won't let him take you."

The young man slunk to the sitting area and curled into a fetal position on the sofa. Pity stirred in Justin. What kind of upbringing produced this type of person, or Phineas, for that matter?

The officer took another step. "We can't do either of those things. I'm afraid the only option is to lay down your gun and come with us. We don't want anyone to get hurt."

Phineas focused on Squire Bishop. "Let me take him. He's responsible for all this. If it weren't for him, I wouldn't have turned to a life of crime."

The squire shook his head. "We each make our own decisions. I'm not taking any blame for yours."

"Come now. You can tell us all about it at the station. We'll be happy to listen."

Phineas' face turned bright red and he jumped to his feet. "Stop talking about going to the station." He pointed the gun at the officer. "Do you hear me? Don't say it again."

With his attention focused on the officer, another constable slipped around behind him and pushed down his arm. An explosive gunshot filled the room followed by cries of pain. Justin maneuvered to see what happened and spotted Phineas rolling on the floor, moaning and holding his foot.

Mr. Atwood slapped Squire Bishop on the back. "Looks like you're off the hook. This will have to go in front of a judge, of course, but you can be assured Higgins no longer has any hold over you or your estate."

Later that afternoon, Justin and Elena sat side by side on a sofa in the sitting room. He held her hand as they took turns naming the good things that had come about as a result of the events of the summer.

"I have my father back." Elena smiled while blinking back tears. "Everything we went through, including my sprained ankle, was worth it." Her smile faded. "I'm sorry for all the extra work our staff, and yours, had to do. We could have done without the rats." She shuddered.

"No one would disagree with that, but I think it did my brother good to help with the cleanup."

Elena wilted next to him, her mouth turned down at the

corners. "Your brother." She gave a heart-felt sigh. "Cleaning may have been good for him, but he hasn't changed any."

He lifted her chin with his finger and turned her face toward him. "I learned a lot about myself on our balloon ride. How I feel about you, what I'm capable of with God's help and that we can trust God with our future, to mention just a few things. I've also spent some time, over these last few days, considering the value of keeping secrets."

She frowned. "You have another secret?"

"One more to share with Mother. Mr. Atwood isn't the only one who can have a trick up his sleeve."

He kissed her forehead and she gave him a hopeful smile. "I'll pray it turns out as well as his."

"Please do, and also pray that we'll both accept it if God has other plans."

Justin fervently hoped God's plan didn't involve India.

After supper that evening, Justin invited his mother to stroll with him in the garden. She looped her arm through his as they ambled along the path between the tea roses. "I'm glad you and Elena settled your differences. I hope we'll be seeing more of her."

"I'd like that too, but Richard thinks I should join the military and go to India where Uncle George is stationed. He says it's a good career for a second son."

"Hmm, in some cases, maybe. I thought you wanted to write a book."

"I do and I want to go to America to do it. In fact, I have two reasons for wanting to go. The first one you know. The second came in the form of a letter from grandmother. She wants me to find a man named Niall Murphy. There are no reasons as to why, however, she said his last known location was San Francisco, California."

"Ah, very mysterious. I loved her dearly, but she liked to make everything a challenge. Life was never dull growing up."

"Mr. Murphy and my father were business partners. I believe

they invested in several ventures, including gold mines. Mr. Murphy did the footwork in America, while Father took care of paper work here. Apparently, Mother thought they had unfinished business and she wants you to take care of it." She stopped and regarded him. "In my mind, this takes precedence over the military. Have you told Richard about it?"

"Grandmother instructed me not to tell him."

His mother gave a short laugh. "She knew her older grandson well. I'm not an expert in the law, but I believe a deathbed letter is legally binding. If she specified you for this mission, Richard can't take it over. Do you mind if I see it?"

Later, Justin and Richard met in Mother's sitting room. As soon as they were seated, she turned to Richard. "I asked Justin, earlier, about his intentions toward Miss Bishop. He informed me you plan to banish him to India, when he has obligations to her here."

Justin's jaw dropped. "I didn't say–"

She held up her hand, cutting him off. "What do you have to say for yourself, Richard?"

Richard glared at him, then turned back to their mother. "I'm certainly not banishing him, and I didn't say he and Miss Bishop can't wed. I think somebody's being dramatic." He gave Justin a sharp look.

Justin held his hands up and shook his head.

Their mother smiled. "Relax, Richard. You'll give yourself a headache. The point is there will be a change of plans. Justin also shared a letter with me from your grandmother, asking him to go on a mission for her. When he returns, if he wants to join the military, he may with my blessing."

Justin smiled fondly at his mother. She was a good ally, but truth be told, he should have stood up to his brother himself. He still had some maturing to do.

"Why didn't you tell me? I could have taken care of it for you."

"This is something Grandmother asked of me specifically. I'm to find a man who was Grandfather's business partner. At the time she wrote the letter, she believed him to be in California. I didn't tell you because she told me not to. I hoped you'd agree to let me go to America because it would be an opportunity for me to fulfill a dream and possibly find new business opportunities for our family."

Richard harrumphed. "When you put it that way, I agree it's the best course of action. I assume you plan to take Elena with you."

Warmth filled him, making him smile. "Yes. She loves a good adventure."

CHAPTER FORTY-NINE

*E*lena gazed at the beautiful white, lacy dress she'd wear for her wedding. Planning the event had helped take her mind off the investigation and trial. She heaved a sigh. Today should be it. Even though Mr. Atwood assured her there'd be no problem, she wanted to see the case closed and Mr. Higgins in jail.

The front door opened and closed, and Papa called out, "Elena, I'm home."

She flew to the stairs and found him waiting, with a big smile, at the bottom. When she reached him he swept her up in a hug. "Justice has been served. Both Higgins and his nephew are going to jail."

The news cleared away the last dark cloud on the horizon. She looped her arm through his and led him to the study. "Come and tell me everything."

On the way, Papa called to Wilson to send tea. As soon as they were seated, he began. "It turns out quite a few people are unhappy with Phineas Higgins. They reminded the police of their complaints, and they will get to have their day in court, too."

"Good. I hope he doesn't get away with anything." It was satisfying to think he wouldn't be able to hurt anyone else.

"My thought as well."

The tea arrived and Papa poured a cup for her and himself. "Higgins has been ordered to pay restitution for money taken during the faro games and for any expenses we incurred as a result of our fraudulent agreement."

Elena mentally calculated a possible sum and shook her head. "Surely he doesn't have the resources to do that."

Papa's smile broadened. "Oh, but he does. Investigators discovered a tidy nest egg in the bank. It should be enough to repay everyone's grievances. When we've figured out how much he owes us, Mr. Atwood will see we get a check."

She closed her eyes and breathed a prayer. "Thank you, Jesus, for your goodness and mercy."

Papa laid his hand on hers. "Amen."

The relief brought a smile to her face. "Now there's nothing to hinder us from moving forward."

He set his teacup on the trolley. "Speaking of that, I want to get your opinion on something."

Her smile faltered. What could he possibly want her opinion about?

"I'm sure you remember Mrs. Turner?"

Elena relaxed and nodded.

"In light of how things have worked out, I've been thinking of renewing our acquaintance." He hesitated a moment. "How would you feel about that?"

"I think it's a wonderful idea." She set her cup down and gave him a hug. "We should invite her to the wedding."

Three months later

Justin replayed the events of the last few weeks as he sat on the porch of their rented house, enjoying the view of the San Francisco valley and the ocean beyond. He marveled at the many faces of

America. The scenery they'd passed on the train ride to California was magnificent and constantly changing. He and Elena wanted to see all of this beautiful country.

Elena had remarked on how society changed the farther west they went. It had a wilder feel to it. They'd been assured it was much more civilized now. He had a notebook full of observations and ideas for a book. The trip had been a complete success on that count.

He stretched his legs out in front of him and crossed his feet at the ankles. It had taken them a while to find Mr. Murphy, but they eventually tracked him down in a little town several miles south of San Francisco, living with his daughter. The man had fond memories of Justin's grandfather, and the things they did in the past, but couldn't recall any unfinished business dealings.

His daughter went through his papers for him and found deeds to gold mines, some in Alaska, that he and Justin's grandfather still owned and records of other ventures that had played out. Only one mine still had any output and profits should have been continuing to find their way to England. He'd have Richard check into it.

Mr. Murphy did have a business tip for Justin. He'd heard talk about building a railroad along California's coastlline. He recommended getting in on it from the beginning. Justin telegraphed the information to Richard later that day.

Then came the surprise his grandmother had wanted him to find. A message from Mr. Murphy told them to come to his home again as soon as possible. His daughter had continued to search and came across a small box containing a key to a bank safe deposit box. A paper folded into the box said the contents belonged to Justin.

At the bank, they'd found a deed to a gold mine in Alaska, that on further investigation showed him to be a wealthy man. A note in the deposit box from his grandmother said she'd set this up soon after he was born. As second son, she wanted him to be independent in his own right. His grandmother was a wise woman.

Elena came out of the house, wrapped in a shawl, and stood beside him. He reached for her hand and pulled her onto his lap.

She snuggled close. "I love you, Justin, and this adventure we're sharing."

Justin kissed her cheek. "I can't wait to see what God has planned for us."

ACKNOWLEDGMENTS

I want to thank God for blessing me with an imagination and the opportunities and resources to tell the stories he's given me. Thank you to my loving and supportive husband. You never let me give up. My daughters are the best cheerleaders a mom could have and my son and grandson are the first ones I call for tech support. Huge thanks to my ACFW critique group. Your comments, suggestions and encouragement were invaluable. You ladies are awesome. I'm grateful to be a member of American Christian Fiction Writers. Answers to questions, direction on best publishing practices and helpful ideas for every part of the writing process are available to any who choose to partake. Thank you to my editor extraordinaire. She told me she would help make my story sparkle and in my unobjective opinion, she did. Thank you, Cathy and Jodie, for putting the final polish on it. My thanks are not complete without acknowledging my friend, author and seemingly inexhaustible source of information given freely and generously. Thank you, Marcia James.

ABOUT THE AUTHOR

Linda Hoover lives in west-central Ohio with her husband, daughter, grandson and a cat who thinks he owns the house. She earned a degree in psychology at Anderson University where she learned the voices in her head were actually characters from stories waiting to be told.

By day, Linda works as a library assistant at a branch of the county's public library system where two of her duties include choosing books for the young adult and Christian fiction areas. As a result, she has a very long "To Read" list. In her spare time, she writes the stories her voices tell her.

Visit Linda at her website: www.LindaHooverBooks.com or www.Facebook.com/LindaHooverAuthor

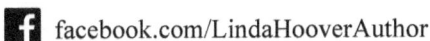 facebook.com/LindaHooverAuthor

ALSO BY LINDA HOOVER

MOUNTAIN PROPHECY

Imagine it's 1918 and your Appalachian relatives are still feuding with their neighbors, still deeply superstitious and still believe in local folklore. Teen twins, Dusty and Darla deal with it every summer when they visit from the city. But this year it's more serious. Hypnotic music comes from an abandoned mine where two young women have disappeared. Yet the mountain families aren't looking for their missing, believing trolls looking for brides are responsible.

Dusty and Darla aren't buying the troll theory—until Darla falls into a trance and starts into the mine. Dusty stops her and vows to keep her from being the next victim. Darla believes she's been called by God to help whoever—or whatever—lives in the mine.

Imagine if your isolated clan has waited hundreds of years in their mountain cavern for a prophecy to come true. A prophecy that vows a heavenly being will come to them, marry the prince and lead them to a better life. After catching a glimpse of Darla, Prince Aidan is sure it's only a matter of time before the prophecy is fulfilled.

Darla is determined to accomplish the mission God has given her, regardless of what Dusty says, but will she be savior or sacrifice?